Making Wishes

Making Wishes

A Novel

Marilyn Holdsworth

AuthorHouse™
1663 Liberty Drive
Bloomington, IN 47403
www.authorhouse.com
Phone: 1-800-839-8640

Published by AuthorHouse 03/12/2013

ISBN: 978-1-4817-0752-7 (sc)
ISBN: 978-1-4817-0751-0 (hc)
ISBN: 978-1-4817-0750-3 (e)

Library of Congress Control Number: 2013900687

By Marilyn Holdsworth

Pegasus

The Beautiful American

Making Wishes

The Portrait of Lady J *(forthcoming)*

For Malcolm

who always encouraged me to wish upon the stars.

PART I

Elloree

Two roads diverged in a wood, and I—
I took the one less traveled by,
And that has made all the difference.

~ Robert Frost

Chapter 1

THE PERSISTENT RINGING OF THE phone shattered the early morning quiet. Even before Elloree could reach the phone to shut off the annoying sound, she felt an intuitive stab, and her hand hesitated before lifting the receiver.

Then her crisp, cheerful answer went across the wire. "Good morning."

It only took an instant for her to recognize the gruff, deep voice at the other end. Not a "Hello, how are you?" or "It's been a long time." But of course it was as it always had been with him. "Hell of a day here, El. I'm up to my ass in work as always. And it's raining—just a sloppy, dreary muck." He made a sort of snorting sound of disapproval.

She had to smile as she pictured him pacing at the other end of the line. She could see his craggy face set with determination as his broad, flat fingers ran restlessly through his coarse, graying hair. My God, hadn't she sat across from him at too many staff meetings to ever forget the intensity in those dark brown eyes?

"Well, I guess the weather is one thing you can't control, Mark," she replied. "But it's good to hear from you," she added, surprised that she meant it. "How are things going?" and there was a question in her voice—not a longing, just a question. She couldn't help feeling curious about a call that had come so unexpectedly, bringing a flood of memories with it.

"Things are not just going, they're growing, and in leaps and bounds," he boomed. "We're about to launch a new promotion that should take us into both national and international markets we've been trying to tap into for a mighty long time."

"I'm glad to hear it, Mark." But still she waited. He hadn't called to tell her idle news about his business growth.

"I'll get right to the point."

Her breath caught in her throat as he said it. Same old Mark—hit it hard, hit it fast, and nine times out of ten, you get what you want. Wasn't that what he'd always told her?

"What I want, Elloree"—he spoke quickly, firing his words into the phone at her as if his rapid delivery would convince her—"what I need and what the company has to have is someone to head up this operation. Someone, not just to work up designs, but to get the goddamned thing rolling like I know it can and must. Someone to handle the artists—kick some temperamental butt, you know, while making them love every minute of it—and then put together some presentations that will knock the balls off those son-of-a-bitch buyers. I need a multidimensional person to get this off the ground and pull the whole campaign together."

Elloree's hand tightened around the receiver. "I know you have a very large and capable staff now, Mark," she said. "Alex Tenner is one of the best, and I read you stole him from Hallmark just last year."

Mark laughed, the deep bellowing sound shaking the phone. "You're right there, but we call it 'making an offer he couldn't refuse.' Yeah, we've got him on our side now. But between you and me, the guy's a light-footed ass who spends too much time thinking with what's below the belt. No, this operation needs someone special."

How very like him, Elloree fumed, pacing the kitchen, still clutching the phone. Today, without warning, one phone call had transformed an ordinary Saturday morning into something that was anything but.

Impulsive, aggressive Mark Williams had always known what he wanted. And as he phrased it this morning, "I want and need you to come back to work, El. This project can't fly without you."

I wish I'd just let the answering machine pick up the call, she thought, *I wouldn't have had to talk to him and hear those persuasive words. Just like that, go back to work. Damn him*. But even as she thought it, she knew she'd made her decision when she'd heard his voice. Still, she answered carefully. "You know I can't just come back, Mark. I would need time." She hesitated and then added, "Time to talk to Tom. And there are things here to work out before I could even think of it." She tried to sound firm and in control, but her heart was racing with excitement.

"Fine, fine; take all the time you need. Call me on Monday with your answer."

She wondered if he could detect the quiver in her voice when she promised to call on Monday.

Elloree stood for a moment staring at the kitchen counter. Mechanically, she rinsed the few dishes that had been left there. "All the time I need," she muttered. "Call on Monday. Time, what does he know about time?" She shook her head angrily.

She could hear the children in the backyard, their voices high-pitched from play. They were still a marvel to her—those perfect little hands and feet, such distinct personalities emerging as they grew. She was always amazed how two boys could be so entirely different. Paul was the oldest, a tall, sturdy, blond boy with piercing blue eyes in a round, cherubic face. Paul regarded the world with a serious curiosity that sometimes seemed too intense for such a small child. Thick, curly hair framed a round, freckled face that was most often thoughtful. His sensitive mouth could be drawn into a determined line one moment and then break into a quick grin the next. But despite all his seriousness, Paul had an infectious laugh. Most children of his age giggled shrilly, but Paul had a deep chuckle that seemed to come from the very depths of his well-worn sneakers.

Timmy was as opposite to his brother Paul as anyone could be. Timmy owed his looks to neither of his parents. In both appearance and personality, he belonged strictly to himself. Although not a handsome child, he had a winsome appeal, and his small-featured face was dominated by ears that protruded abruptly from a mass of carrot-colored hair. From his earliest playpen days, Timmy had displayed two distinct sides to his character—Timmy the comedian and Timmy the crab. He could be laughing one moment and then change swiftly into an irritable whiner the next. Timmy would always have a personality that few would take the trouble to understand.

Elloree abruptly brought herself back to the present. Mark Williams had offered her the career opportunity of a lifetime. She would have to convince Tom that her work at Wishes was important to her. Her love for her work had never been replaced by her roles as wife and mother.

The doorbell chimed, interrupting her thoughts. A messenger from Wishes Inc. handed her an envelope addressed to Elloree Prince. Mark Williams never had accepted her married name. She dismissed the boy with a quick, "Thank you," and tore open the seal. "Need your answer Monday. Come on in; the water's fine," was scrawled across company letterhead in Mark's bold, strong handwriting.

"Just like him to make the decision sound so easy," she muttered. "Damn, he's really pushing hard."

"Hey, Mom. Hey, Mom," came an anxious call from the backyard, and she sprinted for the kitchen door.

Timmy, in his army helmet and cowboy boots, was perched high in the peach tree lobbing fruit grenades at his brother. An overripe one exploded in a direct hit on Paul, who, with splattered pants and injured spirit, hollered his objections.

"He's not supposed to be up in that tree, Mom. Tell him to come down. Timmy, Mom's gonna get you," Paul yelled at his brother, who promptly retorted by tossing another gooey peach that landed squarely in Paul's hair, producing a wail of protest.

Elloree intervened just in time to prevent Paul from shinnying up the tree after his brother. "Okay, okay, let's straighten this war out. Come on down, Tim."

Paul stood angrily at the base of the tree watching his younger, more agile brother swing monkey-like from a limb. Paul's heavier build and more cautious nature usually kept him on the ground, while lithe, little Timmy could shinny up a tree faster than a cat and, once up there, be completely at home. He never had fallen, although he engaged in breathtaking aerial leaps that made his mother shudder. Disciplining Timmy for daredevil tree climbing acts never discouraged him. No one in the Randall household could successfully curtail his death-defying hobby. Everyone had accepted it but Paul, and it infuriated him to have Tim scamper up a tree out of his grasp. It simply was unfair for a little brother to possess such a talent and use it to such unsporting advantage. At this moment, Paul felt keenly insulted and glowered fiercely at the teasing Timmy.

"Aw, Mom, we were only playing," Timmy protested as he landed at his mother's feet.

"Oh yeah! Look at my pants. And I'll bet I've got a bruise as big as a pumpkin on my leg," Paul countered.

"A pumpkin! Boy, get you. I couldn't even throw a pumpkin from up there, and there aren't any around here anyway."

Both boys plodded toward the house at first jostling each other as they went. But as the temporary cease-fire in their war worked its magic, the boys forgot their recent anger and the threesome linked arms and walked across the yard together. Elloree wondered how she was going to tell them about her offer at Wishes, and she knew she could never explain why she would have to leave them. They reached the house, and the boys flung themselves down at the table in the bright, sunny breakfast room.

When Elloree and Tom had purchased the sprawling, old place, the breakfast room had been a dingy green, but she had redecorated it in creamy whites and colorful wallpaper. It had taken months of work for an old German craftsman to strip away the layers of paint to restore the finish of the fine wood floors and paneling throughout the house. Even the high, exposed beam ceilings and rusted, wrought-iron banisters had regained their original luster. And when finally finished, the house had an elegant, stately charm. Ornamental gates across the driveway and a bubbling fountain in the front courtyard completed the transformation of the once run-down, old place. But Tom remained practical to the end, grumbling about inadequate heating and antiquated plumbing.

Months ago, sitting in this very room, Elloree had tried to talk to Tom about her work. She wanted to submit her freelance artwork to some local publications. With her background, she knew she could sell some pieces and begin to build a client base that could grow into her own small company. Tom had listened patiently while she'd outlined her plans, smiled, and then suggested she accept the post of art director for the spring community hospital benefit. He pointed out it would be a perfect outlet for her talents since the hospital would need brochures, posters, and advertising layouts planned. He had stubbornly refused to discuss her wish to work any further, using the boys and their schedules as a final objection. Since there was no financial need for her to work, Tom considered the subject closed. He had patted her shoulder and left the room, reminding her to call the hospital benefit chairman on Monday.

Frustrated and bewildered, Elloree resented his attitude and lack of understanding. In the beginning, Tom had seemed intrigued with her work, but after their marriage, he'd discouraged her from continuing with it. At first, she'd resisted, but gradually, she had given in to him. The last assignment she had done professionally had been six years ago, just before Timmy was born, and now she did have the two boys to consider.

At this moment, Paul was looking at her expectantly, waiting to be reprimanded for the morning's activities with his brother. Both of their smudgy faces turned toward her with large question marks stamped across them.

"Well, Mom?" asked Paul.

"How do you feel about Mrs. Clive coming to live with us for a while?" Elloree plunged in hopefully. Mrs. Clive had been the Randall's part-time housekeeper for several years and would be the ideal one to take over.

"Why?" questioned practical Timmy. The boys eyed their mother, concern and suspicion creeping into their faces.

"Well, I've been offered ..." Elloree's words trailed off and stopped. Those faces suddenly made her very uncertain.

"Are you going somewhere, Mother?" Paul asked seriously. For these adult conversations, he always used "Mother" rather than the less formal and usual "Mom."

The boys looked young and vulnerable sitting there before her, like two helpless puppies, she thought. Instead of the unemotional, factual conversation Elloree had planned, she found herself blurting out, "Oh, I love you both so very much. You must never forget that, no matter what I do." First she hugged Paul and then moved quickly around the table to gather Timmy into her arms for a moment.

"Never mind, boys, it'll keep. Go on outside to your play, but stay away from those peaches."

Timmy and Paul exchanged puzzled glances then raced for the door.

"Beat you to the garage, Shrimp," Paul's challenge echoed after them.

Elloree sat down at the table, cradling her head on her arms for a minute. "Oh God, what will I say to Tom if I can't do better than that with the boys," she moaned.

Chapter 2

It was Sally Wagoner who interrupted Elloree's thoughts about Wishes and Mark Williams later that morning. Her familiar voice came cheerfully across the phone line. "Hi, El, you didn't forget the Art League committee meeting, did you?"

"Oh God, no, Sally. I mean yes, I really did. Was it this Saturday morning? I'm sure I put next Saturday down on the calendar. Shows where my mind has been lately, doesn't it?" Elloree apologized.

"Oh, El, we're counting on you. It's at Aggie Marsh's house at 11:00. You can make it, can't you? There's a light lunch planned right after. I don't think I can get through it without you," Sally implored.

Elloree started to protest but decided it was useless. Besides, she liked Sally Wagoner and hated to let her down. "Okay, I'll be there, Sally. Anything I need to bring?"

"Only your notebook. Marge Lewis and Ann Downs are doing the lunch this time. See you there, El. Bye."

"Bye-bye, Sally. Thanks for calling to remind me." Dejected, Elloree put down the phone. "The last thing I need is a committee meeting this morning," she muttered. "How long ago did I get myself into this?" She shook her head, trying not to remember.

Tom had smiled his approval when she'd told him of her election to the Art League's executive board. "It will be a great creative outlet for you. I know how you've needed something other than the boys and the house," he had said.

She had looked at him sitting at his desk in the library comfortably, surrounded by his books and antiques. "But I don't want to do this, Tom. I'd much rather—"

His words cut across hers. "Not everyone in Oak View is invited to sit on the board. It's something of an honor for someone so young and new to the group to be asked." He shifted in his seat under her steady gaze.

Elloree studied Tom for a long moment. She suspected that he had discussed the matter with his mother, but knowing she would be resentful, he never would admit that he had. The senior Mrs. Randall had spent her lifetime building a network of important friends through her dedicated involvement with prestigious and influential groups. Although her disapproval of her daughter-in-law had been obvious to Tom from the start, he had reluctantly allowed his mother to be more involved in their daily lives than Elloree cared to admit.

But now, although she knew it was useless to disagree, she still questioned,"Did your mother arrange this?" Then, disgusted, she answered her own question, "Never mind, I guess I knew the minute I opened the invitation, or perhaps I should call it 'the summons.'"

"You'll enjoy it," Tom assured her, and the subject was closed between them.

The Randalls were community leaders and patrons of the arts, giving of themselves unselfishly by serving on committees and boards as well as by making substantial financial donations. Although Mrs. Oliver J. Randall III was dismayed by her son's choice in a wife, she felt it her familial and civic obligation to see that Elloree was properly guided into the correct channels. The younger Mrs. Randall needed to be made aware of her family and community responsibilities.

The senior Mrs. Randall's arrival at the house on Pilgrim Road the next day had not been entirely unexpected. Elloree ushered her in graciously, but she was immediately aware of the reason for her mother-in-law's visit. She floated like some exotic bird into the living room and perched herself on the edge of the antique sofa. A faint scent of Chanel followed her into the room, and her perfectly manicured hands fluttered as she spoke. A large, emerald-cut diamond on her ring finger caught the morning sunlight, sending tiny prisms dancing across the Aubusson carpet.

"My dear, this seat on the board is such an opportunity for you. You'll meet some of Oak View's most distinguished women from the oldest and best families. To turn this down would be an insult, out of the question," she added with finality.

Elloree shifted her position on the sofa next to her mother-in-law, struggling to maintain outward composure. *An insult to whom? You? Tom? This is not an invitation for me; it's for you. My service on the board isn't a request; it's a command.* She longed to say them, but the words stuck in her throat, and she could only stare silently at the older woman.

The morning's call from Sally Wagoner about the committee meeting had brought the memories flooding back. Sally was Elloree's best friend in Oak View, but the two young women had little in common. Sally was perfectly happy to be where she was and who she was. Her husband, a partner in the law firm Wagoner, Lewis, and Broad, was the youngest member of the town council. Sally openly enjoyed the prestige his position in the community afforded her, and her life revolved comfortably around the Art League and other civic organizations. This morning she was counting on Elloree's support for her proposal of a new club fundraiser.

Elloree picked up the phone to call Mrs. Clive and then gathered up her notes for the meeting. She took only a few minutes to review them before calling in the boys to tell them of the change in the day's plans. Long faces met her words.

"Aw, Mom, we were going to the park after lunch. You promised," Paul protested. He had a new boat he wanted to try out on the lake.

"Never mind. I'll be home right after lunch. I give you my word on that. Then we'll go. Okay? Mrs. Clive will be here any minute. Now I have to dress."

On the way up the stairs, she heard Mrs. Clive coming through the back door into the kitchen and calling to the boys. Once upstairs in the privacy of her room, Elloree breathed a sigh of relief. She always hated to disappoint the children and especially on a Saturday. She sank down in one of the comfortable chairs by the fireplace for a moment before hurrying into her clothes.

Decorated in soft blue tones, the master bedroom suite with its plush carpet and splendid, antique furniture had a calming effect on her. She spent many of her most peaceful evenings curled in front of the marble hearth reading or sketching while Tom attended one of his many business dinners. Some of Tom and Elloree's happiest moments, times of intimacy and hope, had been shared together in this room, but this morning, she found herself remembering those times with slight bitterness. She moved quickly to her dressing room and surveyed the contents of the long wardrobe closet that stretched the length of the wall. Although the closet was filled with fashionable clothes and racks of shoes, Elloree took only a moment to select a pair of smartly tailored, navy blue slacks and a cream-colored, silk blouse.

Tom always provided her with the latest fashions for his own sake as well as hers. An elegant dresser himself, he admired good-looking clothes. One of the first things that had attracted him to Elloree had been her style. She was a woman who always looked impeccably dressed with her own special flair. She wore simply tailored, sophisticated clothes and seldom indulged in garish prints. Although as an artist she loved bright dominant colors, on herself, she much preferred subtle shades of blue and green or, occasionally, stark black or warm navy blue. Like most women, her state of mind influenced her dress, and today was definitely a navy blue or black day.

She slipped into the blouse, chose a colorful scarf for accent, and selected some jewelry from the carved mahogany box on top of her dressing table. She stepped into a pair of matching navy shoes and reached for her suede coat. She whirled about quickly in front of the full-length mirror to check her appearance, glanced at her make-up and hair, and then hurriedly went downstairs.

Mrs. Clive's ample matronly shape was already wrapped in an apron when Elloree hurried through the kitchen on her way to the garage. The smell of freshly baking cookies filled the air.

"Not until after lunch," Elloree called to the boys as she headed for the back door.

"Just one, Mom, please. Right from the oven is best," Paul protested.

"Okay, but only one," she admonished, looking sternly at Mrs. Clive, who nodded in agreement.

"Only one?" wailed Timmy. "I like 'em best hot so the chocolate's all melty."

"I don't have time to argue, boys. We'll take some to the park with us when I get back." The door closed behind her, and with a twinge of guilt over leaving them, she slid behind the wheel of the sleek, black Mercedes. *I'll only stay long enough to vote with Sally*, she promised herself.

Always a fast driver, Elloree felt a sense of pleasure when the powerful car accelerated as she pulled out of the driveway. The light rain of the early hours had turned to a heavy mist, leaving the streets wet and slippery. As on most Saturday mornings in Oak View, the roads were mostly deserted, with only a few cars heading in the direction of the golf course. It only took Elloree a few minutes to reach the Marsh's house on Oak Avenue. The wide street was lined with large, well-kept homes and many old, gigantic, sprawling oak trees. Many of Oak View's wealthiest families lived in this charming, long-established section of town. Elloree pulled to the curb and stopped in front of a stately, colonial-style house surrounded by perfectly manicured, rolling, green lawns dotted with elm trees.

Several cars already lined the street, and a red Jaguar convertible pulled neatly in behind her. Glancing in the rear view mirror, Elloree smiled as she watched Jan Alexander squirm from behind the wheel and step from the car. Jan waved and called out, "I'm not the only late one this morning I see."

The two women exchanged greetings before starting up toward the house together.

"I almost forgot completely. Without Sally's call, I wouldn't be here at all," Elloree said, wishing for the second time that morning that she had not answered the telephone. Jan waited as Elloree carefully set the alarm on her car. "Can't be too careful these days—just last week, a car was stolen right out of a driveway on Pilgrim Road," Elloree commented before joining Jan on the wide, brick walkway lined with colorful flowers.

Jan patted her short-cropped, dark brown hair. "Cut it because of the car." She waved toward the convertible. "It was always a stringy mess," she said, eyeing Elloree's honey blond, shoulder-length hair with envy.

Vivacious and plump, Jan struggled constantly to maintain her weight. As they walked, she tugged impatiently at her skirt, smoothing the fabric that bunched around her slightly bulging waistline. Even in high-heeled shoes, Jan was short, and the snug, straight line of her dress only accentuated the roundness of her figure.

"I don't suppose you ever have to watch your diet," she said petulantly to Elloree, tall and slender, walking beside her. "I just have to look at a pastry, and I blow up like a balloon. It wouldn't make a difference if I dieted all year, I'd never have your long legs," she said wistfully. Then, not waiting for a response, she continued, "I missed you at the Patterson's last Saturday night." Her tone was casual, but there was a question in her voice.

"Tom couldn't make it home from his business trip in time."

"Too bad. Aggie was in her element. You missed quite a show." She looked over at Elloree for a reaction to her words. Then, seeing none, she said, "You know how Aggie is; she's never forgiven Gerald or the rest of the Marshes either for that matter. As if he could help it that his family all turned out to be such poor business managers," she scoffed.

"Yes, I suppose Aggie does resent it a bit that Gerald actually has to work for a living," Elloree said with a laugh.

"Resent him?" Jan stopped, staring at Elloree as if she had hurled an obscenity at her. "Resent him," she repeated. "I think she loathes him. But then Aggie would hate anyone who cut down her money tree. She's never gotten over marrying wealthy, well-connected Gerald Marsh only to find her checkbook restricted and her social position precarious."

Elloree felt suddenly very tired, and she wished she had gone to the park with the boys. She didn't want to hear more about the Patterson's party, but Jan was determined to share her newly acquired information. Hesitating on the Marsh's front porch, she lowered her voice and leaned closer to Elloree, "Phillip Roth and Barbara are getting a divorce. It's because of his twenty-five-year-old assistant, and Barbara is devastated. Aggie saw them together last week—the assistant and Phil, I mean. Of course, Barbara and Phil weren't at the Patterson's," she confided.

"Naturally. And Aggie would be the one to spread their news. She does savor gossip like a fine wine, doesn't she?"

Jan Alexander ignored Elloree's touch of sarcasm. "You and Tom should have been there. Absolutely everyone asked about you, especially Aggie."

"I can just imagine," Elloree grimaced.

"It was a perfect dinner, catered by Juliette, of course—she always does the Patterson parties—and such a delicious dessert, strawberry cheesecake," Jan patted her hips. "But too, too much food."

"Sorry I missed it," Elloree said without enthusiasm.

"I think Barbara is going to be at the meeting today. At least that's what I heard. So I thought I should warn you—you know, about Phil and everything."

But I hardly know Barbara, Elloree wanted to say but decided it was pointless.

Finally they were at the front door, and eager to end the conversation, Elloree rang the bell. The melodious sound of the chimes interrupted Jan's news report.

The door immediately swung open. "Well, there you are at last," Aggie scolded. "Do come in. The meeting had to start without you."

She took Jan Alexander's arm. "So glad to see you, Jan. Wasn't Saturday night a beautiful party? Simply elegant. Everyone was there," she purred. Then to Elloree, "Too bad you missed it."

Trim and stylish, Aggie Marsh did make a handsome appearance. She moved with a studied grace as she glided across her grand entry hall to usher in her tardy guests.

"You can put your coat in there," she said to Elloree, gesturing toward one of the paneled doors. "I'll just take Jan on into the garden room to the meeting." Her perfectly made-up face hardened with dislike, and her eyes shrank into tiny glittering dots as she looked at Elloree. Then she turned abruptly away, again took Jan's arm, and ushered her through the wide French doors into what Aggie casually called the garden room.

Elloree hesitated for a moment before following them. She stood in the middle of the stately hall's polished marble floor beneath the ornate crystal chandelier that hung suspended from the high, molded ceiling. Elloree looked up and smiled to herself, remembering Aggie's detailed description of the fixture's authentic royal heritage. Although she'd actually purchased it from a Jewish antique dealer of dubious reputation, Aggie boasted it had once graced the stately chateau of a European nobleman. This morning, standing beneath the dozens of sparkling crystals, Elloree shook her head and almost laughed out loud. "Not the only phony thing in this house," she muttered to herself as she opened the French doors at the far end of the hall and followed the other two women into the meeting.

A cascading fountain, its base decorated with alabaster cherubs and surrounded by lush potted ferns, occupied one end of Aggie's garden room. Decorated with designer, white wicker and glass furniture arranged tastefully on an ivory paver-tile floor, the room had the cool, uninviting elegance of its owner. An aroma of freshly brewed coffee mingling with a faint scent of perfume greeted Elloree as she glanced around for Sally. Seated at the far end, Sally was already presenting her motion to the group. Relieved that she wasn't too late to support her friend, Elloree slid into a vacant chair in time to cast her vote for Sally's proposed new fundraiser.

Chapter 3

Across town from where Elloree sat listening to the chatter in the Art League meeting, Mark Williams replaced his phone receiver and stared at it. He had picked it up only to put it down again several times during the last few minutes. It was Saturday morning, and his empty offices were coldly deserted, the heavy silence at once a relief and oppression to him. His old, walnut desk was strewn with unopened mail and unanswered memos, but he sat drumming his fingers impatiently on the work-worn wood.

"Oh hell," he muttered to himself. "I promised I'd leave her alone and let her make her own decision, but damn it, it's a crime for her to even think of passing up this chance."

At forty-five, Mark Williams had a rugged rather than handsome appearance. Even in an expensive, perfectly tailored suit he managed to look slightly disheveled. Thick but already graying hair framed a keenly intelligent face lined and hardened by years of fighting for his business survival. Although only of average height, his broad shoulders and determined air made him appear much taller. Mark Williams had never wasted much time worrying over his appearance or his appeal to women.

He had always been singularly driven by his fierce desire to build his company, Wishes Inc., into a respected, international competitor, and everything else in his life had come second.

He whirled his well-worn, burgundy, leather office chair around and faced the window. It wasn't a pretty view, but to Mark, the sprawling gray industrial area below was the real city, and he loved it. He had turned down several opportunities to move his company from this dreary, unsophisticated end of town. His wife, Sylvia, had urged him to move uptown as soon as Wishes Inc. had begun to grow, but he had stubbornly refused. To him, this was where his life was, and the real pulse of the city could be felt only here. He sat staring out on the foggy, damp cityscape lost in his thoughts of Elloree. Just as he heard the outer office door open and then click shut, he made a silent promise to himself. Somehow, he would get her to accept his offer.

"Good morning, Mr. Williams," came the somewhat formal but pleasant interruption.

"Oh yes, Miss Mills, I forgot I asked you to come in this morning." His thoughts came back to the present.

Joan Mills looked slightly rebuffed by his casual, forgetful tone. She had been his dedicated secretary for many years, and she was what Mark called good people, the kind it was hard to find these days—loyal, hardworking, and unattractive. Long ago, he had decided unattractiveness in a secretary was a definite virtue. Too many of his business acquaintances insisted on window-dressing their offices with voluptuous young secretaries. Their images might flatter male egos, but Mark had heard more than one story of steamy office romance gone sour. Too often, the pretty corporate playmate turned into a bitter adversary, claiming sexual harassment or crying fraudulent tax evasion to the government auditors. For Mark Williams, such entanglements brought risks that would never be worth taking. Hard work and dedication to Wishes were all that mattered in an employee. And although he insisted on total loyalty to him and to Wishes, he rewarded those around him generously when they worked hard to accomplish company goals.

This morning, Mark really looked at Miss Mills for perhaps the first time in five years. She was wearing a charcoal, pinstriped suit with flat, serviceable shoes. The drab color she wore seemed to reflect her personality. Quiet and never prone to giggles or emotional outbursts, Miss Mills was consistently efficient and paid strict attention to detail. Her monotonous wardrobe of gray skirts with matching sweaters or blouses was only occasionally varied by black or dark blue accents. Summer or winter, her shoes were the same sensible, low-heeled black leather and her hair, now streaked with silver, still hung loosely to her shoulders, as it had when she had walked through the door of Wishes on her first day.

It struck Mark this morning that Joan Mills had been unobtrusively growing older with him and Wishes, Inc. It startled him to see just how much she had aged since he'd last looked at her. Although no one could accuse Miss Mills of ever having been pretty, she had an honest, sincere character that reflected itself in her quiet, peaceful expression. Mark couldn't help but think how funny it was that he still called her Miss Mills after all these years, but somehow it would seem almost blasphemous to even think of such an individual as simply Joan.

Miss Mills was busily preparing coffee in the adjoining room. Presently, she reappeared, cheerfully placing a steaming mug before him. The coffee and her quiet smile warmed him as always. Theirs was a special relationship, built on years of trust and mutual respect.

"I suppose we better get on with those letters." He fumbled absently with the stacks of papers before him. "I want to get this off the ground within the next month. I want some beginning designs by the first of November, and the entire line, I'm projecting, will be out on the market before next fall. So we'll have to get moving. I don't want to miss out on any seasonal sales."

"Yes," she nodded encouragingly and waited.

"Damn it," he muttered. "That woman is holding up my whole parade." He flung himself out of his chair, paced up and down for a moment, and then whirled to face Miss Mills. "The size of this promotion demands a special talent," he continued, "not just an artist; they're a dime a dozen. For a job this size, we need a creative dynamo—someone to pick it up and move with it. Sure, we need some idea drawing, but I need somebody to put together a whole package. You know what I mean. Wishes and I need Elloree Prince," he finished, shaking his head in frustration.

"You mean Mrs. Randall," Joan Mills gently reminded him.

"Yeah, yeah Elloree Randall. Goddamn shame she married that provincial bastard," he exploded.

Miss Mills remained stoically silent. Outbursts like these never unnerved her anymore. Years ago, she had learned that Mark needed her as a backboard to bounce his own thoughts off of. It cleared his mind. She knew that, often, her most valuable service to him was just quietly listening. Her patient, undemanding nature had allowed her to survive in his life where his own wife had failed. Joan Mills had suffered through those dreadful days of his divorce with him. She had always been there but had never allowed herself to show him any of her own pain. Inwardly, watching him throw himself away on a reckless, shallow woman only to be plunged into depression and disillusionment for months following the breakup had torn her apart. Secretly, Joan Mills had always blamed Elloree Prince. She was sure it had been because of Elloree's sudden marriage to Tom Randall that Mark had turned to the money-lusting Sylvia in the first place.

The day the break had finally come, Mark and Sylvia had had a terrible row right in this very office. It had started innocently enough but had ended with Mark roaring and Sylvia hysterical.

"Why don't you come home?" she screamed accusingly at him. "Why?" she answered her own question, "Because you'd rather stay down here with some miserable little whore of an artist; and don't think I don't know what you're doing. I do know." Her voice rose to a shriek.

"The hell you do. You just have a suspicious, dirty, little mind, and you always have. I work damn hard to provide you with designer clothes and all those lunches with your alley cat friends," he snarled back.

The final barb was Sylvia's. "You never have loved me anyway," she whined. "You only married me because you couldn't have that goddamn tramp of an artist of yours—that Elloree."

At that moment, Joan Mills at her desk in the outer office heard Mark's voice go icy cold with contempt. "Don't ever speak to me like that again, or of her like that. Now get out. You've said enough." Joan Mills could visualize his colorless, angry face as he fought to control his temper.

"All right, Mr. Self Righteous," Sylvia flung back. "Go to Hell. I'll see you in the divorce court." She slammed the door and flounced out past Joan Mill's desk. "Don't try to be so goddamn discreet. You make me sick," she snapped.

It was a disgusting scene, and Joan Mills had felt as embarrassed as if she had been purposely spying through a bedroom window. She had sat twisting a pencil and then nervously running it through her hair, wondering what she could do for Mark. Then she'd heard his strained and oddly quiet voice call her into the office. "Get my lawyer, Charles Steele, on the phone, and get me a room at the Town Club for the night," he said. He stared at her for a moment as if he wanted to say something more and then turned abruptly away. The matter was closed between them, and neither he nor Joan Mills would ever mention Sylvia again.

Joan Mills had known from that moment that Elloree would always haunt Mark. Yet she couldn't find it in her heart to hate or even resent the artist. During the months she had known Elloree at Wishes, she had never disliked her and had always admired her talent. It had been Elloree Prince's sketches that had first launched Wishes, Inc. Her ideas and hard work had helped build the foundation of the company. Teamed with Mark Williams's uncanny business sense, Elloree's artistic talents had made Wishes thrive.

Their first real break had come when Mark had landed the big account with Mason Hale, one of the leading national department store chains. Soon, more big orders had followed from other leading retailers, and Wishes' designs had spread throughout the country. Now, looking at the prosperous, successful executive seated behind his desk this Saturday morning, Joan Mills found it almost impossible to remember those days when Wishes was such a fledgling operation.

"She's got to come in on this one," Mark continued. "I could turn the whole campaign over to her. It would be fabulous for her and for Wishes. Now that the company is finally growing big and prosperous, she should be in on the excitement when we finally hit the home run that moves us into the major leagues. God, those years she worked to start this thing were nothing compared to what it could be like now. A talent like that tied down, shut off. Christ, what a crime," he muttered.

He looked at the phone longingly for a moment, but knowing that to push Elloree hard would be a mistake, he hesitated. Suddenly, he slammed his hand down on the desk, but Miss Mills never flinched. "Let's get this backlog of letters out. Those New York buyers are going to be looking for some production answers from us."

Joan Mills smiled encouragingly, picked up a file folder, and started for the outer office.

Chapter 4

Thoughts of Wishes, Tom, and the children raced through Elloree's mind as she sat listening to the endless committee reports from the Art League board. Her decision to return to Wishes was not an easy one to make. Although, during the last few months, she had drawn further and further away from Tom, this morning she sat thinking of him as the meeting droned on.

Self-assured, content with his business life and social position, Tom Randall was the image of success. Although his dark brown hair was thinning and graying at the temples now and he had added a few pounds, he still had a distinguished, handsome appearance. He radiated the confidence that comes with the successful running of a prosperous multimillion-dollar company. The Randall Land Development Corporation thrived under his direction. Never content to rely on family name or money, Tom had built the company into a top national organization. And Elloree did admire him for that. He enjoyed the challenge and satisfaction he found in his business life.

But in spite of his obvious love for his own work, he could not accept Elloree's need for hers. She longed to feel once again the thrill of creating and designing, but the children made her choice difficult. She knew it was the boys, not Tom and the life he had planned for her, that held her to the house on Pilgrim Road.

Elloree was relieved when the meeting finally ended and Sally Wagoner crossed the garden room to join her. Sally's husband had dropped her at the meeting on his way to his Saturday golf game, and Sally needed a ride home. She had promised to take her daughter, Annie, to spend the afternoon with a school friend. Eager to take her own children on their outing to the park, Elloree was more than happy to leave early with Sally.

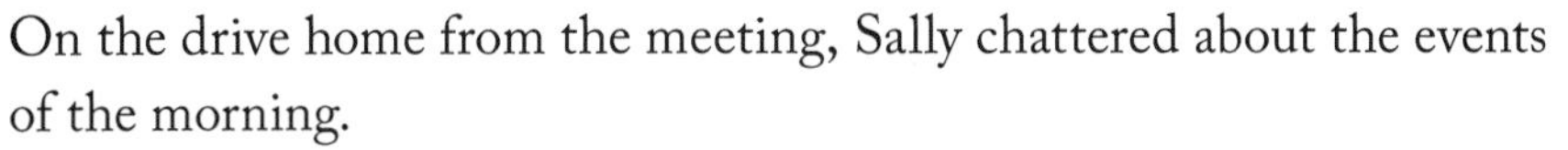

On the drive home from the meeting, Sally chattered about the events of the morning.

"Well, you sure put Aggie on the edge of her chair," Sally said with a laugh. "It looked for a minute like she was going to jump right up and march across the room to make you keep quiet."

"I waited to speak until the president called on me. And I only said what I knew the group should hear about printing expenses if they hope to make any money on their project," Elloree countered. "Aggie just can't allow anyone to have any thoughts of their own or know anything she doesn't. She always needs to dominate the scene, and today I just got tired of pretending to agree."

Sally studied Elloree as she easily maneuvered the big Mercedes through Oak View's Saturday afternoon traffic. Sally admired Elloree's intelligence and ability to speak her mind, but today seated next to her, she sensed her friend's thoughts were somewhere else. It at once fascinated and disconcerted Sally that things vitally interesting to the women she knew always seemed so unimportant to Elloree. Months ago over lunch, Elloree had confided in Sally about her past work at Wishes, Inc. Afterward, she had shown her some of the sketches she still made from time to time. Sally had heard the enthusiasm in Elloree's voice and seen the excitement in her eyes, and she'd been amazed by her friend's talent. So she really wasn't surprised today when Elloree mentioned her thoughts about returning to work at Wishes.

"I really don't know why I'm telling you," Elloree said. "I honestly don't know what I'm going to do yet. It's the children, Sally. I hate to leave them, and I know I would have to work long hours. Children need a mother at home. I do believe that. And Tom wants me there, too," she added unhappily.

Sally smiled encouragingly at her, waited for her to continue.

Elloree was silent for a moment. "But what about my needs as well as Tom's?" she said, asking herself more than Sally. "Perhaps it's possible to satisfy both, but I seriously doubt it. Neither Tom nor his mother would ever accept me going back to work. It would inconvenience them—cause them to make changes they don't want to make. Tom is totally satisfied if I attend the league meeting every Wednesday, volunteer at the hospital on Fridays, and fill in the week chauffeuring the boys to their activities. But I don't think I can do it anymore. There's something inside me demanding expression. Call it a creative force, or maybe just call it a selfish disposition."

Sally said nothing; her face reflected her lack of understanding of Elloree's problem. But she sat dutifully as a friend and listened. She could have participated in the conversation much better had it revolved around the latest hemlines designers were showing or the probable affairs of the club tennis pro. No, Elloree was a different breed that somehow had gotten mixed into her tight, little Oak View circle. But Sally was curious. How had Elloree become a Randall and gotten herself into that beautiful old house on Pilgrim Road? She had heard many speculations, but none of the stories had come directly from any of the Randalls. Today, Elloree's openness gave Sally the opportunity she had been waiting for, and suddenly she blurted, "How in the world did you ever marry Tom Randall in the first place?"

Elloree looked over at her friend, sitting in the seat next to her. She had a small pug nose that tilted slightly upward, and curly, strawberry blonde hair framed her face. Dressed in a perfectly tailored designer suit, Sally was the picture of self-satisfied suburban contentment. Her life was devoted to husband, home, and community service.

"You know, Sally," Elloree replied thoughtfully. "I sometimes wonder how it happened myself. I met him while I was working at Wishes."

Sally's eyes lighted up with interest; perhaps her friend had a scarlet past after all. She'd always had suspicions about Elloree's marriage. Why else would the Randall's be so closemouthed about it? Didn't all artists have loose morals and live bizarre lifestyles? Any girl from Oak View's most acceptable families worked hard enough in high school on her grade point average to get into college and then devoted herself to finding a suitable husband.

"I wanted a career after college," Elloree continued. "I started with Wishes when the company was just getting off the ground. Those were exhausting and exhilarating days. I poured hours of work into the development of the little caricatures that became Wishes' trademark. The idea just popped into my head as I sat doodling at my desk one afternoon. At noontime, I had taken a walk in the park and watched two little children sharing an ice cream cone. Back at work, I sketched them on my drawing pad and scrawled the caption, 'Happiness is sharing with you.' After that, Wishes brought out an entire 'Happiness is …' line, and it went over big. I churned out one card after another and expanded into other products—notepaper, wall plaques, and calendars—all with the same designs. Up until that point, Wishes had been struggling to keep afloat, but that Happiness line brought us our first break."

Listening to Elloree's account of her early days at Wishes, Sally wondered more and more about her friend's relationship with Tom and how the couple had ever gotten together. Growing up in Oak View, Sally had known the Randalls for years, and although Tom had been ahead of her in school, his reputation had been widely known. Always a popular boy with the girls, he had gone on to university only after a crash prep course. Never a serious student, he had devoted himself to fraternity life, seldom missing a party and always turning up with a different girl of dubious reputation. At the end of his junior year, Tom had been on the verge of being expelled. Sally had heard all about it when she was home for summer break. Carol Reynolds had delighted in giving the account at the club dance.

"He broke into the prof's office the night before the chem exam and made a copy of the whole test. He had to pass that exam or be dumped."

"He must have been drunk or high on something to think he could get away with that," put in John Evans.

"Oh, he got away with it all right. The Randall money bailed him out as usual. You should know that, John."

Today, Sally wondered if Tom still enjoyed the story. He used to tell it himself after graduation. Once out of school, he had gone directly into the family business. How he'd happened to marry Elloree was the one thing about Tom Randall that intrigued Sally.

As the two women drove, winding through Oak View's streets lined with stately homes, Elloree continued to reminisce. "Tom just walked into the company one day to see Mark Williams, my boss. Mark was interested in acquiring some property through the Randall Land Development Corporation. I was in Mark's office showing him some of my designs."

"Just like that? Caught sight of you and that was it for him?"

"Something like that," Elloree replied. Sally's look of naked curiosity caused Elloree to hesitate.

But Sally was determined to know more of the story. She had heard many versions but never one straight from Elloree herself. Elloree had been the subject of conversation at more than one luncheon and bridge table in Oak View. Although Sally was as loyal to her as she could be to any friend, she couldn't help wanting to know more. It would give her the edge on Aggie Marsh next time she saw her—not that she would say anything against Elloree; it would be enough just to know something about someone for once that Aggie didn't. Sally glowed with satisfaction, thinking of the few chosen words that she would use to whet Aggie's appetite for gossip. She wouldn't tell her the whole story of course; she'd just give her enough to kindle her interest. Delicious. She smiled smugly thinking of it.

Suddenly, Elloree was aware that Sally was eagerly waiting for her to continue. And at that moment, Elloree felt a repulsion for her friend's obvious look of anticipation and a rush of dislike for her, but for what reason, she wasn't sure. Perhaps it was because she knew she could try for a lifetime and never really belong with Sally in Oak View's inner circle.

"I don't know what it is with me," she said, laughing and steering the conversation back to less serious ground. "I've got everything it appears, doesn't it? Why risk it on some lousy job? I'll tell you, Sally, stay clear of me. I'm a weirdo."

Sally couldn't hide her disappointment at the turn of the conversation. She was immediately impatient, since nothing really interesting was coming out after all. She shifted her position restlessly and turned her head to the window. She knew Elloree would never tell her, now that the moment had somehow slipped by her.

"Oh, you'll come out all right whatever you do," Sally said peevishly. "After all, lots of women do work these days—not many around here I don't suppose, but other places," she added . "Tom will just have to adjust to it, and the kids will survive. You do get yourself worked up over the strangest things, Elloree. Remember the time I decided to try modeling lessons so I'd be sure to be in the league's fashion show? Well, my family adjusted beautifully to that. I had to spend hours practicing." She looked out the window dreamily remembering the triumphant day of the event when she was asked to wear the gorgeous, flowing, blue chiffon gown that everyone in the show was hoping to wear.

Sally reluctantly came back from her reminiscences as she caught sight of her daughter whizzing down the street on her bicycle. "Oh, Lord, there's Annie out in those terrible tattered jeans and old shirt. I told Mrs. Knotts to throw those things away. What a mess she looks." Sally was already halfway out of the car as Elloree stopped at the curb a few houses from the Wagoner's beautiful, rolling front lawn.

"Annie," Sally shrilled, "get right home and change those terrible clothes. What on earth do you think you're doing riding around like that?"

Annie pedaled good-naturedly up to them. "What's all the shouting about, Mom?" Her shirt had a large tear across the shoulder and some smudges down the front from riding through the bushes.

Sally shuddered when her daughter pulled up beside the car.

"Children," she moaned. "I'm having a terrible time with her these days. She doesn't like dancing school. She wants horseback riding lessons instead."

Annie made a face when she heard dancing school mentioned.

Sally turned to Elloree. "Thanks for the lift, and let me know what you decide to do, won't you?" she added halfheartedly. She stood next to the car talking through the open window. Glancing down the street, her eyes rested on a sleek, blue sports convertible parked in the driveway of the house next door. "Now, look at that, Elloree. Margie Taylor has another new car. Parked it right out front, of course. Couldn't put that in the garage. Not Margie." Turning to her daughter, she said, "Annie, let's get you home. I only hope nobody saw you out like that. Why couldn't you have put on that cute little play outfit I picked up for you at Macy's the other day?"

Annie made another face and turned away from her mother. "Ugh," she said. "I hate pink."

Sally ignored her daughter's comment and continued her conversation through the window. "Have you been in Macy's lately, Elloree? They've added a whole new department in sportswear. Really brought in some yummy things. We should go together, have lunch." Sally began to launch into one of her favorite topics, shopping, but Annie impatiently tugged at her arm.

"Come on, Mom. You promised to get me to Patty's by 2:00. I want to go now."

"Not dressed like that, you won't," Sally said firmly, rolling her eyes at Elloree and mouthing the word *kids*. "Get your bicycle, Annie. Bye, Elloree, and thanks again. We'll have to talk soon. Don't forget our shopping lunch," she called over her shoulder.

Elloree smiled, waved, and watched Sally hurry down the sidewalk after the furiously pedaling Annie. She backed the car around, turned into Fair View Lane, and headed home. She felt intensely lonely as she drove the few short miles to Pilgrim Road.

Chapter 5

Tom Randall was spending his Saturday morning in the quiet of his opulent downtown office. Decorated with expensive, heavy oak furniture and oriental carpets, his had been one of the executive offices featured in *Up Town* magazine, and he had been delighted by the distinction. He had selected the fine wood paneling and exquisite antiques himself, although he had asked Elloree to help with the decorating when the new offices first had been chosen. He had thought she might enjoy doing it, since she had so enthusiastically refurbished the old house on Pilgrim Road. But she had declined, and secretly, he had been rather pleased because he had enjoyed doing it himself. He'd always wanted to design his own offices, and while the older Randall was alive, the purse strings were held too tightly to allow for such lavish surroundings. But now that Tom headed the company, things were different. One of the first changes he had made was to move to more suitable office space. For Tom, the company had an image to maintain, and the atmosphere in the Park Street building contributed much more to it than had the old, cramped Mission Road offices.

Tom did love fine and expensive things, but he never allowed his taste (or anything else for that matter) to compromise his ability to make shrewd business decisions. He was good for the company, always bringing in new, aggressive growth. Although much of Oak View's old establishment would always label him a playboy, they had to begrudgingly agree that the Randall Land Development Corporation was thriving. Tom had been one of the first developers to realize that condominiums and townhouses would be the strongest sellers in the coming years. He always had an uncanny ability to change direction whenever necessary to keep ahead of the competition. When other companies were collapsing from dips in the economy, he was husbanding his resources, studying markets, and acquiring huge tracts of land from destitute owners. With small capital outlay, he parlayed the Randall Land Development holdings to cover a vast area throughout the state. Then he set his legal team into action to find ways to change any zoning restrictions that would have prohibited his developments. He moved ahead swiftly, determinedly guiding his company with assurance and discipline.

This morning, Tom was studying a model of a proposed suburban shopping center sprawled on a table before him. He looked at each of the buildings thoughtfully. He would have to see Carl Foster, the head of land acquisition first thing Monday morning. He wanted to get the project underway as soon as possible. He finished writing some notes to himself in preparation for his usual Monday early morning staff meeting that would begin his next week.

"That about wraps it up," he said to himself. "Better head home." He glanced up at the walnut pendulum clock as it struck 1:00. Then his eyes rested for a moment on the photograph of Elloree that smiled at him from its place on his desk. He had always liked that particular photograph of her better than any other. It seemed to capture her allusive nature, holding it still for him for a moment. The soft-featured face was surrounded by cascades of honey blond hair; only the intense, gray-blue eyes betrayed the inner strength that he knew was there.

He stared at her picture, and a rush of emotion surged through him, as it always did when he looked at her. No other woman had ever given him the same feeling of excitement that he felt when he was with her.

Perhaps it was because he would never understand her that she could still evoke such emotions in him. She was his wife, and they had two sons together, but she was no more his now than she had been that first day when he'd seen her in Mark Williams's office years ago.

Tom Randall had hoped to finish off the transactions with Williams in a hurry that day. He had a luncheon date with a very attractive brunette that afternoon, and Mark Williams should have known what he wanted by that time. Williams had had more than enough time to look over the property.

When Joan Mills ushered Tom into the office, a slender, blond girl was standing next to Mark Williams bending over his desk, which was strewn with a mass of colorful layouts.

"Tom Randall," Williams boomed. The blond head came up, and the gray-blue eyes rested on him, and for the first time in his life, Tom Randall felt uncomfortable in the presence of a woman.

"We're just finishing up here, Tom," Mark Williams said good-naturedly. "You don't mind if we finish off. Then Elloree can get this rolling. Excuse me, Elloree Prince, this is Tom Randall."

Again her gaze penetrated him, and then she smiled and the look of challenging defiance gave way to warm, sparkling humor.

"It's nice to meet you, Mr. Randall," she said without meaning it at all and turned back to the drawings. "How about this one?" She was all business as she held up a design. "What do you think, Mark? I think the kid is a little big in the foreground." With quick strokes of her pen, she sketched a rendering on a plain piece of poster board. "That's better, don't you think? Now more color up in the corner. A good line or two to go with it, and what do you think, Mark? Is that a birthday card or isn't it?"

"Great," he consented. "We'll sell a million of 'em!"

They laughed together, and Tom Randall felt a rush of unreasonable jealousy for the obvious relaxed teamwork they shared. Watching them work together in even those few minutes, he sensed the rapport that existed between them. They fit together like parts of a perfectly designed machine.

Then she was moving past the office chair where Tom sat waiting for them to finish. She hesitated only a moment. "It was nice meeting you, Mr. Randall. I hope we haven't detained your business too long."

Awkwardly, he scrambled to his feet. "A pleasure meeting you, Elloree."

She darted him a glance, a look of disapproval that he had presumed to use her first name.

Then she was gone, and turning back to Mark Williams, he remarked, "Striking girl."

Mark's lined face hardened, and he answered softly, "She belongs to Wishes. She makes Wishes run like clockwork, one fabulous design after another. Did you bring those papers I wanted to look over before we go to escrow on the deal?" He changed the subject abruptly back to their pending business.

Chapter 6

TOM HAD CALLED ELLOREE EVERY day for two weeks after that first meeting. Finally, she'd consented to meet him for lunch at the newly renovated downtown François restaurant.

In the beginning, Tom Randall told himself he was just accepting another female challenge. It was a new experience for him to feel ill at ease in the company of a woman, bewildering and irritating. Women always had been easy for him to handle. As a wealthy bachelor, Tom knew all the most sophisticated nightclubs in town and the darkest dives as well. Polished manners and smooth flattery usually got him what he wanted from any one of his current stable of playmates. Rejection was a novelty for him.

Although he carefully planned every detail, the luncheon date did not turn out as Tom Randall intended. Elloree remained coolly aloof throughout the meal. He had chosen the five-star bistro for the occasion. Any woman would have to be impressed by the intimate dining room, softly illuminated by exquisite crystal chandeliers and staffed by chivalrous waiters impeccably serving delectable French cuisine. Tom couldn't believe anyone could be less than dazzled by the sheer splendor of the place. But to his annoyance, Elloree had ignored the opulent setting, and he had struggled vainly to make conversation. The only time she showed a spark of interest was when, in desperation, he steered the conversation to Wishes and her work.

After the delicious meal, when they finally had left, he'd felt let down with a bitter taste of failure in spite of the superb food. He pulled the car to the curb in the front of the old limestone building that housed Wishes on its fourth and fifth floors. He switched off the ignition, depressed by his defeat. *What a damnable woman*, he thought as he turned toward her.

Then suddenly, she was laughing, throwing back that amazing mane of honey hair and turning sparkling, mischievous eyes on him. "Well, Mr. Randall, did you finally prove to yourself what I'm like. And am I your first failure? Don't pout; you look like somebody just stole your favorite toy." She reached out and touched his sleeve, taunting him with her laughter.

Roughly, he grabbed her to him. She felt his mouth on hers and, for a moment, completely surrendered to the rush of passion that raced through him. Then pushing him away, she sat very still; tears laced her thickly lashed huge eyes. "That's the only way you can understand women, isn't it? Like a toy or game to be played for a time and then discarded for a new one."

He felt the stab of rejection, and the truth in her words cut through him. God, what a frustrating woman. Why did she make him feel so goddamn awful? He shuddered and reached for a cigarette. "All right, lady," he said. "Two can play at this." He leveled his gaze at her and answered through wounded male pride. "Sorry if I offended you. I just got carried away for a moment and thought there might be a woman somewhere inside that machine. Guess I was wrong. You're absolutely right. It is a game. But you're much too complicated of a player for me. I just wonder if you even understand yourself." He was suddenly unreasonably angry with her and more at himself for acting such a fool. Hell, if he had taken Carol for lunch, he would be comfortably bedded down in a hotel suite by now. Why the hell had he wasted his time on this irritating girl?

It was an unlikely beginning for a relationship that ended in marriage and children. He thought back on it today for the first time in years. Maybe he should have listened to the inner warnings then. He should have married Carol, like Mrs. Randall had so hoped and planned for him. Carol, from one of Oak View's oldest and wealthiest families, would have been an attractive asset for any man. Redheaded and voluptuous, she was not without physical appeal for him, and they came from the same mold. But perhaps that was why he couldn't marry her. And he had become completely fascinated by Elloree, although he knew life for him with such a woman would be difficult. But he had no choice; his desire for her had been all-consuming.

After their lunch at François, Tom didn't see Elloree for a month, and then their next meeting was quite by accident. He had completely recovered from his damaged ego and was dining at Paul's Steak House on the west side of town. Once a month, he met at that particular restaurant with his old college classmate, Phil Thompson. A certified public accountant and tax specialist, Phil was a trusted friend and a keen advisor on some of the complexities facing the Randall Company. Comfortably married himself and doing well in his field, Phil always enjoyed jibbing Tom about bachelorhood. He frankly wondered how Tom had held out so long, with his mother promoting one after another of the local society daughters. He was about to ask him about the current favorite when he saw Tom staring intently across the shadowy room at the corner booth.

"Somebody from the IRS?" he inquired jokingly.

"About as hard to figure," Tom replied. "Excuse me for a minute."

He eased out of the booth and walked over to where Elloree was seated with Mark Williams.

Immediately recognizing him, she smiled. "Ah, Mr. Randall, you're looking debonair as usual. How's the land development business?" She spoke with amusement creeping into her voice. Wearing a tailored, dark green dress with her hair swept back from her face, she was as strikingly beautiful as she had been the first time he saw her.

"Very well," he replied. "And how's the card game?" Not waiting for an answer, he turned to Mark Williams. "I'm giving a party at the family homestead on Saturday on the twenty-fifth. I'd like you both to come. It's a celebration of sorts," he added by way of explanation.

"An engagement party?" questioned Mark sarcastically.

"Not mine," Tom laughed. "Not yet. It's a special evening and I'd really like you both there if you can make it. I'll give you a call during the next week to confirm it." Satisfied with the impression he had made and that Elloree was sufficiently curious to possibly come, he returned to his tax discussion with the waiting Phil.

When Tom called the following week, Elloree had many excuses. Why, it would be impossible for her to attend the party. Convinced the main one was Mark Williams, he became even more determined that she would accept. At last he decided to gamble, "You really must be there because Carmen Lanz is coming, and I think you'd really like to meet her."

"Carmen Lanz?" He was pleased by the amazement in her voice. "I've always wanted to meet her. I didn't know you knew any artists. Somehow you don't seem the type," she said.

"There you go, always typecasting, aren't you? I'll pick you up at eight. Tell Mark he'll have to escort himself," he added abruptly, hanging up the phone before she could protest.

Carmen Lanz did agree to come to the party. After selling him three of her highest-priced paintings to decorate the offices of the Randall Land Development Corporation, she could hardly refuse an invitation to her benefactors' champagne dinner. The party marked the end of another triumphant year for the Randall Company. Unlike his penurious father, Tom believed it was important to reward his personnel for a job well done. The lavish affair at the family estate offered the perfect setting for the benevolent king image he liked to project. Although he seldom visited the palatial mansion, he did enjoy acting as a host at these corporate parties.

After the death of Tom's father, Mrs. Randall had begged her son to move into the huge, sprawling house, but Tom had wanted freedom from her ever-prying eyes. He had moved out following his graduation from university and stubbornly refused to return. Tonight, although tastefully decorated and polished for the occasion, the house seemed a final mockery of all his father's dedicated work. Built in the senior Randall's declining years to satisfy his wife's ambition to own the most splendid home in Oak View, the house had always seemed cold and unfriendly to Tom. And he avoided it as often as possible but never could deny his mother one of her greatest pleasures—her opportunity to be the reigning queen for the night. Mrs. Randall was playing her favorite role when acting as hostess for all the loyal Randall subjects.

The house stood as a colossal symbol of his mother's triumph, and Tom knew she enjoyed all the prestige it provided. Tom's father had been her trophy husband, and the house was her final prize. Never one for pretense or ostentatious display, old Oliver Randall opposed the construction of the mansion as long as he lived. Although he finally gave in to his wife and built it, he refused to share the enormous master bedroom suite with its elaborately draped canopy bed she imported from Europe. Stubbornly, he set up his own private quarters in the east wing of the house and surrounded himself with mementos from his travels.

Always an outdoor man, Oliver Randall filled his rooms with gun racks and souvenirs from his many hunts. In his later years, he had escaped the pressure of city life more and more, leaving the business to Tom while he tramped into the wilds. Many of his treasures he had stuffed, and they hung from the walls as reminders of the life he really loved—where a man could pit himself against the odds of nature and cleanly win or lose. Mrs. Randall was appalled by his vast taxidermy collection that he so proudly displayed, and the east wing always remained shut off from the rest of the house.

On this particular evening, Tom felt drawn to the vast, deserted chambers, where thick dust coated the once fine wool carpeting and dingy sheets covered the furniture. A moose head protruding from the end of the wall stared down forlornly on the cold, uninviting room. Tom stood staring at the bleak surroundings and remembering earlier years. His mind flooded with memories of his father, a short, dynamic businessman possessed by a dream to build a corporate giant. All of his life, Oliver Randall had remained focused on accomplishing his goal, although he was constantly harassed by his wife's own visions of success. Obsessed with attaining social position, Clarice Randall pursued and courted every wealthy, prominent personality in Oak View. And the acquisition of the proper possessions to reflect her rising station became her lifelong quest.

Tonight, Tom spent the moments before the guests arrived prowling that closed-off east wing, and he felt Oliver Randall's presence. Suddenly, he wanted to surround himself with recollections from the past, sensing similarities between his father and Elloree Prince. Perhaps, if he had really known his father, he could better understand this unusual girl. But his only memory of his father was of a man too busy building an empire to share time or thoughts with a lonely little boy. And to escape the fashionable world that his wife so openly wooed, Oliver Randall had turned his back on her parade of prosperous, well-connected friends. He refused to engage in any of her social networking and spent his hours away from his work tramping through the wilderness. Tonight, the vacant room seemed to echo with the old man's words. "*It's a hell of a lot simpler for a man to pit himself against nature than society.*"

Tom heard a door slam and his mother descending the stairs. His thoughts interrupted, he came reluctantly back to the present. He pictured her sweeping regally down to the kitchen to give last-minute instructions to the swarm of smartly uniformed maids.

Always on stage, Clarice Randall moved through life like an actress giving one glowing performance after another, and tonight, he knew, she would be playing one of her favorite roles. He could hear her calling to him, but he had a sudden inclination to stay where he was and let the party go on without him. He wanted to take Elloree by the hand and leave them all behind, but he knew he never could. With a last look at the empty rooms, he closed the door quietly behind him and went to greet the arriving guests.

Chapter 7

Carmen Lanz was the first to arrive for the party at the Randall estate. Prompt and outlandishly dressed, she appeared alone at 7:30 as the invitation had requested. With short, blunt-cut, straight, white hair and wide flowing black palazzo pants topped by a purple sequined blouse opened to the waist, she was a startling sight. She wore no makeup, and her skin had a chalky pallor, relieved only by a slash of bright magenta lipstick that outlined her thin mouth. She gestured dramatically, lisping slightly as she greeted Tom in a husky, throaty voice. Tom considered her one of the most unattractive women he had ever met, but he was grateful she was there. When he excused himself from the party and went to pick up Elloree, he felt smugly pleased with himself for ensuring the presence of Carmen Lanz. "She may be a free-spirited artist," he muttered to himself, "but she sure as hell knows its money that buys paint and canvass."

Elloree greeted Tom at the door of her smart, uptown apartment with a warm smile. Dressed in a sapphire blue, silk dress that accentuated each smooth curve, she looked sophisticated and appealing.

As he helped her slip into a silver fox jacket, he felt a stab of eager anticipation for the evening ahead. They chatted easily together as he guided his vintage sports car through the heavy Saturday evening traffic toward the quiet streets of Oak View's Mayflower District. Large, imposing stone pillars marked the entrance to the area, and a gently curving road wound into the exclusive hills. Named years ago by the community's founding fathers, none of whom Tom suspected ever had arrived on the Mayflower, each of the streets boasted signposts that reflected the historical past. Tom turned the car into Plymouth Rock Road and followed the winding lane to its end in front of two wide, wrought-iron, electric gates. High brick walls surrounded the property, and a long, narrow driveway lined with giant oak trees was the only entrance. Tom punched in the security code and then switched the car's headlights to high beam as he steered through the blackness.

Rounding a slight turn, he heard a small gasp from Elloree as Mayflower Manor suddenly loomed before them. Fashioned after a southern antebellum mansion, its towering, sculptured columns supported a sweeping veranda that wrapped around the entire front façade. Two long lower wings stretched outward from both sides of the colossal center section of the house. Situated on a slight rise, it appeared even more massive from the approaching drive.

"What a spectacular house!" Elloree said.

"You got that right. It's a spectacle. It's a damn dinosaur. Costs a fortune to heat and takes a staff to keep it up," he told her. "It was the last thing my father built, and it's an ostentatious atrocity, but my mother loves it. Won't listen to reason and move into something smaller. She lives in it alone now that the old man's gone." He shook his head in disgust.

"Well, it is grand," Elloree said to him as a smartly uniformed parking attendant opened the door of the car for her. Immediately, Tom was by her side, taking her arm and guiding her up the wide marble front steps through a majestic portico. A chandelier hung from the stately entry hall's second-story ceiling like a giant, golden candelabra ablaze with tiny crystal tapers that sent prisms of light dancing across the polished terrazzo floor. Somewhere at the rear of the house, a combo was playing dance music, and Tom guided her though the crowds of guests toward the sound.

Throughout the evening, Elloree's charming good humor encouraged Tom. For the first time, he thought that she might warm up to him after all. Discussing art with the lisping Carmen Lanz was one of the evening's highlights for her, and the two were deep in an analysis of Salvador Dali's work when Mrs. Randall gave her son a beckoning glance from across the room.

Tom worked his way across the floor to his mother. Elegant in a pale beige gown, Clarice Randall strategically had seated herself in front of the fireplace, where its warmth gave a glow to her subtly made-up features. She wore an exquisite pearl and emerald necklace with matching earrings, and on one hand was a ring with an enormous diamond set in Florentine gold and surrounded by a spray of smaller stones. The jewels sparkled as they caught the firelight.

As he approached her from across the room, Tom had to admit his mother was a handsome, aristocratic figure. Although taller than his father, she had always stood erect and proud by his side. Blonde and very pretty in her youth, throughout the years she had preserved her appearance with faddish diets, expensive facial treatments, and arduous exercise programs. Now with piles of snow-white hair done high on her head, she looked elegant and far younger than her years. For Clarice Randall, a woman's most valuable assets were her looks and her social connections.

Married to Tom's father after a brief whirlwind courtship, she expected to enjoy the prestige that she assumed his position would award her. But marriage for her had been a few brief years of passion that had faded quickly, leaving her with a hard-hitting business tycoon husband and one son. Isolated from a man driven solely by the insatiable demands of his work, she retreated into the only world she ever really understood. She poured more and more of her energies into becoming more beautiful and desirable for society. She created a lifestyle for herself that was built around grand entertaining, playing bridge, and attending charity clubs, to which she generously devoted her time and money. She provided her only child, Tom, with the right schools and social background to ensure him a successful life and marriage to a nice, moneyed girl from a respected family. Elloree Prince did not fit in with her plans for her son at all. A hint of a frown clouded Clarice Randall's charming gracious manner when she spoke to her son, not waiting for him to sit down next to her.

"Who is that young lady in blue? Someone I should know?" she questioned abruptly.

"Not really, Mother," he answered flatly. "She's nobody you'd know—just the girl I intend to marry, that's all." Immediately he regretted saying it. But her prying always irritated him, and although he'd said it to provoke her, he found he meant it.

Mrs. Randall turned her full, imposing gaze on her son. "What about Carol? You know the Lawrence's have been friends of mine for years. It will be awkward for me," she said it so simply he just looked at her and laughed.

"Awkward for you? God! Marrying Carol might be more than just awkward for me."

He set his jaw, and Mrs. Randall saw the same stubborn look that she used to see on her husband's face when she tried to convince him to attend an opera opening or some gala benefit. It was perplexing to see that same trait appearing in her son. Tom always had been so easy to guide into the right places. Obviously, the girl in blue had some unfavorable affect on him, and she stared across the room at Elloree, already disliking her immensely.

"I'll introduce you to her when I'm ready, Mother. Now let me alone. I'm a big boy now." He walked away from her, knowing he had confused and frightened her.

His mother wanted him to marry into the suitable Lawrence family, not necessarily for his own sake as much as hers. Talking to her friends about the marvelous match would keep her going for years. For the first time in Tom's life, he thought he clearly understood what had driven his father to build the sprawling giant of a company that became the Randall Land Development Corporation and then leave it all to tramp the wilderness alone.

On the drive home from the party, Elloree was relaxed and talkative, and Tom found her warmth and charm engulfing him. They enjoyed laughing over Carmen Lanz together.

"What a phony," Elloree pronounced. "I've never met anyone so disappointing in my life. That just shows how you can't go by what the art critics say. She copies; she doesn't create. I missed her opening at the Fallbrook Gallery, and now I'm glad I did. Thank you for a truly enlightening evening." Her wide blue-gray eyes were fully upon him, and he felt an intense stab of emotion. He looked longingly at her, fighting a fierce desire to take her in his arms. But he knew to rush her now would be to lose all the ground he'd gained, and he desperately wanted to hold onto what he perceived as his newly acquired position.

He only smiled at her. "I wanted very much to see you again. I'm very happy you came, and I hope you had a good time. Perhaps we can make a fresh start. I'd really like that." His eyes caught and held hers, and he hoped she wouldn't shut him out again.

She looked at him for a long moment, and he was afraid she was going to laugh at him or mock his sincerity. But she was very serious when she replied, "I did have a good time, and yes, we might try again, Mr. Tom Randall, if you really want to. Call me at work next week. We might try lunch again, but please not François this time. Some place simple would suit me far better." And suddenly, she was laughing, but this time it was a warm bubbling sound that filled him with happiness. "What a terrible time you must have had that day. Poor you, I wasn't kind," she said.

Then suddenly, she was in his arms, and he felt the marvelous deliciousness of her mouth on his and the thrill of her body pressing close to him. And he knew at that moment he had to have this woman completely; he wanted to possess her very soul.

After Tom left Elloree's apartment that night, he didn't go directly home. Although it was very late, he drove through Oak View's deserted streets thinking of the evening and especially of Elloree, and he promised himself that somehow he would have her. He knew he wanted her more than he ever dreamed possible to want any woman.

During the next six months, the only thing that marred Tom's happy moments with Elloree was Mark Williams. He was suspicious of the relationship between Mark and Elloree but Elloree refused to discuss it. Tom suspected her attachment was as much to Mark as it was to Wishes, but she always steered the conversation away from any discussion of their personal relationship.

It tormented Tom to think of her working long hours at the company with Mark Williams by her side, and he began to build a deep resentment of Mark and Wishes, Inc. Both the man and his company became his rivals. Although he feigned interest when Elloree bubbled excitedly over designing some new line at Wishes, inside he felt a growing hatred for this bond that excluded him. He had no place in it, and he wanted to be an important part of all of her life. Determined to marry her since the evening of his company party, he became more obsessed with his desire for her each time he saw her.

Then unexpectedly, one day a call came from Elloree to Tom at his office. She never had called him at work before, and he was surprised and alarmed at the urgency in her voice when she asked him to stop by her apartment that evening. For the rest of the day, he was worried and had a vague sense of dread as he drove across town to see her. Was she going to break off their relationship? Had she chosen Mark Williams after all?

But when he arrived a half an hour earlier than expected, Elloree greeted him warmly. Inviting him in, she ushered him over to the living room's white leather sofa. "Would you like a drink?" She offered to pour from the decanter of wine on the coffee table before them.

"Yes, maybe even two or three," he tried to sound casual as he accepted the glass she handed to him. "Salud," he lifted his glass and waited for her to speak. But when she said nothing, he could not endure the tension a moment longer. "Hey, I'm here now. What's so all-fired important?"

"I'm going to New York with Mark tomorrow. There is a chance for Wishes to land a really big account with the Wellington chain, and Mark thinks he'd stand a better shot at selling them with me along. I just thought I'd better tell you myself rather than have you find out I'd suddenly disappeared."

A slow, burning rage replaced the alcohol's mellow, warm glow. He stared into his crystal wine glass, turning it back and forth in his hands as she talked on about the trip.

"Mark says our newest line could work into all kinds of other great products if this outfit will go for it. It could really turn the tide for Wishes. It would be terrific to get into that arena. I'm really terribly excited about this trip. Worked up tons of new designs for the line."

She stopped, suddenly looking at Tom twisting his empty glass angrily in his hands. "Tom," she said softly. "It's as bad as that, is it?" She didn't mock him; she just sat there looking at him.

"Goddamn it," he exploded. "You know it is. You know how I feel about you, Elloree. And you just sit there telling me you're going off for two weeks with him." He couldn't even bring himself to utter Mark Williams's name. "You're going to shack up with him for two weeks," he jealously accused.

She stared at him in disbelief. "That's what you think. That's how well you know me?"

He knew she was angry, but he would not, could not let her go. "I've treated you like no other woman I've ever known," he raged. "I love you and want to marry you. You must know that. How can you tell me you're going off with him just like that?"

"So it's marriage, is it? Not just the big conquest anymore?" Her sarcasm hung heavily in the anger-filled room. "I thought we were playing a game, weren't we? Who gets Elloree to bed—you know the one. Isn't that the way it goes?"

"Stop it!" he was shouting now. "Stop it! I'm not playing a game with you. I want more than just your body; I want all of you to belong to me. Can't you understand that?"

She shuddered, withdrawing in the face of his fierce anger.

"Why can't you just let me love you?" he rushed on. "God knows it's all I've wanted for all these many months now. Don't go to New York with Williams. Stay here. Marry me, Elloree. Please." He felt at that moment that his very life hung on her decision and knew that, if she went with Williams, he would lose her.

She sat studying him for a long moment before answering. "All right, Tom. You win. I won't go if it means that much to you. You must know how it is with me—I can never belong to you completely. Still, you want to marry me anyway. You'll never possess me like you do your land, you know, or perhaps like you might another woman. It would be much simpler for you with someone else. But if you're sure, we can give ourselves more time and see how things work out."

"I don't want anyone simpler. And yes, I am that sure. I want to marry you and the sooner the better."

Chapter 8

Tom's Jaguar was parked in the sweeping circular driveway when Elloree arrived home from the Art League meeting. Switching off the ignition, she sat silently behind the wheel for a moment, wrestling with her thoughts. She had made her decision. She was going back to Wishes, and she knew she would call Mark Williams on Monday morning to tell him yes, to get her old office ready for her. *No matter how difficult it is to deal with Tom and the children*, she promised herself.

"This afternoon's outing will have to wait," she muttered, eyeing Tom's car. "It's now or never."

The boys exploded through the front door, long-legged Timmy the first to reach her car. Tugging on the Mercedes' door handle, he complained, "You were gone so long. He took my new dump truck out in the sandbox and jammed it all up." He pointed an accusing finger at Paul.

"I did not. You told me you wanted to take it out there. Boy, you're somethin' else, Tim." Paul stood in the center of the driveway glowering at his brother.

"Okay, boys, let's not start that. I need to talk to your father before we do anything together this afternoon," Elloree said, reaching for Paul's hand.

With his chubby fingers clamped tightly around hers and Timmy bounding ahead of them, she felt a rush of doubt. But once she was inside the house, her determination returned, and she went in search of Tom. She found him in the library with a pile of business files heaped on the floor at his feet.

She poked her head in the door, and Tom looked up from his comfortable leather chair by the fireplace and smiled at her. The logs crackled, giving a warm glow and wood scent to the room. Late afternoon sunlight filtered through the leaded glass windows that flanked the hearth. The library was Tom's favorite retreat in the house. Although masculine with dark walnut paneling and a high-beamed ceiling, the room was warmly inviting when a fire blazed in the big, brick fireplace. Although Tom always grumbled about the poor heating in the old place, he secretly enjoyed its inadequacy, since it gave him an excuse to build a fire on these chilly afternoons.

He greeted her with the special look that came into his eyes whenever she entered the room. "How was the meeting?" he asked.

"The same. Dreadfully the same," she answered, crossing the room to the fireplace and turning to face him. "Tom, I have to talk to you about something."

Hearing the intensity in her voice, he put down his papers and waited. But when she hesitated he prompted, "It sounds important. Let's have it."

As always, Tom got right to the point. He always responded swiftly to gain an immediate advantage. He liked being in control, and his direct approach often caught his business adversaries off guard. And suddenly Elloree's tone made him suspect he might need some leverage. This conversation was not going to be about friends and the morning meeting.

Faced now with the task of telling him about her decision, Elloree felt a rush of panic. It was silly to be afraid of Tom, but again she hesitated for a long moment. Maybe it was not of him but of herself she felt the fear, knowing her decision would change the lives of them all.

Tom would never accept her return to Wishes. After all this time, he still showed signs of resentment toward the company and Mark Williams. It was foolish and unjust for him to dislike Mark so intensely, to feel such fierce jealousy. Elloree admired and respected Mark, but she'd never thought of marrying him. They would have destroyed each other's talent if emotions had gotten in the way. Only by working completely free from entanglements could their genius flourish. They did love each other and always would, but not as lovers. Their devotion to and pride in making Wishes grow and thrive was their love. Wishes was the child that Mark would never have, and it had been theirs together.

Then she heard the sound of her own voice, strained, high-pitched. "I've heard from Mark Williams again. Wishes is finally ready to move into the big time." Tom's jaw tightened, but he sat quietly listening as she plunged on. "They're starting a whole new line, not just cards but gift books, dolls, and all kinds of related products. It's really going to be big, and if it goes over well, it will put us in line not only to go international but even perhaps eventually to take the company public. It's what Mark has always dreamed of us doing."

"Us?" he questioned, looking very hard into her flushed, excited face. "What do you mean by 'us'?" He knew, perhaps always had known, the day would come when Elloree's work would call her away from him.

"I mean, he wants me to come in and kick off the whole thing, set it up for him. It's the career opportunity of a lifetime. The company needs me. Maybe just for a few months, to get it started," she finished lamely.

The only sound in the room was the crackling of the fire as she waited for Tom to say something. *He'll forbid me to go*, she thought, *and I'll have to go anyway*. Suddenly she was angry with herself and with him. "Don't you see I have to go, Tom? And I will go, with or without your blessings."

He looked at her standing before him, twisting her fingers nervously as she spoke defiantly. Those eyes that could be so softly beautiful now stared at him coldly. He knew this time she would leave him completely if he tried to hold her. Perhaps she would anyway, but at least if he let her go easily, she might come back, and he knew he would have to gamble.

He held his emotions in check as he answered steadily, "I'm sure you've given it all much thought before this."

She nodded.

"What about the children?"

The question hung in the air and he knew she was fighting to hide her feelings from him. They both knew her drive and ambition would take over the moment she walked through the door at Wishes. There would be long hours, and a job that demanding would take its toll.

"It isn't necessarily the amount of time you spend with children, Tom. It's the quality of the time."

"Is that a quote from some child-rearing article written to ease the conscience of America's working motherhood?" he spat sarcastically.

"Mrs. Clive is the perfect one to step in with the boys," Elloree rushed on, ignoring his comment. Quickly she outlined her plans, schedules she would prepare to run the household smoothly. She was breathless when she finished, relieved and trembling.

Tom listened, waited until she finished, and then rose from his chair abruptly. "I guess that's it," he said simply. "How soon will you start?"

She stared at him in disbelief. No sarcasm, no attempt to change her mind. And oddly, she felt deflated.

"I'll spend Sunday with the children, make out their schedules for Mrs. Clive, and go into Wishes Monday morning. I'll see Mark, hear his offer, and look over what needs to be done to get started. But I'll only stay a few hours that first day," she said, assuring herself as much as him.

"I'll expect you home for dinner then on Monday," he said. And closing the door quietly, he left the library.

She listened to his footsteps as he went down the hall to the playroom, and she heard the children's muffled voices calling out to him. She sank into a chair, relieved to be alone and suddenly very tired. The fire had burned down to smoldering embers, and the afternoon light was fading. Monday morning, Wishes, Mark. It all seemed unreal, but the chill that swept through her wasn't just from the coldness of the room.

"He'll never accept it—no matter what he says now. And it won't be the same for any of us," she whispered into the shadowy dusk.

Chapter 9

A satisfied smile spread across Aggie Marsh's perfectly made-up face. Elloree Randall had submitted her resignation to the Art League, and with the news, Aggie's ordinary morning turned into a day filled with promise. Sally Wagoner's call was a welcome surprise.

"Back to work?" Aggie shrilled with disgust and triumph in her voice. "I always knew there was something depressingly common about her. What about Tom? He'll never agree to that, nor will old Mrs. Randall. I give that marriage about six months at the most," she purred.

All the malice she had felt for Elloree for so long and stifled because of Mrs. Randall senior's influential social affiliations now could pour out. Aggie would enjoy spreading and elaborating this story. Already her mind was working to weave a much more titillating tale than just going back to work. She would arrange a luncheon at the country club with Sandy Waters and Cathy Fisher to get the rumors started.

For years, Aggie Marsh had resented all of the Randalls, especially Elloree. To her, Tom Randall would always be just a rich man's playboy son who'd inherited the family business. But somehow, he had turned it into a huge financial success. Tom Randall should have failed and had to struggle, like Aggie's own husband, Gerald, whose poor decisions and weak management had almost bankrupt Marsh Enterprises.

"Not fair, not right," Aggie muttered aloud as she jerked a stylish outfit from her closet and began dressing for her luncheon. "All that money and every worthwhile social connection just because she married a Randall. Not fair. Not fair." Then she smiled, reminding herself of her plans for the day. "We'll just see how old Mrs. Randall likes my rendition of the 'Elloree Goes to Work' story. By the time it gets to her, it should be really good."

The chiming of the hall clock reminded Aggie of the hour, and this was one time she didn't want to be late. Checking her appearance, she smiled at her reflection in the mirror, gathered up her handbag, and slammed the bedroom door behind her.

Oak View's oldest, most exclusive country club was located at the far east end of town. A small, unpretentious, bronze placard marked the entrance to the club grounds. A long oak tree-lined drive wound up from the main road. A velvet green golf course spread off to the right with a pool and clay tennis courts to the left. Spacious lawns, lush gardens, and outdoor dining patios surrounded the club's restaurant facilities.

Established before the turn of the century, the Oak View Country Club's membership still depended more on birth and family than bank accounts. Aggie felt the same smug sense of pride she always experienced when she turned her cobalt blue Lincoln into the club's driveway. She found it very satisfying belonging here, since only the most influential and old-moneyed families could be found listed in the membership roster. Just last month, the board of directors had met and rejected the club's latest applicant, a Jewish doctor who had recently purchased one of Oak View's largest estates. Although Dr. Bersteirn had been assured a place on the club's waiting list, he was sure to tire of the wait and join the many others at the brassy new Colony Club on the outskirts of town.

Cruising toward the parking lot behind the grand old colonial style buildings that housed the club's offices, dining, and meeting rooms,

Aggie shuddered with disgust. The spaces were filled with shiny new Mercedes, BMWs and an occasional Rolls Royce. Her Lincoln was at least four years old now, and Gerald had flatly refused to get her a new car. Patiently he had explained the precarious financial position of Marsh Industries and why purchasing any other vehicle this year was simply impossible. He had finished by reminding her that club dues and school tuitions were going up, as well as everything else that contributed to their gracious style of living.

No amount of nagging on Aggie's part had done any good. Although for years Gerald Marsh had given into her, this time he had to hold out. Lately, he was spending much longer days at the company and after hours trying to unwind in the bar across the street. Gerald Marsh had developed heavy lines, sagging jowls, and dark circles under his eyes. His once smooth-faced, prosperous appearance had disappeared, and he looked much older than his years. The strain of holding Marsh Industries together was showing, and it disgusted Aggie. She hated the business. "Nothing but a grubby plant filled with dirty, oily machines and smelly workers," she muttered aloud as she slowed her car "He's always down there, for all the good it does me," she said bitterly, pulling into a parking space beside a burgundy Mercedes 450SL.

Opening her car door, she grimaced as she looked at the sleek imports on either side of her aging Lincoln. "Damn him," she hissed. "He's so tight." But then catching sight of her two friends approaching, she brightened, remembering the purpose of their meeting.

With her chic, feather-cut, ash-blond hair and dressed in a royal blue pantsuit, Aggie looked stunning when she greeted Sandy Waters and Cathy Fisher at the club's entrance. Her guests smiled warmly, anticipating an entertaining and informative luncheon as they walked through the spacious lobby.

Aware of the appreciative glances that followed them, the three attractive young women crossed to the club's main dining room. With its soft beiges accented by deep rose tones contrasted by antique walnut furniture, the room had an elegant but inviting atmosphere.

Once settled at her favorite table by a window overlooking the manicured first tee, Aggie ordered white wine for them. Scanning the fairway below, she suddenly caught a glimpse of Brian Coleman, golf clubs slung across his shoulder, striding toward the men's locker room. Perhaps if her timing was right, after lunch she could manage to run into him.

Tall, muscular with dark wavy hair and an impeccably trimmed moustache, Brian was a top insurance salesman for Crowes and Broad Life. The company founders encouraged their key salesmen to use the club facilities for business luncheons and dinners. They knew the value of a game of golf in closing a deal. Many millions in insurance had been sold between Oak View's first and eighteenth tee. Brian lunched at the club at least once a week and Aggie had seen him only last Wednesday. They had accidentally bumped into each other; at least she had made it appear that way. They had shared a drink on the terrace, and she had enjoyed his company immensely. She had assessed his charms then and decided he might be interesting. After all, she was tiring of Tony Richards, and besides, Gerald's suspicions were growing. It was definitely time for a change.

A smartly uniformed waitress served their drinks, and Aggie gazed out on the emerald carpet below, sipping her chilled vintage chardonnay contentedly. The day was turning out better than she could have expected. Her two friends were amazed by her Elloree Randall story, and they all concluded the marriage could never stand the strain.

"What's Tom going to do?" Sandy purred. "A husband like that shouldn't be left alone. He's so successful. You know somebody is bound to snatch him."

Aggie winced, feeling a barb had purposely been directed at her own Gerald's lack of success. "Oh, Tom Randall's nothing. I've never thought he had much. Old Mrs. Randall controls things," Aggie said peevishly, twisting the stem of her second glass of chardonnay.

Her guests continued their speculations on Elloree and Tom's marriage, and Aggie glanced across the room to where Brian Coleman was just sitting down with two other men. He looked over at her, a slow sensuous smile spreading across his handsome suntanned features, and she felt an immediate stab of excitement. Yes, this luncheon was going to be very pleasant. After the salad and seafood crepes had been served and enjoyed, Aggie and her friends lingered over coffee.

Brian Coleman exchanged more glances across the room with Aggie, and when at last he'd finished with his tiresome clients, he ushered them outside to their cars. He waved and smiled as they drove off. It had been a very profitable afternoon. He was satisfied that both had bought his pitch for a substantial raise of their insurance coverage. He glanced at his watch impatiently. She should be coming out at any moment and if he knew women, those looks only meant one thing. Damn, he wished she'd hurry. He had an early evening appointment, but there might be just enough time.

Minutes later, Aggie stepped through the door, and she looked even better to him than she had from across the room. She had been teasing him for the past month with chance encounters and seductive looks. Maybe this afternoon he'd get lucky. At last she had bidden her friends good-bye, and he walked over to her.

Aggie watched him approach, her eyes eagerly devouring his trim, athletic good looks. She greeted him, "Brian, what a surprise! Did you enjoy your lunch?" she asked coquettishly.

"Very much. Especially the view." He smiled, allowing his eyes to travel down her sleekly clad, curvaceous body.

Aggie felt a warm tingle. The glow of the wine, the afternoon sun, and his deep, husky voice made her feel pleasantly aroused.

"I've been admiring you all through lunch," he said easily. "Do you have plans for the rest of the afternoon?" He leaned closer to her, and she caught his musky, masculine scent.

"Nothing that can't wait," she answered, smiling.

Brian stroked her shoulder affectionately as he guided her over to his car. "Nice day for a drive," he said, opening the convertible's door for her. She throbbed with excitement as the engine roared to life and they sped down the drive away from the country club.

Their short drive ended at his apartment, high above the city overlooking the valley. Once he had ushered her inside, Brian moved with the experience of an expert. Lovemaking was something of a second occupation to him, and Aggie Marsh was the style and age of woman he enjoyed most. He took her in his arms swiftly, kissing her, his tongue probing her eagerly parting lips and then drew her into the bedroom.

Aggie had never met a man who could keep up with her, but Brian Coleman proved to be her match. Again and again, she felt the surge of wild passion as his hands and body brought her to the edge of ecstasy. When at last she climaxed in violent, shuddering waves, she lay spent in his arms, drowsy and fully satiated.

He rolled away from her, propped himself up on one elbow, and smiled that same slow, sensuous smile. "Pretty good," he said patting her round, smooth, bare hips.

Suddenly she hated his insolence and pushed him away, tugging the sheet around her.

"Come on," he said. "Don't be that way. We're two of a kind, Aggie. You and I are just alike. So don't expect more from me than you do of yourself. Okay? We can have all we want of each other, but no strings." And he reached for her again. She felt him stiffen and harden as he pressed his body close to her, kissing her neck, stroking her thighs, and sliding his hand between her legs, massaging insistently.

She pulled away from him and sat up, swinging her long legs over the side of the bed. "I have to get dressed," she said irritably, standing up and reaching for her clothes. She stepped into her panties and impatiently tugged her slacks up over her hips. "Damn zipper's stuck."

He sat up next to her, ran his hand up her leg, and loosened the tangled fabric. He reached up, stroked her back, and slid his hands around to her bare breasts, cupping them; he pulled her back down on the bed. His tongue caressed her nipples and she moaned softly. "Again, next week, lunch and again," he whispered as she pushed him away.

She smiled coyly and teased, "Why don't you call me, and I'll see if I have time. Now let me get dressed. I've still got to go back to the club and pick up my car."

Maneuvering her Lincoln through rush hour traffic toward home, Aggie reflected on her afternoon. The entire day had turned out beautifully. She smiled to herself and checked the time; she was right on schedule. Her children would be finishing their piano lessons, and Gerald would be calling within the hour to let her know what time to expect him.

Chapter 10

Monday morning, Elloree watched the first rays of sunlight slant across the bedroom carpet. She slipped quietly out of bed and dressed hurriedly without disturbing Tom. Although they both had been restless throughout the night, he was sleeping soundly when she closed the bedroom door. In the silence of the warm kitchen, she sipped steaming coffee from a mug as she went over the boys' schedules one final time. Yesterday, she had outlined the week for Mrs. Clive and posted a calendar on the kitchen wall, noting all the dates of the children's upcoming activities. She had given the housekeeper a list of suggested menus, along with notations of chores and deliveries. She finished her coffee and smiled. She was ready for her first day at Wishes.

"Just routine," she said as the boys burst into the kitchen.

"I don't want cereal," Timmy announced. "I don't like that kind."

"Yes you do. It's your favorite."

"Is not."

"Yes, it is." Elloree handed him a pitcher of milk.

Pouting, he splashed the milk into the bowl, flooding the cereal until it slopped over the sides.

"It's all mushy, and I don't like it," he whined.

"That's because you put too much milk on it, Dumbo Timbo." Paul glared across the table at him. "The stuff's floating in it. Mom, Tim's used all the milk and made a mess."

"I didn't. Did not," Tim shouted back.

"Boys, please finish your breakfast. You know I have to leave early this morning." She forced a smile.

"How long are you gonna be gone? Until dinnertime?" Timmy asked, still pushing his cereal around in his bowl. He shoved an enormous spoonful into his mouth and then wiped the back of his hand across his face and down the side of his pants.

"Use your napkin, Tim." Elloree tried to sound patient. "Your napkin," she repeated.

"Whose gonna take me to baseball practice?" Timmy asked, wiping his face with his hand again.

"Didn't you listen at all last night, stupid?" Paul cut in, pushing a paper napkin across the table at him. "You're going to ride with the MacKenzie's. Mother explained it all to us last night. You're supposed to wait after class for Stevie MacKenzie, go to the gym with him, and get your baseball stuff out of your locker and then wait out front for Mrs. MacKenzie. Don't you remember anything, dum-dum?"

"Don't call me dum-dum."

"All right, all right." Elloree felt her temper flaring with the two of them. "Paul, that's enough."

As Tom sauntered into the kitchen in search of his morning coffee, without a word of warning, Timmy flipped a spoonful of cereal across the table into Paul's face. Squealing with indignation, Paul flew from his chair, but Elloree grabbed his arm in time to ward off the punch directed at Timmy's eye. With Paul's arm in one hand, Timmy's in the other, and cereal splattered all over the table, she looked up to see Tom watching from the doorway. His look told her more than any words ever could.

She dropped her grip on Paul. “Clean it up,” she snapped at Timmy. “Then go to your room until it’s time for school.”

She turned away from him quickly, not wanting to see his face cloud up with tears. She didn’t think she could bear to see him cry, not this morning of all mornings. She had promised herself last night that everything would run smoothly today. She had resolved to go over every detail, but already things were in a mess.

Without speaking to Tom, she poured herself another cup of coffee and headed for the upstairs. From the hall, she heard Paul consoling Timmy. Whenever she disciplined one of them, the other always rallied to his brother’s defense.

“Never mind, Timmy. I’ll help you.” Paul was reassuring the sniffling Timmy. “You’ll be all right after school. Stevie’s mom will be there. Don’t worry.” Paul’s voice trailed up to her

Elloree closed her bedroom door to shut out their voices.*My God, only breakfast Monday, and already I’ve failed them.* Disgusted with herself, she impatiently dabbed on fresh lipstick and brushed her hair into place. “I’ll be all right once I get to Wishes. Things will fall into place when the routine gets established. It’s just routine,” she repeated. “Just routine.”

Once behind the wheel of her car and turning out of the driveway, Elloree forced the morning’s breakfast scene from her mind. “Focus on the positive,” she told herself. “Mrs. Clive arrived on time and took over with the boys. She’s capable and great with the children, and they like her. She’ll get things organized in no time. Nothing to worry about. It’ll take a little time, that’s all,” she reassured herself. But a vague sense of doubt still remained with her when she pulled into the parking area at Wishes.

For a moment, Elloree sat in the car, staring at the gray, stone building that housed Wishes, Inc. It looked just as she remembered it, solid, unpretentious, like the man himself. Mark Williams still refused to move the business uptown, although the company now was prosperous. No corporate images would ever concern Mark. *Keep the overhead low, watch costs, cut to the bone, no fat.* She could hear his words echoing from the past. Mark was a one-of-a-kind businessman, and suddenly, she was eager to see him again.

She hurried up the steps and through the wide, glass doors. She pushed the button for the elevator and waited impatiently, but when the doors slid open she hesitated. Suddenly she was uncertain; a stab of fear shot through her.

"My God, what if I can't really do it? What if I can't create anymore or the job's too big for me to handle and I fail? I can't go crawling back to Tom now. I won't," she vowed. The doors snapped shut, and the car jerkily ascended to Wishes' corporate offices on the fifth floor. *"Of course I can handle it,"* she reassured herself for the second time that morning.

Filled with anticipation and anxious to see Mark and hear all his plans, she stepped out of the elevator.

He was in his old office waiting for her when she opened the door.

"Hi," she said, and all the years fell away. He grinned back—his crooked smile that seemed to break his craggy face into a million pieces.

"Goddamn it," he roared. "I thought you'd never come out of that stifling hot house you sold yourself into. Now we can get to work. Make this baby fly."

That was Mark's way of saying I'm glad to see you, you look great, and that's a terrific outfit you're wearing. He was just the same, and so was she after all. She threw back her head and laughed with him, feeling a surge of excitement for the work ahead.

"Well, I'm here, Mark. Let's get started."

"You bet. We're gonna work like hell and love every minute of it, El." He punched the intercom button and bellowed, "Miss Mills, bring me those last letters from our New York buyers and all that background material I put together over the weekend for Elloree."

Elloree shook her head staring at him in disbelief. He had known she would come back to Wishes, just as she had known she would, and it was as if time had stood still for them.

PART II

Wishes

When you work you are a flute through
Whose heart the whispering of the hours
Turns to music …
It is to charge all things you fashion
With a breath of your own spirit …

~ Kahlil Gibran

Chapter 11

Wishes had undergone many changes since Elloree had left the company, and she found that she had a lot of catching up to do before she could begin her real assignment. Each day, she started early and worked past the dinner hour. By the time she finally fell into bed, she was too exhausted to think about anything or anyone. Overnight, her life had become, once again, Wishes and her work.

Elloree was happy to be creating again, filled with ideas, and impatient to begin designing a bold new line. Mark had outlined his expectations during her first week, and she was determined not to let him down. The two of them were always the first to arrive at Wishes and the last to leave. Most of their days finished with a final meeting in his or her office to review their progress and make plans for the following morning.

Three weeks after her return, Mark Williams stopped by Elloree's office for their usual late evening meeting. He hesitated in the open doorway for a moment, silently watching her working at her desk. Her hair was tightly pulled back from her face, and her brow was furrowed in deep thought, but her features were softly feminine, even in the harsh florescent light. She had an aura of gentle helplessness about her that had always intrigued him, but he knew how strangely misleading it was. Beneath that delicate beauty was more strength, purpose, and determination than he found in most men. She looked up and caught the look of puzzlement in his eyes.

"Hard to figure, eh, Mark?"

"Can't get the layout together? Well, it can wait."

"No, it's not the layout. I mean … I mean … me." For the first time since her return, she brought something personal into their conversation.

"Hell, it's not so hard to figure why you came back. No human being with a brain can stand to have their thinking stopped. It was inevitable you'd resent it. I'm glad you finally hauled yourself together and had the guts to get back to what's important. You'll be better off, happier."

"Will I, Mark? I don't know. Sometimes I wonder if I should have come back. I love it so much, the work I mean. I'm shutting my family out more and more each day. They don't have any place here." She spread her arms in a wide arc. "This is my world." She waved her hand toward the piles of sketches strewn across her desk. Her eyes searched his face.

"So, you leave the bastard. You shouldn't have married him in the first place." Mark spoke firmly, quickly his mouth set into a hard line, his chin stuck out defiantly.

Elloree knew it would be useless to deny his words. Anyone who interfered with Mark William's grand design for Wishes had to be eliminated, and he would never understand why Elloree couldn't do the same.

"Leave Tom out of it for a moment, Mark. There are the children. I do love them and I am responsible for them."

Mark's powerful hands gripped the edge of the desk, and he leaned across to her, his features an immovable mask.

"A mistake—the whole damn thing was a mistake. For God's sake, can't you see that, even after these last few weeks? You belong here, Elloree, at Wishes. Don't let them get in the way." His palms came down hard and flat on the desk, sending pencils and pens clattering to the floor.

That's how it was with him and how it had been with his own wife Sylvia. How swiftly he had set her aside when she'd interfered with Wishes. Clear-cut, simple—all that was good for Wishes on one side and everything else on the other. Mark would never allow himself to become emotionally involved with anything or anyone who might affect his work. But Elloree knew no such simplicity would ever belong to her. Her life could not be like his, and she stared at him with a feeling of envy mixed with pity.

Suddenly, she felt disgusted with herself—guilty, selfish—and for the first time in weeks, she wanted to go home. Hastily, she scooped her drawings into a pile, pushed back from her desk, and stood up.

"I'm going home now, Mark. I'll have to work these things out for myself. But I won't let it interfere with my work. We'll be on schedule. Talk to you in the morning."

He put out his hand, awkwardly stopped her, and forced his words. "I'm sorry, El. I had no right to talk to you that way. I know it's a tough time for you." His eyes softened, and he patted her arm gently.

She nodded and walked toward the door. His sudden emotion at once touched and alarmed her, and she would wonder about it for days afterward, but tonight she had to go home.

"Thanks, Mark. I'll see you in the morning."

"For God's sake, don't be late. We've got a staff meeting first thing in the morning. Need your sketches and presentation," he roared after her retreating back.

The old house on Pilgrim Road was sleeping in the moonlight when Elloree let herself in quietly through the back door. She hesitated as she crossed the hallway; one of the French doors leading to the side patio was ajar. She could see the patio's colorful Mexican tiles and tiered terra-cotta fountain outlined in the dim light. A faint scent of jasmine filled the still night air. She had always loved the courtyard. It usually reminded her of peaceful haciendas and lazy siestas in the afternoon sun, but this evening, the sight of it brought her little comfort.

Why couldn't I have been content here, never left them? she asked herself.

As she headed for the stairs, the light under the library door told her Tom was still up. Often on these nights, he worked later than she did. The later she worked, the later he worked.

"Childish. Whatever you can do, I can do. How childish," she muttered and her wistful nostalgia vanished. "Let him sulk in his study all night." She tiptoed quickly across the polished hardwood floor, hoping to avoid him.

Suddenly, the library door jerked open, and disheveled and unshaven, Tom swayed in the doorway. Elloree froze and stared at him in disbelief, stunned by his appearance and the strong smell of alcohol.

"Ah, there she is." His words slurred, and he lurched forward. "The powder puff tycoon. Home at last. How was the office, dear?" he sneered and belched loudly.

"Tom, keep your voice down," she pleaded. "You'll wake the children."

"Christ, listen to that. Wake the children," he mocked. "Why the sudden spurt of motherly concern? You've hardly seen them for weeks."

"Tom, it's late, and I don't want to talk about it now." She turned toward the stairs. His arm shot out to block her path, and she could smell his whiskey breath.

"Well, I do want to talk. Now," he glowered.

Elloree stood very still looking at him, her resentment rising. What right did he have to wallow in his own self-pity, pass judgment on her?

"Get out of my way, Tom," she snapped, climbing the first two stairs. "You're in no condition to talk now about anything."

He gazed out of his fuzzy drunkenness at her. "You, lady, disgust me, but you're going to listen to what I have to say. You're going to stand here and listen to me if I have to hold you. Your children need you. They didn't ask to be born. You chose to marry me and have them. Now you decide to leave us. Just like that—walk out to a more rewarding job," he snarled. "Turn your back on your responsibility."

Shaking with anger and exhaustion, she reeled away from him. "Stop throwing the children at me, Tom. It isn't them that you're worried about. It's you. You can't stand for me to do anything. It's some kind of threat to you and your whole suffocating way of life. Well, I won't be smothered anymore."

For one awful moment, she thought he might actually try to slap her into submission. Instead, he jerked her roughly toward him, forcing her to lean far over the banister until his liquor-swollen face was close to hers. "You're my wife. Tonight, you're my wife." Then with one quick bound, he was standing next to her, and tightly gripping her arm, he forced her up the stairs.

In the soft, gray dawn, Elloree woke and rolled over to see the clock, grateful Tom was already gone. Clothes were scattered about the bedroom, and an overturned glass reminded her of the night before. Slipping out of bed, she shuddered, wrapped herself in a robe, and then went down the hall to the boys' rooms. Both of them were sleeping soundly—Paul sprawled across the bed twisted in the blankets and Timmy curled into a ball like a contented cat. Satisfied that they were all right, she hurriedly dressed for work, remembering her early morning conference. Mark was depending on her, and more than ever, she was determined not to let him or Wishes down.

Quickly, she jotted down some daily instructions for Mrs. Clive before she climbed into the Mercedes and headed across the still drowsy city. As she drove, thoughts raced through her mind. She could not erase last night's ugly scene—Tom's bitter words and angry passion. Oddly enough, she had no hatred for him; perhaps she understood him better than she did herself. Some of the things he said were true. The children were the important ones, even if he did use them to cover his own need.

Still lost in her troubling thoughts, she pulled into her company parking space. Switching off the motor, she sat for several minutes staring up at the familiar old, granite building. Then reaching for her briefcase, she jerked open the car door and stepped into the chilly morning air. *The children will have to adjust, and Tom will have to accept it. I'm not giving up Wishes.* She hurried across the nearly deserted lot and up the steps. Mark would be waiting for her, eager to see her presentation of her new line. And if he approved like she thought he would, she would be ready to start production immediately. A tingle of excitement raced through her as she anticipated the morning ahead.

Chapter 12

THE ELEVATOR GROUND ITS WAY up to the fifth floor, and Elloree impatiently checked her watch. She was right on time but knew Mark already would be waiting for her. She pushed through her office door, dropped her briefcase next to the desk and hurriedly gathered together her portfolio of renderings for Wishes' fall promotions. She had designed a series of cards around one winsome caricature she named Little Susie. After first sketching the curly-haired, blond figure with an endearing, angelic face, she was convinced Little Susie would be a success. She had drawn her in many appealing poses with old-fashioned costumes and whimsical animal friends. She had used bright colors and bold lines on a plain white background. Quality textured stock, simple captions, and short clever verse gave the cards a unique, handmade appearance. Susie captured the universal enchantment of childhood, and Elloree was counting on her to launch Wishes into the international marketplace. She called the line Best Friends Best Times Greetings, and she was sure not a mother or grandmother alive would be able to resist the rosy-cheeked little girl dressed in sunbonnets and petticoats.

But this morning, Susie's perky, smiling face staring out from each layout only reminded her of past picnics in the park and trips to the zoo with her own children. She felt a sudden twinge of guilt as she scooped up the drawings along with her notes for the morning staff meeting.

I can't think about them now," she told herself. "Mark's depending on me. My presentation has to be good. I'm going to need everybody's help if Susie's going to be a winner. And she's just got to be, she vowed as she started down the hall to the meeting.

When she slid into the chair next to Mark, she felt the tension in the room. Already gathered around the conference table were Wishes' top designers and major department heads. Looking into their expectant faces told her how important the new line had become to them all, and she knew each would play a key role in Susie's success.

Mark listened impatiently to division reports, insisting production was lagging and unit costs were too high. "Find some cheaper stock, go out of state, overseas, just get the goddamn cost down," he growled. "And do it fast. We have to be ready with every sample of the complete line by the time that New York gift show opens. We gotta have the inventory to fill orders and guarantee fast delivery—boxed, shipped, out the door. All products, display items, and sales promotions ready no later than the fifteenth. That means T-shirts, banks, calendars, dolls—the works."

His broad, flat fingers drummed the table, and he turned to Elloree. "Okay, El. You're up. Let's see what we're all going to bust our asses over for the next months."

He smiled at her reassuringly, and she stood to introduce Little Susie to the group. As she placed each rendering on an easel next to her, she suggested other ideas and products that might be added to the line. Her enthusiasm for Susie was contagious, and she could feel the excitement growing around the table with every design.

"I've called the series Best Friends Best Times Greetings," she said, concluding her presentation. "I chose that name rather than Little Susie because it's broader and might make it easier to expand and add additional lines later, but it's up to you, of course Mark."

"I like it. Best Friends Best Times Greetings—it's good, very good, and we can use the Little Susie name, too." He beamed his approval.

Nods of assent went around the table, and Elloree sat down, relieved that Susie had taken her first step.

Pleased with Elloree's presentation, Mark surveyed the room quickly. Although he was eager to begin working on their new line, they needed to review the other lines that were already in production. For a moment, his gaze rested on Alex Tenner, who shifted uneasily under his employer's penetrating stare.

"How's that book series coming, Alex?"

Alex Tenner's long, perfectly manicured fingers fidgeted with the notebook before him. Then he smiled confidently. "We're ready for final editing on the lead four now."

"Elloree already approved the first draft?"

The question brought a frown to Alex Tenner's usually smooth, effeminate features, but he nodded, looked over at her, and forced a smile.

"They all look good, Mark," Elloree assured him. "I especially like the seasonal idea. The Autumn Is, Winter Is series. Each book is very cleverly done."

Alex forced another tight-lipped smile.

"How about envelopes? Are we offering them as a gift card book package or individual thin volumes? You were going to get back to me on that the other day." Mark waited impatiently for his answer.

"Envelopes. Bright, multicolored to match the book binding. Like this." Alex Tenner produced a sample and passed it around the conference room.

"Eye catching. I like the logo on the flap," Mark said, turning to Elloree. "You happy with that look? Colors okay?"

"Very nice, Alex." Elloree smiled at him again.

He stiffened. He didn't need her praise. And he dropped his head and studied his notes to hide his resentment. If she hadn't come back to Wishes, this would have been his campaign featuring his own designs, not that bitch's Little Susie. It was what he'd worked his tail off for these past five years. Damn rotten break, having her put in over him to take all the glory that should have been his. He sat studying Elloree and Mark Williams, trying to assess their relationship. Office gossip said the link went way back, but he hadn't been able to dig up anything juicy. Still, he wondered. Begrudgingly, he had to admit she was a good-looking woman and full of talent. Although today, dressed in a charcoal pinstripe pantsuit, he thought she was showing the strain. Her eyes looked tired, and her manner was tense.

She's gonna make a mistake, stub her toe sometime, and I'm gonna be right there—take back what's mine, he silently vowed, his mouth drawing into a thin, determined line. *God, I'm gonna love watching her topple off that damned pedestal Williams has her on.*

Alex shifted in his chair and continued watching Elloree from across the room. The air was crackling now, with Mark barking assignments and due dates. *Strange pair*, he thought, looking from one to the other. Rumor has it she has a husband and two kids. He listened to her crisp voice discussing easily with Mark Williams the company's production schedules.

What the hell is she doing messing things up here for me? She belongs home with a dust mop and her brats. He smirked at the thought. *Maybe men are her weakness.* For a moment he considered asking her out for a drink one night after work—a little wine, some shoptalk, see what slips out. But then, looking at Mark bawling orders, he decided not to chance it without more snooping around. She wasn't worth the risk. Women never were—like cuddling up to broken glass, all of them.

Suddenly Mark stood up, signaling that the meeting was over.

"Next week, same day, same time," he announced.

Like each of them had been jolted by an electric shock, the Wishes staff bolted from the room. The company would be in a frenzy of activity for the next seven days. Not one of them wanted to fail to meet Mark's production goals.

"Teamwork. That's what it's all about. Now let's get Little Susie off the drawing boards," he roared to the already emptying room.

"Have to admire that bastard, Williams," Alex muttered walking down the hall back to his own department. *Drives 'em all into the ground but no more than he does himself. The guy's a goddamn machine, but they all love him for it.* Reaching his office, he flung himself into his chair and tossed his notebook on the desk. Long hours. He was looking at some very long days between now and next week.

Okay, bitch, I'll have to play it your way for a while. No way I'm gonna antagonize Williams over you—not yet. No, I'll just wait, but maybe another jab at the company grapevine might dig up some useful ammunition. Time to call in a few favors, help with the digging. He scowled, reaching for the phone.

Chapter 13

In his rumpled suit, tie hanging loosely around his opened collar, Mark Williams showed the stress of the past months. He sat glaring across his cluttered desk at Elloree. His deep frown and silence told her how unwelcome her request was. Angry and frustrated, he studied her closely before answering. How could she even think of taking a day off when their final deadline was so close? They had crews working around the clock. Of course she had put in long days, but they all had. He knew that better than anyone. The entire Little Susie line had been developed with remarkable speed and was outstanding, the best his company had ever produced. The greeting cards and every related product reflected the dedicated, tireless efforts of the Wishes staff. He and his staff were proud of them.

"It looks like hell for the rest of the outfit to have my key designer and top project coordinator pull out for even a day," he grumbled. But looking at her in the late afternoon light, he saw the signs of fatigue etched on her face. Her usual bright, sparkling eyes and warm smile were dull and forced. Instinctively, he knew to push her too hard now would be a mistake. If he lost her, he'd lose the best chance Wishes had to move into the major markets he had been courting for years. Carefully, he measured his words. "Have you told him about the trip to New York yet? You know I'm counting on you. The whole damn company is depending on us to bring home some trophies."

"Oh for God's sake, Mark, don't be so melodramatic. You'll pull it off with or without me now. The hardest part is done. You and I both know that." She spoke quickly, angrily. "You have what you wanted. Little Susie has been conceived and delivered. She's a reality, and she's great, just needs a few finishing touches."

"Elloree, you know these guys are some of the shrewdest, hard sell sons of bitches in the business." His soft tone failed to disguise the iron will behind his words. "I'm counting on the gimmick of bringing them the artist on a platter to tip the scales. We can offer them whole promotions around you—nationwide store appearances with signings of original sketches to give out to their customers. Build a fan club. I know the public will eat it up, and the buyers will too. But I have to have you there with me to—"

"Sell," she finished the sentence for him. "You intend to sell me as well as the line? You never even discussed it with me. That would mean traveling coast to coast, year-round advertising." She stared at him, her eyes wide with disbelief. "I can't fly all over the country for Little Susie, you, or anybody, Mark. I'm married, have a family, remember? Get somebody else. You'll have to, that's all."

"Who?"

The question hung between them, and they both knew the answer.

"We can't send some green designer to handle those wolves, and besides, most of the artists on our staff are men. We need a woman for this job, and you know it," he said.

"What about Carolyn Miller? Her Ad agency does great promotions," she asked hopefully.

"We're stretched tight now with extra production costs. Hiring anyone else or bringing in an advertising agent is impossible. The people we need to sell are tough and sales savvy. All that they're going to buy is the original—you." He stretched his arms out in front of him, placing his opened palms flatly on the desk, resting his case. For a moment, only the ticking of the wall clock broke the silence in the room .

"Okay, Mark, this one time, for Little Susie. She deserves her chance."

"You both do."

"You mean you do, Mark," she said tiredly. "You win. I'll go to New York. But I have to have a day or two off to arrange it."

"Take two. Take three, but get packed."

Mark Williams smiled to himself as his office door closed behind her. He had won his first important round in his fight for Wishes. With Elloree at his side, he would have those bastards begging for Little Susie. She had said they would go to New York together, but he knew he wouldn't rest easy until the plane left the ground with her in the seat next to him.

Chapter 14

Tom Randall leaned back in his overstuffed leather office chair and studied the face of the man sitting opposite him. The man shifted uncomfortably under the scrutiny of his employer. Carl Foster had been in charge of land acquisition for the Randall Development Company for six years, and never had he lived through a more grueling month than the one just past. Randall had been driving his entire management relentlessly for weeks, and according to rumor, he had trouble at home. But looking at his boss this morning—confident, immaculately dressed—Carl Foster thought it impossible to tell.

But something sure as hell is eating on him. God, I've already spent fifteen minutes explaining to him why that Pine Bluff acreage isn't desirable. Still, Carl Foster patiently tried again. "Too hilly, too remote, just not a good bet for the kind of development you're proposing."

"Don't tell me that. I've seen it, Carl. It's exactly right for us. I want it. It's just that simple. You get it and for a good price. I know that land. I've hunted up there with the old man. It's a perfect site for a mobile home development. It'd be great for retirement people or weekenders looking for affordable housing and country living."

Carl Foster started to protest once more, but Tom impatiently cut in, "Don't tell me that rancher who owns it won't sell. He'll sell if the deal's right. He's ornery as hell, I'll grant you that, but he'll listen to a bargain. Offer him a bigger down payment. Cash always talks to these old guys. They remember the days when a dollar was a dollar."

"But I can't even reach him to talk about buying the property. No mailing address, no phone. How the hell am I supposed to contact him? Old geezer that reclusive won't be easy to approach, let alone convince," Foster complained. "Let him rot out there. He spells trouble. Why not go after that parcel out by Rainbow Ridge? It's in a great location. Some improvements are already in, and I know I can get it for a good price. Already talked to the owners, and they're ready to deal."

Tom Randall held on to his temper with visible effort. These people always knew your business better than you yourself did. At that moment, he wished he could fire them all and go out and tramp the wilds like his father had done. Instead, he leaned across the desk, his manner controlled, but his eyes bored into Carl Foster riveting him to his chair. "Use your imagination, Carl. I want that land, so you figure a way to get it for me. Don't try to sell me on some pile of shit I've walked away from for ten years."

For a long moment, both men stared at each other without speaking. Hostility mingled with respect in Carl Foster's eyes. His employer could be tough and unyielding, but he was enormously successful. Positive, determined to have things his own way, Randall was seldom wrong. And Carl knew to keep his job he would have to find a way to get that land.

"Tell you what, Foster, take a few days off, go up there," Tom Randall suddenly offered, smiling generously. "Look the place over again; study the situation. Take the family, go fishing on the lake, but remember, I'm counting on you to catch that big one I want." The smile vanished and his eyes narrowed, locking with Fosters.

Carl squirmed nervously, twisted a pen in his fingers, and then brightened. He'd enjoy a few days away at the company's expense. He and Janice hadn't had a vacation for a long time, and things hadn't been good between them lately. What the hell? He'd tried to talk sense into Randall, but he recognized the ultimatum. Without that Pine Bluff property, he'd be finished at the Randall Land Development Corporation anyway.

"Okay, I'll take a trip up there soon as possible. Leave the first of the week," he promised.

Back in his own office, Carl Foster sat dejectedly considering his position. He knew Tom Randall would never tolerate his failure to deliver the land. He'd have to find a way. He sat brooding at his desk, examining possible schemes. Maybe he could pull off the eminent domain angle he'd used to get them into Paradise Valley. Get the government boys involved, grease a few palms, and sell the Pine Bluff county officials on a plan for a fairground, a park, or some damn package for the good of the community. Get them to seize the land and then cut a deal with them. "Might work, but geez, I'd need time," he muttered aloud, shaking his head. "And I don't have time. Randall only understands the word, *now*. Gotta be a way." He stared ruefully at his calendar. At least Randall hadn't given him a deadline. "Not a spoken one anyway—not yet," he groaned. "But I know when that guy wants something done, he doesn't mean today or tomorrow. He means yesterday."

Long after Carl Foster had left his office, Tom Randall sat staring out of his office window. He was sure the Pine Bluff property would be bought; his message had been clear. Foster was no fool. He was cunning, hard to like maybe but a master at digging up the right information to persuade stubborn landowners to see things the company's way. Carl Foster would do his job if he wanted to keep it.

Suddenly, his thoughts were interrupted by his secretary. "Mrs. Randall senior on line one."

For a moment, he considered avoiding his mother and then changed his mind, knowing she would only call again.

"I'll take the call," he told the trim, efficient young woman. "Hello,

Mother, what can I do for you today?" He hoped his brusque tone conveyed his lack of interest in idle chatter.

"You know very well why I'm calling you, Tom. This business with your wife is all over town. It's a dreadful embarrassment to me, as well as a worry."

"A worry, Mother? Why should you be worried about Elloree and me? You've never worried about anyone but yourself in your entire life." He hadn't meant to sound so bitter, but he was tired, and it was the end of a long, hard week.

"All right, just what is on your mind?" he asked, hoping to make the conversation as short as possible. He always hated a confrontation with his mother; neither of them ever accomplished anything.

"Isn't there something to be done, Tom? What about the children? I went by yesterday after they'd come home from school. This whole ridiculous situation is very hard on them."

"What do you suggest, Mother?"

"Either tell her to come home and stay home or divorce her. You could request custody of the children on grounds of desertion. I spoke to Sam Grant about it. She couldn't touch a thing."

All Tom's resolve to be patient with her disintegrated. "Just what did you tell Sam Grant, Mother?"

"Why the problem, of course. He's a good legal council, even if you don't like him. He's been a great help to me since your father died."

"Sam Grant is an ingratiating, shrewd son of a bitch."

"Tom, he's my friend," Mrs. Randall said, sounding greatly offended.

"Now you hear me and hear me good, Mother. If you so much as breathe another word of my private life or anything else about me to that scheming bastard, I'll walk out on this precious company that keeps your bills paid. You need me to run this monster of a business. Without me, it'll come down around your ears. So back off." He slammed down the receiver.

Still angry and upset, he jerked open the door to the outer office. "Let's wrap it up for this week, Denise. I want to get out of here," he said to his secretary. And he found he meant it.

But walking toward his car in the cool evening air, he felt lonely and depressed. Going home to the empty house on Pilgrim Road was not going to console him on this Friday night. He slammed his car door, twisted the key in the ignition, and the powerful motor roared into life. The Jaguar screeched as he sharply turned the wheel and headed out of the parking structure for the Oak View Country Club.

Chapter 15

IT WASN'T BY ACCIDENT THAT Aggie Marsh ran into Tom Randall at the Oak View Country Club that Friday evening. She had been trying without success to bump into him for weeks. When her friend Char Miller called her from the club lobby that night, she couldn't conceal her delight.

"Aggie dear, how are you? You'll never guess who I just saw walk through the door?" Char asked and then added without waiting for her reply, "Tom Randall, and he's *alone.*" Char Miller emphasized the word alone, hesitated for effect, and then continued, "I just had to give you a little ring. How are things with that latest friend of yours? Whatever is his name? I can't remember. Oh well, I guess names aren't the important thing to you anyway."

"Brian Coleman," Aggie replied with a laugh. "You might like him. You're such a good friend of mine, I'll introduce you to him."

"Any friend of yours could be a friend of mine." Char giggled. "Don't forget lunch on Wednesday."

"Thanks for the call and the reminder," Aggie said, eager to end the conversation.

It took Aggie only minutes to select a smart, black, silk dress from her wardrobe. Hurriedly, she added a gold necklace with matching earrings and stepped into a pair of strappy, leather, high-heeled pumps. "Finish at the club," she said, shoving a hairbrush and makeup into her purse.

Cruising into the Oak View Country Club parking lot, she smiled to herself and planned her approach. She had waited a long time for this moment, and nothing must spoil it. Brian had been fun for a while, but that relationship had begun to bore her. At first he had been independent, passionate, but now the challenge was gone. And she was weary of his nagging demands. Last week, he had called her every day, pleaded with her to meet him again. Yes, Brian was getting possessive and tiresome. She needed something new and exciting in her life.

Breathless with anticipation, Aggie pushed through the club's ornately carved entry doors and quickly crossed the polished marble floor to the ladies' lounge. She paused before a large, Venetian, gold gilt-framed mirror and studied her reflection, checking every detail of her appearance. The soft, clinging fabric of her dress hugged every curve, accenting her lush figure and her sleekly styled, ash-blond hair framed her face. Satisfied and confident of her appeal, she gently patted and smoothed the silk down over her hips, smiling at her image. A tingle of excitement rippled through her as she thought of what the night might bring. Tom Randall was attractive enough, but much more importantly, he was Elloree Randall's husband.

Tom was seated at the far end of the grill room, nursing a scotch and soda. Thick, plush, rust-colored carpeting; bleached Pine paneling; and comfortable leather tub chairs gave the room a warm, masculine ambiance. Handsomely framed oil paintings of championship golf courses decorated the walls, and a long oak bar stretched down one side. Above the rows of crystal glasses and imported liquors hung the picture of a distinguished, white-haired gentleman clad in tweed plus fours, driver in hand. "Founding member, Colin Smith-Jones, Hole in One, 1896," identified the portrait.

Tom glanced up at the painting. *Just like the old man. Proud and tough*, he thought, looking at the picture and then around the room at the various members gathered there. Usually the relaxed, friendly atmosphere cheered him, and he enjoyed swapping golf stories with friends. But tonight he wanted to be alone, and he was grateful that the others in the room were strangers or only casual acquaintances.

The conversation with his mother had depressed him, and the thought of Elloree working late again with Mark Williams infuriated him. It was Friday night. She should have been home with the boys, even if she did want to avoid him. Maybe his mother was right—he should let her go. But he knew he never could. He still wanted and needed her. She belonged with him, to him. He twisted his drink in his hands; his thoughts focused on Mark Williams, and his jaw tightened. "Never liked the goddamned bastard," he cursed under his breath. "Why in the hell, if she wanted Williams, didn't she marry him, save everybody a lot of misery?"

He swallowed the last of his drink, but the alcohol was no help tonight. He still felt lousy, and suddenly he was bone tired after his exhausting week. He pushed back his chair roughly, but before he could rise, he felt a hand on his sleeve, and a woman's voice interrupted his thoughts.

"Why hello there, Tom Randall. I haven't seen you for ages. How are you?" Aggie Marsh stood by the table smiling down at him and toying with an empty wine glass.

Still lost in his thoughts of Elloree and Mark, he gazed up at her, and then recognizing her, muttered, "Hello, Aggie. How are things?"

"Just fine, Tom," she purred. Not waiting for an invitation, she slipped into the chair next to him.

Even through the haze of the scotch, Tom Randall was aware of Aggie Marsh's flirtatious play for him. She smiled warmly and hung on his every word as she asked about his children, skirting discreetly any mention of Elloree.

He was lonely, and he knew she was waiting for an invitation to join him for a drink or dinner. *Good-lookin' woman*, he thought. *Easy to understand why she has no trouble finding new friends. Well built, nice tits, tight little ass.* His eyes slid appreciatively over her, but suddenly, the thought of an evening with Aggie Marsh repulsed him.

She eyed him impatiently, confident of her allure and his unhappiness. *Perfect timing. Char Miller will always be my friend*, she thought, twisting her glass and smiling at him. Suddenly she prompted sweetly, "You look tired, and I sure am. Why don't we leave, Tom? Go some place more relaxing."

Tom looked over at her, a boyish, slightly intoxicated grin spread across his face. "Right, why don't I get out of here? It's been nice seeing you, Aggie." He scrambled clumsily to his feet and said with finality, "Good night."

Rising quickly from her chair, she took his arm. "My place is closest. Gerald's out of town on business, and the kids are on a school trip. Come by for a nightcap," she coaxed, running her fingers up and down his sleeve provocatively.

He reeled back from her. "I already said good night, Aggie. You aren't my style. I don't like socialite whores, even if they are cheaper." He flung the stinging words at her and stalked toward the door.

The cold night air cleared his head, and his temper subsided. But he felt drained, annoyed with himself for lashing out at Aggie. Slumped in his car, he sat waiting for the engine to warm up, and a sudden wave of loneliness engulfed him. *What the hell's the matter with me?* he mumbled. *I should have gone with her, for Christ's sake. I hate going home to that house.*

Dejectedly, he wheeled the Jaguar around; headed down the dark, tree-lined drive; and roared out through the entrance to Oak View's most exclusive club.

Chapter 16

Elloree spent three days at home with the boys before the New York trip. On their last day together, she planned a special outing for them at Oakfield Park. The morning was sunny and the landscape already dotted with joggers and picnickers when they arrived. Timmy and Paul dashed ahead of her, searching for the right place for their well-worn picnic blanket and lunch hamper.

Breathless and with crimson cheeks, Timmy raced through the trees and back across the grass to his mother. "The wind's gonna be perfect," he panted, holding up his new kite for her to see. "It's a beauty, isn't it? Dad got us each one. He was gonna take us out to fly 'em, but somethin' came up." His small face puckered into a frown, remembering the past weeks of broken promises and lonely times.

At the mention of Tom, Elloree looked quickly away to hide her emotions from Timmy. Only yesterday, she had asked Tom to come on this outing to the park with them, but he had refused, using his work as an excuse. She had hoped to have a chance to talk to him in a more relaxed environment. Lately, they had settled into a world of silent acceptance, both of them coming and going from their work, seldom exchanging more than a few words. Their times together were awkward, strained, and Elloree even had considered moving into an apartment. But the thought of leaving the children was unbearable, and she clung to the hope that soon they would all begin to accept the changes in their lives.

"Here's the best spot, Mom," called Paul, standing beneath the leafy branches of a towering elm tree. "Let's put our stuff down here."

"I wanna be over there, next to the slide," Timmy whined, pointing to a cluster of picnic tables across the park.

More contrary than usual these last weeks, Timmy argued over everything. Often, he burst into tears or lashed out verbally to get his way and then sulked for hours if he didn't. But it was for Paul that Elloree felt the most concern. Paul had always kept things inside himself, but lately, he was spending long hours in his room alone with his books and music. He showed less and less interest in his school activities and his friends. Whenever Elloree tried to talk to him, he withdrew into a stony faced silence.

Today as she looked at Timmy pouting petulantly and Paul scowling sullenly, she found herself praying silently for some miracle to bring back their laughter. She desperately hoped the bright, sunny day here in the park would somehow magically bring smiles to their cloudy faces.

"I think we'd better stay here under this shady tree, Tim. By noon, the sun is going to be too warm over there, and besides, there are too many people by the play equipment," she overruled him.

"Oh, okay." Timmy begrudgingly gave way. "Let Paul have his way as usual." He scowled, kicking a pile of dead leaves toward his brother.

Before Paul could retaliate, Elloree quickly intervened, determined not to let their bickering ruin the day before it even got started. "Paul, spread out the blanket, please. And, Tim, put the lunch basket over there," she said firmly, ending the debate. "Now you can go over to the swings and slides, Tim, if you want to."

His recent anger forgotten, Timmy dashed shrieking across the park toward the play equipment. "See ya later, Paul dork." His gleeful shouts floated back after him.

Paul plopped down on the blanket and stared after his retreating brother. Sitting down next to him, Elloree reached for his hand to draw him closer, but he edged away. Fumbling with the folds of the blanket, he sat silently, looking across the park where Timmy was already perched atop the highest slide.

"Would you like an apple now? Or would you rather wait till lunch?" Elloree opened the conversation, suddenly feeling awkward with her own son.

"I'll wait."

Patiently she tried again. "How have you been doing in Miss Wilson's class these past few weeks?"

Paul usually liked to talk about his schoolwork, enjoyed discussing his assignments and class activities, but this morning he answered shortly. "Everything's okay, I guess."

"How did your book report turn out?" she continued to try.

He looked at her inquiringly, "Which one?"

"You know, the one on the history of California and the gold rush days."

"I did that weeks ago. I got an A."

Weeks ago—the words hung in the air between them. It had been weeks since she had taken the time to ask about his school life.

But it was Paul's next words that caught her completely off guard. "What's going to happen, Mom? Are you and Dad going to stay together or what?" He raised his eyes and peered intently at her.

She wanted to turn away from the anguish she saw on his troubled young face, but she knew she had to answer him as truthfully as she could. "I don't know, Paul. I honestly don't know right now."

"Why did you go back to work and leave us?" he persisted. "Don't you want to be our mother anymore?"

Stung by his words, she could only stare at him for a moment, unable to speak. He looked so miserable, young, and vulnerable, unable to understand why his life had so suddenly changed. She reached out to pull him toward her, but he jerked away.

"I'll always be your mother, Paul. I love you very much. You're very important to me. Both you and Timmy are."

"Then why don't you stay home with us?" he shouted angrily. "Why did you go back to Wishes? Wishes is a stupid name for a company anyway. Wishes don't come true. It's dumb to make 'em. You aren't coming back no matter how hard I wish." Then he was up, running across the grass to join his brother, and tears burned her eyes as she watched him go.

During lunch, both of the boys seemed more the sons she remembered. Laughing and joking together, they devoured their sandwiches. Munching on handfuls of Mrs. Clive's home-baked cookies, they talked about flying their new kites. They had saved this event for last because the afternoon breezes were always more blustery and bound to send their kites higher.

"Shall we try to get two up or just work with one?" she asked.

"Two, Mom. Let's do two," they both squealed with excitement.

"Let's have a race to see who can get his up fastest," Timmy suggested impishly, knowing his long legs would give him a distinct advantage.

"No way," countered Paul. "I'm not racing you."

"We'll all have an ice cream afterward no matter who gets his kite up first," Elloree promised.

"Double scoop chocolate," Timmy chimed.

"If that's what you want," she answered. "Now you two better split up. We don't want any collisions in the air or on the ground." She wanted this day to end happily, not with broken kites and tearful boys.

Timmy was off at a run for the wide clearing beyond the trees, shouting back to them, "I still bet I can get mine up first."

Paul turned to his mother. "I'm not going to race him," he said disdainfully. And then added with a sheepish grin, "What's the use? I wouldn't win anyway."

Laughing, she pulled him to her, hugging him tightly. And this time, he didn't pull away. "I'm so glad you're my son and we're here today," she said, folding her arms around him.

"Me too, Mom," he said, hugging her back.

Then he was racing across the park, his chubby legs pumping like pistons with the brightly colored kite bobbing along behind him.

Had there been a race, Timmy would have won. It wasn't any time before his yellow and red kite was a soaring speck in the sky, and with Elloree's help, finally Paul had his up too. Paul was smiling happily as they walked together, letting out the string carefully and playing it back and forth to avoid the treetops. The clear, blue sky sprinkled with puffy white clouds and the stiff breeze made it a perfect day for boys and kites.

"Look at all the clouds, Mom. Gosh, they're lucky to be just floating around up there. My kite gets to fly, but it's gotta come down 'cause it's on a string. I guess only the clouds are ever really free. Do you think so, Mom?"

She smiled at him. "I think you may be right, Paul."

"I think it'd be nice to be a cloud. Don't you, Mom? Do you ever wish you could be something different? I do." His flushed young face turned earnestly toward her.

"Yes, sometimes I think it'd be nice, but I'm afraid we're all a little bit like your kite. We have our own strings. You just can't always see them because they're in our hearts."

A sudden gust of strong air caught the tiny colorful dot flying high above them and sent it into a spiraling dive.

"Mom, it's going down. Do something quick."

Both of them started to run. Elloree grabbed the string, held it high above her head, and jerked it back and forth frantically, trying to stop the kite's descent. But it plummeted downward, and nothing she could do would send it back up into the sky.

"It's no use, Paul. It's down."

"It's broken. I know it's broken," he wailed as he ran toward the pile of plastic, sticks, and string. He stood looking at the crumpled ruins at his feet, tears rolling down his smudgy cheeks.

She knelt down before him, taking his hands in hers. "Don't cry, Paul. I'll get you another. We'll get one just like it or better."

"I don't want another kite. I want this one. It was special. It flew highest, even higher than Tim's. What made mine dive, Mom? They're lots of others here, and they're all still flying." He waved his arm at the many bright specks bobbing and fluttering above them.

"It was the wind, Paul. Sometimes things happen, and we just can't do anything about it. You did your very best to save it. We both did. Maybe we can repair it," she said, bending down to pick up the shattered kite. "Tell you what; we'll stop at the toy store on the way home. Pick out something else if you don't want a new one."

He brightened a little at her suggestion. "What about the ice cream?" he asked, wiping his eyes and reaching for her hand.

"Double scoop," she laughed. "Even triple if you want. Now we better go round up Tim. Is Candy's all right for the ice cream? Or would you rather go someplace different?"

"Candy's. I want to go there. It's my favorite."

Hand in hand, they crossed the park in search of Timmy and his high flyer.

Chapter 17

MONDAY MORNING, AMERICAN AIRLINES 8:00 a.m. flight 469 bound for New York's John F. Kennedy Airport departed on time. As the sleek jet taxied out onto the apron, Elloree tugged at her seat belt and fastened it securely, preparing for take-off. She watched the two trim, efficient young flight attendants pass through the cabin checking that overhead compartments, trays, and seat backs were in place. Once airborne, she knew she would relax, but the last moments before actually leaving the ground always made her nervous.

Sitting next to her, Mark Williams sensed her mounting tension and patted her hand reassuringly. "We'll be in the air in just a few more minutes, now. What's holding these guys up?" Impatient to be moving, he shifted in his seat and peered up the aisle, as the plane slowly began to move along the runway.

Moments later, they raced down the long ribbon of concrete, and Elloree tightly gripped his arm until the aircraft lifted easily into the air.

"Sorry, Mark, but there's always a moment when I wonder if we're really going up," she said, relaxing her fingers and dropping her hands into her lap.

"Don't apologize. These big babies never cease to amaze me. My God, to look at 'em, you'd never think they'd fly."

Elloree smiled over at him, adjusted her seat back, and settled herself comfortably, now ready to enjoy the trip. From her window, she looked out on a blanket of fleecy white clouds stretching beneath the wings. It didn't seem possible that only yesterday she was flying kites in the park with the boys. But gazing out on the frothy sheet below, her thoughts turned to home. Both boys had seemed happier last night, and for the first time, she had seen a glimmer of hope for their adjustment. But Tom was another matter. Resentful, withdrawn into his work, he had remained in town over the weekend.

That's a problem that no outing in the park is going to remedy, she thought, laying her head back against the seat cushion. Closing her eyes, she listened to the monotonous droning of the engine, and the miles began to fall away as they cruised smoothly toward New York.

Mark Williams sat contentedly next to her. A faint, satisfied smile played across his face as he looked over at her. He had won, just as he had known he would. Her presence in the seat next to him was evidence of that. He had convinced her, finally made her realize what was really important to her, to them, and most especially to Wishes. He studied her resting quietly beside him. Her shoulder-length, blond hair was pulled back, held neatly in place by a wide, tortoise-shell barrette. She wore a smart, black pantsuit; a pale pink, silk blouse; and small, gold earrings. The rosy hue of the fabric complimented her delicate features, and he sat watching her silently for a few moments. He felt a sudden rush of relief, remembering the awful moment in the airport when he thought she might change her mind about going.

"Almost lost me at the boarding gate, didn't you, Mark?" she said, reading his thoughts, her wide blue-gray eyes focused on his craggy face.

"Gotta admit you gave me a bad moment or two back there. Important thing is we're on our way now, and Wishes is on the way with us," he said with satisfaction. "I feel like celebrating already." He leaned out into the aisle to check the progress of the beverage trolley.

Over white wine accompanied by a lukewarm lunch, they talked, mapping out their strategy for capturing the big accounts essential to Little Susie's success.

When their meal trays had finally been removed, Mark stretched and turned to Elloree. "What do you think that was supposed to be? They always give the stuff they serve some damn fancy name, and it always tastes like warm cardboard, no matter what it's called," he said, reaching for his briefcase and snapping it open.

"Chicken Alfredo, Mark. Chicken and noodles," she said laughing.

"You mean that sticky mess under the cardboard was supposed to be noodles. Beats me why these airlines don't wise up and quit trying to dish out some gourmet concoction. Hell, I'd settle for a sandwich and a bottle of beer," he snorted. He pulled a sheaf of papers from his briefcase and handed them to her. "Top one's the first day's schedule. Take a look. We're going to have to haul ass to fit it all into one week. But I'm sure you, we can do it." He beamed reassuringly.

Mark's enthusiasm was contagious, and Elloree felt her own excitement mounting as they talked, drafting their agendas together. When the fasten seat belt sign flashed in preparation for landing, they both wondered where the hours had gone. She had been completely absorbed in their business planning, and only when the plane began its final descent did Elloree glance at her watch.

Paul's school baseball game was that afternoon. It was the last game of the season, the play-off between two tough rivals, and she wouldn't be there to watch him cover first base. She closed her eyes, picturing him biting his lip to hold back tears of disappointment when she had told him. She had promised to call from New York to hear about the game's outcome, but now she dreaded making the call. She didn't want to hear Tom's icy, disapproving voice or the boys' whiny complaints. The sudden jolt of the plane as it touched down pushed the thoughts of home from her mind.

Mark was already in the aisle retrieving their belongings from the overhead bin before the plane had reached the terminal. As soon as the doors opened, he propelled her through the crowds and into the airport toward the baggage claim area.

"Damn waste of time," he complained as they stood waiting for the luggage to drop down onto the carrousel. "I should've known to bring just a carry-on. Change of underwear, shave kit—all I really needed," he fretted, pacing up and down and searching for their bags.

Elloree smiled, looking at his rumpled slacks and sport jacket, but she knew he was probably right. The driving force of the man would make the difference in their success, not his stylish appearance. Minutes later, he had retrieved both of their bags from the revolving piles circling slowly in front of them.

"Can be tough getting a cab in this city, but maybe we'll get lucky," Mark grumbled as they pushed their way through the throngs of travelers. "Can't be shy here," he said, cutting around a young couple dragging two huge suitcases on wheels, followed by three dawdling children.

"Must be hell herding that bunch across country," he muttered as they finally reached the curb.

A battered blue and white taxi nosed in between the line of cars and shuttle buses disembarking passengers. The back door of the cab flew open, and a young man in blue jeans and sneakers clutching a ticket leaped out. He pushed past them and raced for the terminal.

"Hop in, El, before this clown takes off," Mark commanded, grabbing the car door. She slid across the tattered seat as he shoved their luggage between them and jumped in next to her.

"Hey, I ain't supposed to pick up no curbside fares. Gotta get my rides at the stand. We got rules," the driver complained, leaning over the front seat and glaring at Mark.

Mark smiled broadly. "We'll remember that next time. Now let's get outta here."

The driver glowered into the rearview mirror. "Gonna cost ya, buddy," he said, gunning the motor and swinging the cab out into the heavy stream of traffic.

"That it is. It's gonna cost just what's on that meter," Mark replied cheerfully, settling back against the scruffy upholstery.

"This here thing ain't reliable. Sometimes it works; sometimes it don't. When it don't, I gotta figure the charge." The cabby smirked, tapping a stubby forefinger on the clicking meter.

"Fairfield Hotel," Mark said. "I make this run every week, got the miles figured down to the penny—got to, for the expense report." He winked at Elloree.

"Maybe ya do, maybe ya don't. Routes change, traffic, detours. Makes a difference. Ain't always the same." He smirked again, leaned on the horn, changed lines, and then braked so abruptly their pile of bags slid to the floor.

"Stuff should've been in the trunk," he muttered.

Mark smiled good-humoredly. "Right. Like you say. Rules. I'll just bet you've got a tough-ass supervisor with his rules. Customer satisfaction, safety, fair charges. Dumb stuff like that."

The cabby eyed him again in the rearview mirror. "Okay, buddy. Where'd you say you was goin' in such a piss-off hurry?"

"Fairfield Hotel. As the crow flies."

"Only thing flyin' around here is all that shit they're flingin' at us from Washington," the cabby snorted. "Middle Eastern peace talks my ass. It's all about oil and money, man. Them towel heads only want the big bucks, not no promises from no White House jerk who can't even keep his pants zipped. Price at the pump is what keeps these babies rollin'." He smacked the dashboard with authority. "Simple as that; gas goes higher, we strike. Paralyze the whole damn city, whole damn country." His eyes bugged out, and he smiled, relishing the thought. "See what Mr. Fancy Politician does about that."

Mark and Elloree exchanged looks but said nothing, not wanting to encourage the political commentary. For a few blocks, they drove in silence, weaving in and out of the busy Manhattan traffic. On both sides of the street, towering skyscrapers jetted up into the low-hanging gray clouds. Suddenly, a large black cargo van cut directly in front of the cab, and again their driver stomped on the brake, tossing them forward.

Cursing under his breath, he rolled down the window, stuck out his hand, and flashed an obscene salute at the other driver.

"Ain't no courtesy on the streets these days. Cut you off, pile you up. Nobody cares."

The cab swerved to the right and turned into the entrance to the Fairfield Hotel. A smartly uniformed doorman stepped up to the dilapidated vehicle and helped Elloree from the car. Mark leaned across the seat and eyed the meter.

"As the crow flies," he said, pulling his wallet from his pocket and handing the driver some bills. "That should cover it." He opened the door.

The cabby studied the money in his hand. "You got lucky today, pal. Not much traffic, no detours."

"I thought I just might," Mark answered, dropping their bags onto the waiting luggage trolley and taking Elloree's arm. "Nice ride; welcome to New York." He laughed as they stepped through the revolving entry door into the hotel.

Elloree sat down in the lobby to wait while Mark signed them in at the reception desk.

"Two adjoining rooms, sir. Tenth floor." The desk clerk looked over at Elloree and raised an eyebrow. "Luggage will be delivered to your rooms shortly. Complimentary continental breakfast daily 7:30 until 9:30. Hope you enjoy your stay with us."

Some use the separate room routine, some the phony names—silly to think they're fooling anybody, he thought handing Mark the two keys.

"That old goat at the desk thinks I'm a woman of sin," Elloree whispered to Mark when the elevator doors had snapped shut.

"Maybe he's right. You look pretty wicked to me. Better not let him see that scarlet letter you're wearing." He grinned.

When the car stopped at the tenth floor, they stepped off into a long, carpeted corridor and, in minutes, found their rooms. Mark unlocked both doors and handed her a key.

"Luggage should be up in a minute. Then we'll talk about dinner," he said, disappearing into one of the rooms.

Decorated with old-world elegance, each suite had a sitting area and a large bedroom with adjoining bathroom. With its 1920's architecture and reproduction period furniture, the Fairfield had remained, through the years, one of New York's most charming landmark hotels.

Elloree stepped through a wide entry lined with closets into a spacious room with a high, molded ceiling. A small, plush sofa; coffee table; and two comfortable chairs occupied one end, and a four-poster double bed filled the other. A carved Armoire that had been converted to an entertainment center stood along one wall. A Victorian writing desk and polished mahogany dresser with gilt-framed mirror completed the furnishings. From one window, she had a view of the city; from the other, the hotel's garden courtyard. And to her immense relief, she found the marble bathroom was equipped with an oversized porcelain tub as well as a stall shower. She was looking forward to a long, soothing soak in a hot bath to restore her spirits and was about to turn on the faucets when a loud knock on the door from the next room interrupted her.

"Open this damn door, will you. It must be locked on your side as well as mine," Mark bellowed.

She smiled to herself; nothing clandestine about Mark. She fumbled with the lock, twisted the stubborn latch, and swung the door open. They stood facing each other, and he looked down at her, suddenly awkward as a schoolboy.

"Sorry, I didn't mean to bang. Just thought you might join me in a little scotch. It's been a long, tiring day." He produced a bottle and two glasses from behind his back. "If you like, you can have dinner sent up, or we could go to the hotel's restaurant. It's pretty good."

"Yes to the scotch and no to the hotel food. Don't you know some local spot with atmosphere and jazz where a girl can unwind?"

"Now you're talking, El." He poured the scotch and settled into a chair. "Here's to us and that goddamned beauty, Little Susie. She's going to make it for all of us." Mark smiled broadly at her.

After their long flight and the week's many pressures, she knew he must be tired, but he was in high spirits. His rumpled designer clothes hung on him like the sheet of an unmade bed, but he was alert and eager for their coming challenges.

They finished their drinks, and he stood, smiling at her, "How long will it take for you to be ready?"

"Ready for what, mister?" She mimicked his gravelly voice swinging her hips and grinning impishly.

Surprised by his swift reaction, she backed against the wall. His arm shot out catching hers in his firm grasp. "Don't fool around with me like that." The warm camaraderie of the day vanished with his harsh, cold tone. But then, just as suddenly, he was smiling again and apologizing. He reached for her hand. "Sorry, El. It's been a long day and even longer week."

"It's okay, Mark. It's been a stressful time for both of us."

"Just tap on the door when you're ready." He hesitated. "That's if you still want to go with a gruff, old bastard like me."

She nodded as the door closed behind his broad-shouldered, powerful retreating back, and she was left wondering about this side of Mark Williams she did not know.

Chapter 18

The Medium Rare was small, intimate and a good choice for Elloree's first night in New York. Casual, with an appealing menu and live music, the atmosphere immediately cheered her sagging spirits. Specializing in aged beef, fine wines, and mellow jazz, the restaurant was a favorite with local New Yorkers.

"I thought you'd like it." Mark beamed with pleasure over her smile of approval. "Better be careful on these stairs; not much light, and they're steep." Holding her arm firmly, he guided her down the uneven stone steps into the dim, cavernous interior.

Elloree blinked to accustom her eyes to the darkness. Used brick walls, pine beams, and rough-hewn plank flooring gave the Medium Rare the look of an old European wine cellar. Wrought-iron racks filled with vintage bottles lined one side of the room, and a huge oaken keg occupied the corner next to the bar. At the far end on a small, raised stage, a man was adjusting sound equipment and lighting. A diminutive young Asian woman in a black leather miniskirt and stiletto heels appeared from a side door and ushered them to a table.

Once they were comfortably seated, Mark scanned the extensive wine list. "Red or white?" he asked.

"Usually I prefer white, but since this place seems to be known for its steaks, I think the red sounds better."

"There's a Bordeaux from the Loire Valley Vineyards—good year, good winery. Let's try it." He flagged the waiter and gave him their order.

Minutes later, the server returned with a bottle, offering it to Mark for inspection before removing the cork. Mark swirled a small amount of the burgundy liquid in his glass, enjoying the bouquet before sampling it.

"Full-bodied but not heavy. I think you'll like it, El." He motioned to the waiter to fill their glasses. "Two Caesar salads, two medium rare sirloin steaks, two baked potatoes everything on 'em. Okay with you?"

Elloree nodded, and the waiter disappeared, leaving them alone to sip their wine and enjoy the music.

On the small stage accompanied by a guitarist, a tawny complexioned young woman with long, straight, coffee-colored hair began singing a blues ballad. Her rich, husky voice drifted through the restaurant. Seated on a stool next to her, head bent in earnest concentration, her accompanist strummed his instrument. His wispy, pale hair hung about his slight shoulders, and his bony fingers picked at the strings. One narrow, pointed-toed boot tapped to the rhythm of the singer's sultry notes.

Mark peered through the darkness as the vocalist's final plaintive words drifted back to them. "Girl's got a voice, but that fagot guitarist plucks that thing like a damn ukulele. She better look for some better backup if she's gonna take that act on the road," he snorted. "This place used to bring in the top talent. Great horn players, big names. Hell, where'd they get that pair?" He leaned across the table, pouring more wine into Elloree's glass. "Where's that waiter with those steaks? We want 'em for dinner not breakfast." Impatiently he searched the dark corners of the restaurant for their server. "These guys are masters at disappearing just when you want 'em."

"He's coming, Mark, and it looks like he has our order."

Across the room, their waiter was weaving among the tables

balancing a large tray. Mark followed her gaze, watching the waiter make his way toward them. "My God," he muttered, his eyes resting on the couple seated directly across the room from them. "Look over there, Elloree. That's the guy we have to sell, right there."

In the semidarkness, Elloree could make out few details, only a man and a woman talking together over dinner.

"That's Leonard Polouski?"

Mark nodded. "That's him. The man controls the buying for a vast international empire of retailers. He came up the hard way and sure enjoys his power—uses it to make everybody sweat. But even the guys who hate his guts the most gotta admit he's one shrewd, successful son of a bitch. He's almost doubled profits since he took over—a record he's proud of—and he's gonna be a tough sell for us. I know him and his reputation." Mark sipped his wine, studying his adversary.

Suddenly he said to Elloree, "This is a good opportunity for you to meet Polouski, size him up. Maybe get an idea for the best way to handle him. We'll stop by his table on the way out."

She nodded in agreement.

They enjoyed their steaks and wine, chatting about the coming sales meetings, but Mark's eyes never left Polouski's table.

"Don't want the bastard to slip out before us," he said, hurriedly paying their bill when they had finished.

They wound through the crowded restaurant toward Polouski's table. "Remember, no Polish jokes, El," Mark whispered. And she smiled, her tension easing.

Then Mark was introducing her, and Polouski was on his feet greeting them. Although not as tall as he had appeared from across the room, Leonard Polouski stood very erect. His dark hair was smooth and glossy like shiny black marble. Elloree assessed him and his dinner companion quickly. Muscular, in his late forties, Polouski's most striking feature was his steely gaze. His eyes seemed to bore through to the very core of everything and everyone. His hooked nose and wide mouth made him more sensuous than handsome, but with an animal attraction Elloree suspected must appeal to many women. Introduced as his assistant, the young woman seated next to him was coolly pleasant, and Elloree immediately sensed a romantic attachment between the two.

"Lunch tomorrow. Rainbow Room twelve o'clock," Mark confirmed as they said their good-byes and he eased Elloree toward the door.

"Looking forward to it," Polouski extended his hand, detaining them. His eyes brazenly traveled down Elloree's curvaceous figure. "See you both tomorrow." His words were insolently polite.

Turning to his assistant, Elloree forced a smile. "Nice to have met you, Miss Collins. Will you be joining us for lunch too?"

"I have another engagement." Her response was quick, her tone icy.

"We'll make it another time, then," Mark said, taking Elloree's arm and ushering her toward the restaurant's exit.

On the cab ride back to the hotel, Mark was jubilant over their encounter with Polouski. "You made a hit with him," he crowed. "I've never seen the guy so courteous. My God, he even got up from the table to meet you. There's definitely hope for us, for Wishes to score big."

But the more enthusiastic Mark became, the quieter Elloree grew. She too had appraised their meeting with Polouski, and she knew bargaining with him was not going to be easy.

That night, Elloree lay awake for a long time thinking of the incident in the Medium Rare and what capturing Polouski's business would mean to Wishes. She couldn't erase the memory of his cold, gray eyes vulgarly surveying her, enjoying her discomfort and his assistant's hostile glare. She knew there would be no simple dealings with the man.

Finally she drowsed, and after reminding herself to call home in the morning, she slipped into a fitful sleep.

Polouski arrived promptly and impeccably dressed at the Rainbow Room for lunch with Mark and Elloree. He wore an expensive designer suit accented by an imported silk tie and Italian leather shoes. He greeted them both cordially, shaking hands first with Mark and then reaching out to Elloree. His fingers closed around hers, squeezing gently, and his lips curled into an arrogant smile. His steely eyes slid from her face to the curve of her neck and the round fullness of her breasts.

"Nice view," he said releasing her hand and turning toward the window. "Clear day. Don't get many in the city. How long you here for?" he asked as they settled themselves at the table.

"Long as it takes," Mark answered. "We're here for the show, but a week isn't long to do all we've scheduled."

Elloree sat across from Mark and Polouski, listening to their small talk about the show as they studied the menus. All of Manhattan spread out below her, but the sunny day and the spectacular sight of the city's skyscrapers did little to brighten her mood. Polouski's friendly manner and polished image had not changed her first impression of him—hard, ruthless, a man used to making and breaking others. *A womanizer of monumental stature*, she thought, returning his smile and listening attentively to his conversation.

"What'll it be? Drink? Bottle of wine? What's your pleasure, Leonard?" Mark asked, snapping his menu closed.

"Dry martini straight up, no olive."

"And you, Elloree?"

"A glass of white wine will be fine."

"Maybe we should order a bottle with lunch," Mark offered, looking over at Polouski.

"No wine for me," he said. "Stuff always makes me sleepy, and bedtime ain't on the agenda yet." He gave Elloree a slow, sensual smile.

"Maybe we should order our lunch when the waiter takes our drink order," she said looking around the crowded room.

"Good idea. Steak sandwich for me," Mark responded.

"Cobb salad," Elloree added quickly.

"I'll leave the greens for the rabbits and take the steak sandwich with ya," Polouski said, lounging back in his chair and surveying the restaurant. The tables were filled mostly with businesspeople with a sprinkle of tourists and society matrons. But he spotted the sales group from one of Wishes' competitors seated across the room and gave them a smiling nod. He glanced over at Mark Williams for a reaction and was pleased to see a scowl had replaced his host's jovial smile.

Polouski had been sizing up Mark Williams and Elloree Randall from the moment they had met. He knew the growth history of Wishes and how much the company needed the fat contract he could provide. But how much he could expect the transaction to be sweetened for himself was what interested him. If they had a good product, he'd buy big; he'd already decided. He needed to introduce sharp new designs to create this year's look throughout all his stores. Besides, he was bored with all his major suppliers. They always sent the same string of salespeople peddling the same lines, offering the same tiresome string of bonuses for him—fountain pens, booze, girls for nights on the town or just nights, always the same stuff. He wanted a blockbuster product but one that came with some fresh new perks—something to make the game interesting.

Mark Williams suddenly interrupted his thoughts. "Want to introduce you to Little Susie. You'll see our whole display at the show, of course, but thought today would be a good chance to give you a sneak preview."

Leonard Polouski's face was a mask of indifference. Like a poker player, he never showed a hint of interest in any sales pitch. He remembered bitterly his early days as a young buyer for a small retail chain in Chicago. He'd been a little too eager, and it had proved a huge mistake. A long-legged blond with great tits easily maneuvered him into a contract without a take-back clause. His overstocking lost him his job, and he never forgot the lesson.

Mark placed half a dozen greeting cards on the table and continued his enthusiastic presentation, but Polouski ignored the Susie samples and stared coldly at him.

"That's it? What's so special about pictures of kids," he cut in acidly. "Hell, every damn company in the business does kids. Why didn't ya do dogs or cats or, if you had to do kids, how 'bout ethnic ones?"

Mark Williams shifted in his seat, and Polouski smirked. This was the part of the business he liked the best. Make the tough, ambitious bastard squirm, work a little for his sale. Be good for him to know and remember just who Leonard Polouski was and what he represented. A little ball crunching was what these guys all needed—teach 'em a bit of respect for the man at the top. He was about to stand up to leave, but Elloree's soft, persuasive voice made him hesitate.

"Kids always sell. People identify with them. Maybe because we're all kids at heart or would like to be. Or maybe because of childhood memories or wishes—the ones that came true or the ones we're still wishing." She smiled over at him, and the tension at the table eased.

He shoved back his chair, frowned, and then reached for one of the colorful designs. He studied the front of the card for a moment, flipped it open, and read the message. His silence and sullen expression gave them no encouragement. Abruptly, he tossed the card on the table in front of Elloree. "There's a point to that. Gotta admit, kids do sell."

"Little Susie is really quite a unique kid, and so is the whole line," Elloree plunged ahead; her words tumbled out quickly, enthusiastically. She saw a glimmer of interest, and she was determined to make the most of it. Talking about Susie was like talking about a member of her family. Throughout their lunch she told Polouski about how she had first created Susie, and why she would appeal to a large buying public.

Mark Williams watched Elloree's laughing, animated face as she described the antics and pranks they had captured on paper of their creation. But most importantly, he saw she had Leonard Polouski's complete attention.

"So, you developed the line yourself?" Polouski asked. His impregnable scowl had given way to an insidious smile as he listened to her.

"Yes, she did." Mark jumped in with his ideas for promotion, and Polouski listened thoughtfully.

"I like the approach; this meet-the-artist thing's got some appeal. You prepared to travel as part of the deal?" His steely eyes riveted on Elloree. "I represent retailers all over the United States and abroad—London, Paris, most of Europe, as well as Australia."

She hesitated only a moment before answering. "Yes, I'll travel to promote Susie if necessary."

Polouski pushed back his chair and stood up. "I'll look at the whole line. No promises."

He turned to leave, hesitated. "Thanks for lunch."

Silently, they watched him stride confidently between tables toward the door and the waiting elevators.

"You'll buy," Mark Williams muttered to his retreating back. "You're gonna buy truckloads of the whole goddamned line. That bastard is going to put us on the map big time, El." He brought his hand down hard on the table to seal his solemn declaration.

"And me, too. Is he buying me with it? Am I part of the package now, Mark?" she asked quietly, already knowing the answer.

Chapter 19

Mark and Elloree put in an exhausting first day at the gift show. Polouski was only one of the big buyers they had scheduled to meet. They worked tirelessly through the days and evenings, talking convincingly to the stiff-faced, tough sell men and women who bought for the most prestigious national retailers. Working together, they made a successful marketing team, and as the week wore on, sales mounted. They landed large orders from all the major chains, and as Mark had predicted, only Polouski was holding out on them.

Although they lavishly entertained him, guaranteed prompt shipping, and offered extra cost breaks for volume, he still made no commitment. As the week drew to a close, Mark and Elloree grew edgy under the pressure. His account was essential for Wishes' growth and their expansion plans for the next year. Without Polouski's international outlets, their profit projections would be significantly off. Financial targets would not be met, and many of Mark's plant development projects would have to be slowed or tabled.

"He's holding out for something. And we both know what it

is," Mark said, jerking his tie off angrily and slamming the hotel room door. "We've got everyone of the major players but that bastard Polouski."

Elloree sank down into a chair, kicked off her shoes, and bent to massage her tired feet. Even her jaw ached from talking and smiling. "I'm so damn charming I can't stand it," she muttered, wiggling her toes. "Our sales team, aside from ourselves at this show, has reported big orders coming in from all over the country, Mark. Wishes is doing well. Maybe we can live without Polouski." She was tired, bone weary and especially of Polouski. But even as she said it, she knew Mark would never give up.

"You know damn well my answer to that. We came here to get that account, and we don't go home until we have it," Mark snapped. "He's just being an ornery son of a bitch. I know he likes the line."

The telephone rang, sharply interrupting their conversation, and Elloree reached to answer it. "Must be an emergency to call at this hour," she said, glancing worriedly at Mark.

He watched her closely knowing he should leave the room, let her talk privately if it was news from home. But he stayed, pacing restlessly, resenting the intrusion. The last thing he needed now was any kind of distraction for her. She had worked hard, brilliantly with him for the last four days. He couldn't have her upset now when their last big fish was about to be hooked.

"Yes. I'll meet you tomorrow in the Fairfield Tap Room. Noon will be fine." Elloree slowly replaced the receiver. "That was Polouski," she said flatly, staring at Mark.

"My God, he finally must be ready to buy. He called us." Mark was jubilant. "I knew you'd get him, El."

"Oh, I got him all right. He wants me to go with him for a few days over to Bermuda. He says he's done all the buying he's going to do in New York and wants to take a few days off to plan promotions. He says he wants my creative input, the artistic touch he calls it. I guess our order depends on my answer."

Mark hesitated only a moment. "Say yes. Go."

"You're telling me to go?" she asked incredulously. "You actually want me to go to Bermuda with that man?"

Mark wheeled away from the window, his jaw set, his tone commanding. "I want that account. I can't afford to care how I get it." His face hardened, and he glared directly at her.

"So that's the way it is. I guess I'm not really surprised." She stood up and their eyes locked.

"You're a big girl, Elloree. He's taken a fancy to you. So you play along for a couple of days, and we go home on our way to building an international giant." His level gaze assessed her. "Just keep him dangling until you get that order. Then pull out."

"Now who's being naive, Mark? You know he might never sign."

Mark was quiet for a moment. "I know, and I also know you'll do it. Wishes means too much to you. You've put yourself on the line. Your marriage is finished, and it's your life now as much as it's mine. Cheer up. Maybe Leonard won't be so bad."

Elloree felt a cold shudder run through her, followed by a wave of nausea. "What kind of man are you, Mark Williams? I thought I knew you." She jerked open the door and fled down the hall to the elevator.

When the doors snapped shut and the car started its decent she was seized by panic.

She hurried across the hotel lobby and pushed through the wide, revolving doors. A line of cabs stood waiting, and for a moment, she thought of taking one to the airport, running. She wanted to run from Polouski, Mark, Wishes—from them all. The cool night breeze caught her hair, blowing it across her face. Angrily, she brushed it aside and started to walk, slowly and then briskly, shaking her head to blot out the scene with Mark, the telephone call from Polouski, all of it.

Head down, hands pushed deeply into her jacket pockets, she walked through the hotel grounds unaware of her direction. In the distance, she could hear the sounds of the city traffic. The wind picked up, and leaves swirled across her path. Small lanterns that lined the walkways blinked in the darkness. She thought back to the beginning, the wild, crazy days when she and Mark had worked around the clock to build the foundation of Wishes. Then she thought of her crumbling relationship with Tom and Mark's own failed marriage that had unraveled into a bitter divorce. And she knew Mark Williams would never allow anything in his life to obstruct his future plans for Wishes—not her, not anyone.

She stopped by the edge of the hotel's garden swimming pool. Fountains gushed from the surrounding rock foundations and splashed into the dark water.

"I'm just another marketable item. Part of the deal," she muttered. She thought of Polouski's eyes crawling over her and shuddered.

It was a game Polouski was playing with them. Little Susie was good, and she was sure he would buy. The businessman in him would see the potential, and he'd buy, but he'd make them sweat first. She stared down into the black water. How important was Wishes to her? Was Mark right?

Slowly, she climbed the steps to the pool terrace and walked back toward the hotel entrance.

Once back in her hotel room, she slipped into her robe, brushed out her hair, and sat down at the desk. She flipped open her daily planning notebook and wrote in large bold letters, "12:00 noon – Polouski."

A knock at the door interrupted her thoughts. Wearily, she called out, "Who is it? Maid service? I don't need anything else tonight."

"It's the worst son of a bitch of them all," came the rasping reply. "Can I come in?"

She swung the door wide, and Mark strode past her, a faint scent of scotch following him. She knew he had come to apologize, and she shook her head. "Don't, Mark. It isn't necessary. You don't need to say it."

"The damn truth is, I meant every goddamn word I said, El." He stared at her helplessly. "I want that account. It's the only thing between me and what I've been working for all these years."

"I know how much it means to you, to all of us at the company. We'll get it. I won't let you down."

His face broke into his crooked, craggy smile. "Okay, go get the bastard. Beat him at his own game. Sell him so much of Wishes he'll have to expand every department in every damn store."

"I will," she said, catching his enthusiasm. "Now get out of here so I can get my beauty sleep."

At the door, he hesitated, looked intensely into her eyes, and then placed a rough hand on her shoulder. "Go after him, El, but strictly business. Promise me that." His eyes softened for a moment, and a look of tenderness crept across his weathered face. "You're a special kind of woman, Elloree."

And the door closed softly behind him.

Chapter 20

At noon, Elloree waited impatiently in the Fairfield's Tap Room lounge for Polouski. He was late, and she eyed the door nervously, sipping a cup of strong black coffee. *Where is the guy? Just like him to try to add pressure by being late.*

A relaxed and confident-appearing Mark Williams sat sipping a beer at the bar. He smiled over at her, but his encouraging nod did little to ease her mounting tension.

Twenty minutes later, Polouski strode through the door. In dark gray slacks and a long-sleeved polo pullover, he was obviously dressed for vacation. He hesitated, his eyes swiftly scanning the room before spotting her. Then he was standing next to her, his sensuous mouth curled into a smile as his steel gray eyes arrogantly drifted from her face to the gentle curve of her breasts beneath her soft, silk blouse.

"Ready to go? Car's out front. Got an overnight bag or do you sleep in the raw?" He snickered loudly.

"I don't need a bag. I'm not going anywhere," she answered. Although she felt numb and cold, her voice did not waver. "I'm sorry if I led you to believe that I came with any dealings you make with Wishes. I want those accounts, but not that badly," she told him flatly, her voice icy.

"What's the matter lady? Too good for me or afraid you're not good enough?" his eyes flicked appraisingly over her trim figure.

Elloree's face flushed with embarrassment, but she maintained her composure and stared contemptuously at him.

Suddenly, Polouski's wide mouth twisted into a broad grin, and he tossed a stack of papers onto the table in front of her. "Go on, look 'em over," he snapped, impatiently. "It's what you wanted. All there. The agreements to buy your entire Susie line for all my domestic and foreign outlets with only a few minor price changes. Do you want to sign 'em or have your big brother over there do it?" He gestured toward Mark at the bar.

Speechless, she stared up at him for a moment before a wide smile spread across her face. "You really do play a tough game, don't you, Polouski? And it's a game all the way." She shook her head, laughing now.

"Yeah, I play tough, always to win," he said flatly, his eyes glinting in the light. "Won from the start. I knew how far you'd go." He wrapped his knuckles on the papers; his insolent manner suddenly vanished. "You're a talented lady. Stick with your pallet of paints and don't try to swim with sharks. Underneath all that icy efficiency stuff, you're too soft. It shows."

Elloree stared at the sheaf of contracts stacked before her without answering.

"Nigel Harrison from London will want you to contact him. I represent him and bought for his string of stores, too. All the information you need is there." Polouski pointed at the pile and then turned around abruptly, almost colliding with a rapidly approaching Mark Williams.

"Williams," he snapped, "you might be interested in these. Could've bought them for a bargain." He tossed a dozen cards onto the table. The resemblance to Wishes' designs was obvious. "Without her, I might've been tempted, but I want the genuine article for my promotions, and she's it," he said, pointing at Elloree. "But if I were you, Williams, I'd do some heavy housecleaning when I got home. Looks like somebody's stealin' your ideas, and sellin' 'em for a hefty price is my guess."

Mark stared at the designs, a slow rage beginning to burn inside him. "Damn right. I'll sure as hell look into it. And if it's really one of my people, you'll be smellin' fried ass all the way from California. You'll get what you're paying for with Wishes, Leonard, I guarantee it. And I'll be in touch with Nigel Harrison as soon as we get back."

"See that you do," was the terse reply.

Then Polouski was gone, striding confidently across the lounge to the door, where he was joined by his assistant.

"Elloree watched as the two of them disappeared into the crowded hotel lobby. "What a man, what a game. He never intended to take me anywhere. He had Miss Crisp all ready staked out for this trip."

"He bought. Goddamn him. He bought, El. Just look at all these gorgeous contracts." Mark roared with delight. "Just look at this. The numbers are staggering. He's making us his top promotion across the whole damn country and abroad."

Elloree hardly looked at the papers as Mark shoved one after another in front of her with mounting enthusiasm.

"A drink, that's what we need to celebrate." He beckoned to a waiter. "What'll you have?"

Her pale face showed the strain of the past days. "Anything will do, Mark. I really don't care. All of a sudden, I really don't care."

"Champagne, the best in the house," Mark bellowed.

When the waiter had retreated, he turned to Elloree. "What the hell do you mean, you don't care? How can you say that after we've finally made it? Wishes is going to be on the map. We're going to be big, El. Big." He stared at her, frankly puzzled. "You're just tired now." He reached over for her hand and squeezed it gently. He poured a glass of champagne from the chilled bottle the waiter had placed in an ice bucket next to them. "To us, to Wishes." He raised his glass. "And most of all, to you."

She raised her glass and smiled, sipping the sparkling wine and catching a little of his enthusiasm.

"After a rest, you'll be ready to pitch back into it. We'll have to come up with another great line. You'll have to start working up new designs immediately." He raced eagerly on, outlining his plans.

Suddenly Elloree felt exhausted, let down, and strangely detached. Perhaps Mark was right; all she needed was a good rest to feel as impassioned as he did. But right now, she only felt enormously tired.

"We'll get a flight back as soon as possible," he continued. "Our work here is finished." He reverently patted the stack of papers Polouski had dropped on the table. "On the plane, we can toss around some new ideas. I've been doing some thinking myself."

"Okay, Mark, that's fine. But if you don't mind, I'd like to go up to my room now, start packing. And I'd like to go home as soon as we get back." *Home*—it had never seemed so far away.

"Home?" Mark's face clouded. "I thought we'd celebrate with some of the crew when we get in, the old-timers who've worked so hard for Wishes. They'll be expecting us to host at least a few rounds of drinks. I'll call ahead to Joan Mills, have her set it up. After all, something this big only happens once in a lifetime."

"Yes, this is big for you, for us. That's true, Mark. All right, you make the arrangements."

Mark Williams watched her retreating back with a sudden twinge of resentment. How could anyone think of anything but their success right now? Miracles had been accomplished in the past months, and this was their moment of triumph. How could she think of going home? She didn't belong at home. She belonged by his side guiding Wishes. They would return from their trip triumphant gladiators, heralded by the entire staff.

Minutes later, that picture clear in his mind, he made the calls to arrange their flight and the company celebration.

Chapter 21

Mildred Clive hung up the phone and looked over at the boys. Seated at the kitchen table, dressed for school, both sat silently staring at their unfinished breakfast.

Anxious faces turned toward her.

"Was it Mom calling from New York?" Paul asked.

"When is Dad coming home for dinner? Why does he eat out so much?" Timmy demanded.

"Your father has to work late hours these days. And I don't know when your mother's coming home." She frowned.

Mildred Clive cared for the children and was trying to meet their needs, but it was becoming more and more difficult. The boys constantly bickered and complained when they were at home together. Their schoolwork was getting done but with no enthusiasm, and even their once-loved sports programs seemed of little interest to them.

"I don't wanna go to swim practice today," Timmy whined this morning. "I don't feel very good."

"Aw, you're just trying to get out of it," accused Paul.

"No, I'm not. I don't wanna go, and I won't." Timmy's lower lip jutted out belligerently. "You can't make me."

Mildred Clive watched him nibbling on his toast.

"I'm not hungry," he protested.

No matter what she prepared to tempt him, he ate little, quickly covering the untouched food with his napkin and returning it to the kitchen. Even his favorite dishes were rejected. But it was the other one who worried her the most. Although Paul's appetite seemed about the same, he was communicating less and less and spending more and more time alone. On the few evenings when his father had been home, Paul had retreated to his room right after dinner.

Concerned, Mildred Clive had tried to talk to Tom, but he had answered curtly, saying the boys were just adjusting to their new routine. But now with the boys' mother in New York and no opportunity to talk matters over with her, Mildred promised herself she would call Tom Randall at his office. She hated to intrude, but Timmy really was not feeling well, and she knew she should discuss the situation with his father. If the child's lack of appetite persisted, he was bound to get the flu or something worse.

Across town, Tom Randall pushed back from his desk, rose, and paced his office for the third time that morning. Since Elloree's return to Wishes, he had poured himself into his work. He started at dawn, worked late into the night, and often stayed in town so he could return to the office earlier the next day. Today, he was determined to end a yearlong deadlock with the city planning commission over a high-rise condominium complex he had proposed. He had turned his entire legal force onto the project, and Carston Kramer, his shrewdest and brightest attorney, had finally found the loophole they needed. He knew he should be pleased, satisfied to be punching it through after so many months of opposition, but instead, he felt dejected. He had won the battle, but now the challenge was gone, leaving him with the drudge of the actual construction.

"Never used to feel this way," he said, turning his back on his office window's panoramic view. "Couldn't wait to see a building go up. Watch it grow from foundation to finish." He shook his head. "Gotta quit thinkin' this way. Get hold of Kramer. Got a long way to go yet on this condo deal."

The shrilling of his private phone line interrupted his thoughts. Mrs. Clive's call was an unwelcome intrusion, but he listened to her. "Yes, Tim should definitely see the doctor this afternoon," he agreed. "But Paul, a visit to the doctor isn't the answer." He felt a twinge of guilt. The children had seen very little of either of their parents for months.

"Maybe Paul needs some counseling," Mrs. Clive persisted. "A talk with the school psychologist might help. I think it's time to get some help."

"Good God, Mildred, lots of kids have to adjust to far worse circumstances," he said impatiently. "But I'll come home early Friday, and we can talk about it then. I can't make it tonight, but I'll break away Friday. I'll take the boys out for pizza. You can tell them to be ready to go about six. And, Mildred, you were right to call. Thanks for the suggestions about Paul. I'll look into the counseling idea." He hung up the phone thinking he really would be glad to see the boys. A change of pace would be good for him too.

He intended to call the school right away for an appointment to discuss Paul when a knock on his door intervened. Carston Kramer rushed into his office, his usual smooth, placid features distorted with anger. "That lousy Jeff Talen's the roadblock, and I can't move him."

"You showed him the figures? Spelled out our position, what we've already invested?" Tom inquired.

"I did, and if he holds out much longer, some of the others on the council are bound to get into it, take sides again, and we'll be right back where we started—nowhere. If they vote to change the zoning of that area, we're dead. There's already been talk about making it single family only. If Tallen stands firm and the others get on board, you'll never see those condos go up."

It only took a moment of reflection for Tom Randall to react. "Get that Tallen on the phone. Set up a meeting. From what you tell me, we've got to act on this now. It can't wait. Another thing, Kramer. I haven't heard from Carl Foster about Pine Bluff. He's up there to get that going. If both deals fall through, our profit projections are in the tank."

"Right, I'll call right away. Let you know what I work out with Tallen. But I haven't heard from Foster. Don't know about that one." Kramer started for the door.

"Put the pressure on Tallen and get me that meeting," Tom Randall called after him. "I'm not going to let one nitpicking, small-time politician queer this deal or some half-assed, has-been cowboy squirrel the other."

Carston Kramer called at 9:30 that night with the news that Jeff Tallen had finally seen the wisdom of supporting the Randall Land Development Corporation's proposal.

"Those condos will go up now," Tom Randall said with certainty. "We've made a believer out of Tallen. Just took finding the magic number. He'll say the check's a donation for the City Beautiful fund or some damn thing. Doesn't matter how he covers. What he skims is his business. But that Foster has yet to bring in the Pine Bluff property. If I haven't heard something positive from him by tomorrow, I'll have to lean on him harder. Gotta find a way to squeeze that good old boy up there who owns that land. Foster must've talked to him by now and failed to convince him, or I'd have heard. I want to see you first thing tomorrow about this, Kramer. Like Tallen, Pine Bluff can't wait. We've gotta get it moving."

Early the following morning, Carston Kramer and two other attorneys met in Tom Randall's executive board room. Kramer's shrewd, cool eyes met his employers. "I think we've covered all the angles, Tom," he said reassuringly.

And the others nodded in agreement.

"Some of Foster's methods may be a little unorthodox, but he always comes through. I wouldn't worry. Foster gets what he goes after. He stays just between the lines, so there's never anything to question. He'll get that land for us," Kramer said with confidence.

As top legal advisor for the Randall Land Development Corporation,

Carston Kramer begrudgingly respected Carl Foster's success, but he didn't like the man's methods. "One day, that guy's going to get caught on the wrong side of the law," he warned. "And there won't be anything any of us can do. I just don't want you and me there with him when it happens, Tom."

Carston Kramer studied Tom Randall seated across from him at the polished mahogany board room table. His face showed the strain from weeks of hard work. *Funny, with all that inherited money and a thriving business, you'd think he'd be having a hell of a good time enjoying life*, Kramer thought, silently continuing to study the man opposite him. *Damn workaholic, expects everybody to put in the same hours he does.*

"Don't assume it's in the bag, Kramer," Tom Randall barked, tapping his pen impatiently on a stack of files. "Follow up on Tallen. See that he doesn't get religious on us and have a change of heart. I want everything on paper, signed by the first of the week. I want all the preliminary soil tests, surveys, the works done so we can break ground next month. I'm meeting this afternoon with the rest of the management team to get it all rolling. You work on this one, and I'll contact Foster."

Carston Kramer nodded in agreement. He recognized an ultimatum had just been delivered that would turn his next weeks into grueling days.

Late that evening, the two men rode the elevator together down to the company basement parking area. Silently, they walked through the dimly lighted structure to their cars. Carston Kramer watched Tom Randall slip behind the wheel of his sleek, black Jaguar and roar out of the garage, tires squealing as he turned into crosstown traffic.

"Damn funny guy," he said aloud, shaking his head. "You'd think he'd be crowing after winning over Tallen and nailing down that deal." Kramer walked over to his own car and checked his watch. "Hell, another evening buried under a pile of corporate shit," he muttered gloomily and then brightened, remembering his kids would be in bed by now and, if he was lucky, maybe Lois had waited up for him.

Chapter 22

Carl Foster turned his dark blue BMW onto the busy interstate highway and headed north. A flood of pleasure raced through him as the car accelerated with a burst of speed. He'd overextended himself when he'd bought the car. The payments were higher than he really could afford, but he needed a prestige car. The car was an important part of his image. The tightwad company refused to lease it for him. They only provided small economy cars for a few employees. He grimaced at the thought; the BMW was what he needed. So he bought it by padding his expense account every month. He never took amounts that would attract attention, but by reimbursing himself monthly for fictitious lunches and dinners, he accumulated enough funds to make the car payments. "Screw the scrooge company," he muttered as he raced down the highway.

Glancing over at his wife sitting next to him, Carl was glad he had insisted they come alone. She hadn't wanted to leave their son with a babysitter, but in the end, she'd agreed. He knew she'd be grateful to him once he got her away. Perhaps she'd even forget that evening two weeks ago when he'd come in late, smelling of booze and stale perfume.

God, what was a guy supposed to do anyway? Janice just didn't understand; she piled pressure on him all the time. Hell, he needed a little recreation now and then. He deserved it after all he had to pay the bills. Bills, Christ, they just kept mounting up. He shifted in his seat, eyeing his wife. She looked relaxed, with her head back against the cushion and her eyes closed. *Sure hope she sleeps*, he thought. *I need time to plan my strategy*. They rode in silence as the miles slipped away.

The car climbed into the highlands once they turned off the main highway. Grudgingly, Carl had to admit it was pretty country; rolling hills populated by thick clumps of trees dipped down into deep valleys. As they drove, the bright midday sunlight reflected on the water of the many small lakes that dotted the landscape.

Janice stirred beside him and sat up abruptly.

"Not much farther," he said. "Just over that next ridge, and we'll be almost there."

She peered out the window. "Lots of trees, but it sure looks dry."

"Yeah, they've been fighting a drought up here for months," he replied. And I intend to use it to my advantage. Hell, can't expect a great price for a dried-up hunk of dirt. Good timing, man," he complimented himself. *I'm gonna make an offer at just the right time; I know it.*

"I didn't think it'd be so hot up here," Janice complained. "I don't think I brought the right clothes."

Carl looked over at her. "You'll be fine," he said. *God, always thinking about clothes.* Keeping her out of stores and malls was a monthly challenge for him. He'd raised hell with her over last month's bills, threatened to cancel all their credit cards. "This isn't the fashion center of the state," he told her. "Anything you brought will do, believe me." *Besides you won't be needing much*, he thought smirking to himself. He hadn't brought her with him to do any goddamn sightseeing.

"There it is." He pointed down the road to the Pine Bluff Lodge. "Only place up here. There's not much choice yet. Rural, unspoiled I guess you'd call it." He laughed, trying to lighten her mood.

Petulantly, Janice stared out at the Pine Bluff Lodge as they approached. A big wagon wheel marked the entrance to a gravel driveway leading up to the main building, and low, single-story bungalows stretched out on both sides. Carl pulled the car up in front and parked beneath a large sign studded with horseshoes.

Minutes later, the two of them pushed through creaking wood doors and entered the lodge's rustic lobby. They walked past a huge stone fireplace toward the small reception desk at the end of the room. Janice flopped down into a well-worn, overstuffed chair and waited for Carl to register.

Not gonna be much night life in this place, Carl thought as he signed the registration card.

The desk clerk, dressed in jeans, plaid shirt, and leather bolo tie, handed him a large key dangling from a red plastic cowboy boot stamped number 4 and inscribed Gene Autry Suite across the toe.

Impatiently, Carl scanned the lobby. "Real Hicksville," he muttered. "Not even a bar." An alcove with a few wooden tables covered with red-checkered cloths flanked by straight back chairs made up the Pine Bluff Lodge dining room.

"We'll get to the room and then I'll have to check out the town. Has to be a watering hole someplace, and that's where the local information center's bound to be," he said to Janice, motioning for her to follow him.

Bungalow four was directly behind the lodge. It had a split rail fence on both sides of the gravel path that led to a sun-bleached door. Carl parked the BMW in front and hauled their bags up the walk. He fumbled with the key and kicked the door wide. Banging through the narrow entry, he dropped the luggage to the floor and tossed his jacket on the bed.

"God, they call this hole a suite," he said, looking around the sparsely furnished room.

Faded floral chintz curtains hung at the windows, and a threadbare hook rug covered only a portion of the rough plank flooring. A small knotty pine dresser stood against one wall, and a pair of matching nightstands hugged the sides of a sagging, iron-framed double bed.

A multicolored quilt lay tossed across the foot of the bed, and a large picture of a lone cowboy on horseback hung above the headboard.

"Jesus, is that supposed to be Gene Autry?" Carl grumbled. "Who's their decorator? Maybe Randall can line 'em up to do the model units for his project." He smirked at his own attempt at humor.

"It's hot and stuffy in here, Carl," Janice whined, collapsing on the bed. She rolled over, scrambled up on all fours, and reached over to twist the knob of a dilapidated window air conditioner. The resulting tepid blast did little to stir the heavy air. A smell of cheap lilac deodorizer and stale cigarette smoke clung to the room.

"God, open a window, Carl. It stinks in here. You said this was supposed to be their best suite."

Angrily, Carl tossed the boot key ring across the room to the bed. "Look for yourself. That's what it says. This is it, Janice—bungalow four, the Gene Autry Suite."

Janice scowled at him and wriggled out of her pullover, jerking it over her head and exposing her plump midriff.

Carl sullenly watched her, and a sudden rush of sexual desire swept through him. He needed to relax, deserved to relax. He moved over to the bed and reached out for her. She'd been holding out on him since that last argument just to punish him. She'd forgive him now; he'd bring her around. He sat down next to her and slid his hands across her breasts, squeezing her nipples until she winced and turned away from him.

"Not now, Carl. I don't feel like it."

His hand shot out and clamped over her mouth, stifling her words. "You want me. You always want me." He forced her down on to the bed. The springs groaned under their weight as he fumbled with the buttons on her blouse and the zipper in her slacks.

She twisted under him, but his bulk pinned her beneath him. He pulled away her clothing, tossing it to the floor in one quick movement. He entered her swiftly, plunging with urgent deep thrusts until he released with a powerful shudder and then lay still beside her.

Seconds later, she heard his heavy breathing and moved away from him, careful not to wake him.

"Where are you going?" Janice was still lying on the bed with the quilt drawn close to hide her nakedness. "Are you going out?"

She had dozed off and awakened to hear the shower running. Now she was watching him standing over his opened suitcase, rummaging through its contents. Carl shook out a sport shirt and pulled it over his head.

"Damn," he muttered as he tossed one and then another shoe to the floor.

"Yeah," he answered. "Gotta see a guy. That's what I came up here for, you know. Can't just screw around with you. I won't be long. Wait for me." He slid his hand under the quilt, felt her smooth, warm flesh and wanted her again. Angry and aroused, he forced himself away from her. "I'll be right back," he promised, slamming the door behind him.

Janice pulled the bed cover up to her chin, turned her face to the wall, and squeezed her eyes shut to stop the tears.

Chapter 23

GRAVEL SPRAYED OUT FROM UNDER the BMW's wheels as Carl backed and then spun the car around and headed toward the main road. More a lane than a road, the narrow, potholed asphalt ribbon was lined by towering pines and populated by only a few curious squirrels. Impatiently, Carl twisted the radio dial to a local news station, but loud static drowned out the report. Disgusted, he switched off the annoying sound and drove the short distance into town in silence.

"God, how'd they get a place like this even on a map?" Carl scoffed, reading a small placard that boasted, "PINE BLUFF – PARADISE FOUND. POPULATION 875." Paradise found, more like lost. Jesus, some local crackpot poet must be the chamber of commerce out here." Carl quickly surveyed the signs down the single street that was Pine Bluff's town center—a few stores, a gas station, and at the far end, Nellie's. "Must be the local grub and grog parlor," he muttered. "Bet it's a real hot spot."

Carl braked the BMW, pulled to the side of the road, and stopped in front of the ramshackle eatery. With its flat, corrugated tin roof; peeling paint; and rough wood siding, Nellie's did not have curb appeal.

Carl pushed through the creaky, faded green doors that opened into

Nellie's dingy interior. He hesitated to let his eyes adjust to the dim light and then strode across the uneven planked floor to the bar that stretched the length of the room. A dozen wobbly wooden barstools stood in an uneven row and were empty except for two lone customers. The rest of the room was lined with tattered, red Naugahyde booths. At the far end, two shabby pool tables were illuminated by a pair of florescent bulbs dangling from the rafters.

A heavyset, whiskered man stared at Carl from behind the bar. "Can I help ya?"

Friendly enough, Carl thought as he asked, "You Nellie?"

The bristly face broke into a wide grin. "Nope. She was my old lady. Lost her two years ago. Named this place for her, and didn't have the heart to change it."

Carl walked up to the bar. "Amazing what people do for true love," he said. Suddenly, he was very thirsty. A good drink was what he needed. "Got any decent whiskey?" he asked, eyeing the rows of dusty bottles. *Stick to the straight stuff*, he warned himself as he watched Nellie's love pour a double shot into a glass.

"Don't get a whole lot of business this early," Nellie's proprietor said apologetically, looking around the room. "Most come in later in the evening. Name's Mac," he added, sticking out a stubby-fingered paw. Carl winced as the calloused fingers closed around his hand and squeezed tightly.

"Staying in town awhile?" Mac inquired dropping his vice grip. "Don't get many visitors here."

"Out at the lodge," Carl answered, taking a careful sip of his drink.

"Up from the city for a vacation?"

Better get right to it, Carl decided. *Mac's twenty questions might take awhile.* "No vacation. Here to see a guy by the name of Packard, Silas Packard. Does he come in here often?"

Mac studied him for a moment and then said, "Nope, not much. Old Silas keeps pretty much to himself out at his spread. Comes in maybe once or twice a month for supplies."

"How do I get out there, to the Packard ranch, I mean?"

"You don't", was the reply. "Silas don't much like visitors."

Carl was silent for a moment. Twisting his glass around on the bar, he regarded Nellie's proprietor. *Tough old boy, not about to be helpful*, he thought. "I want to talk to Packard. Came out here just to see him," Carl persisted.

Mac peered intently over the bar at him as if he was taking a liquor bottle inventory. "Don't know how you'll do that. Silas is kinda hard to talk to. Sticks to himself out at the ranch mostly. Once in a while, as I said, he takes the truck into town for supplies; that's about it. Too bad ya came out here for nothin', if that's all ya came for. Want somethin' to eat?" Mac inquired, considering the subject of Silas Packard closed.

"No, but I'll take another drink."

Mac poured another double, and Carl gazed around the room. The whiskey found its mark, and he felt better as its comforting warmth spread through him. In the far corner, a couple of men sat drinking and playing cards. He watched them for a moment and then decided to try again.

"How far is it out to the Parkard ranch?"

"Don't matter how far it is; nobody goes in there. Got it fenced, gated, and patrolled by dogs. Told ya, old Silas don't want no company."

Jesus, getting information out of this old bastard was harder than getting a whore to confession, Carl thought to himself. "Well, put it this way, if he did want company, how far would it be?"

"But he don't," Mac stubbornly repeated.

Carl switched tactics. "Where's your phone book?" He looked toward the back where a pay phone hung on the wall.

Mac squinted his eyes and shook his head. "Not in it anyway. Silas, I mean."

Carl considered this latest bit of information. No way to get to this guy at all. *God, this could take months, and Randall doesn't wait months*, he thought grimly.

"When Silas Packard does come to town, does he come in here?" Carl persisted.

"Sometimes yes, sometimes no; it depends."

Knowing it was useless to ask what it depended on, Carl finished his drink and said farewell to Nellie's. Once out on the street, he gazed up and down, wondering where his next lead might be. He hadn't noticed Nellie's two card players leave their drinks and game, but one of them slouched up to him now.

"You lookin' to talk to Silas Packard?"

For a moment, Carl considered not answering, just leaving. He didn't like the man's insolent tone and malevolent demeanor. Instead, Carl nodded and waited for a response.

"I know Silas," the card player said confidently. "Done work for 'im on and off."

Carl carefully regarded his informant. Dressed in soiled jeans, a grimy T-shirt, and dusty cowboy boots, he was shifting his weight nervously from foot to foot. His stringy, brown hair hung over the dirty, sweat-stained neck of his shirt, and his eyes darted restlessly back and forth.

"Name's Dan Lester," he volunteered before Carl could ask. "Done jobs for old Silas," he boasted. "Silas don't mind me comin' out to see if there's work out at the ranch," he added to further convince Carl of his acquaintance with the reclusive Silas Packard.

Carl hesitated and then questioned, "You planning a trip out to the Packard place soon?"

Dan shifted his position and leaned back against the wall of Nellie's. "Well, it all depends," he answered.

Seems to be the standard response around here, but this time it depends on how much, or I miss my guess, Carl thought to himself. "Okay, Dan. Let's get down to it. I want to go out to the Packard place and meet with Silas Packard. You think you can get me there to do that?"

"Sure. Piece of cake. Told ya I done work out there."

Carl sized up the situation quickly. What'd he have to lose but a few bucks that'd go on his expense account anyway? The guy looked shifty as hell but probably wasn't really dangerous, and if he could do what he said, he'd at least get out to the ranch to talk to the old guy.

"Fifty bucks," Carl said flatly.

Shifty shrugged and looked off into space without answering.

"Okay, a hundred. I'll pick you up here. How far is it anyway?"

Carl had the other man's attention now. "About twenty miles, I guess. Meet ya here at Nellie's—9:00 tomorrow morning. Drive out there. Deal?"

"Deal," Carl answered and then repeated, "Nellie's, 9:00. Don't be late."

Shifty grinned. "I'll be here, but you ain't goin' nowhere if I ain't, right." He shuffled his foot in the dirt, nervously kicking pebbles.

"I see Silas Packard or no deal. Payment after I meet him," Carl said.

"Okay, gotta finish my game."

Dan Lester sauntered through the door of Nellie's, and Carl Foster walked back to his car.

The phone call came at 10:00 that night. Carl had finished dinner at the Pine Bluff Lodge and was still listening to Janice complain about its many faults. The interruption was a relief, but the ensuing conversation quickly turned his greasy meal into acid indigestion. The voice on the line was crisp, demanding.

"Foster, have you met with Packard yet?" Tom Randall barked.

"Tomorrow," Carl answered. "The guy's some sort of damned hermit, but I've got one of the locals lined up to take me out there in the morning. Swears he knows Packard, has worked for him. Promised to get me in the door. I'll go from there."

"I'm more convinced than ever that the location up there is right for us. Easy access from the city, ideal for retirement living. We won't have to put in many improvements. Just throw together a few model units, get some publicity going, and do some promotions. Fly 'em up there for a look and buy. You know the routine, Carl. It can't miss, but we gotta get that land to do it. Call you tomorrow to hear how you come out. But don't tell me he won't sell. Build a fire under him if you have to."

His stomach churning, Carl Foster hung up the phone. *God, I gotta rely on some shifty-eyed barfly to get me in to see this guy. Jesus, what if the bastard doesn't know Packard after all? Randall's really breathing down my neck.*

He hardly heard Janice as she whined at him. "Well, what am I gonna do all day? There's nothing to do here. I thought this was going to be a vacation. We were going to do things together, have some fun."

"Get off my back, Janice. You'll figure something out," he snarled, reaching over to switch out the light. "Gotta get some sleep. It's gonna be a bitch tomorrow."

Chapter 24

Dan Lester was slumped against the front door of Nellie's when Carl Foster drove up promptly at 9:00 the next morning.

"Get in. Let's get going," Carl dropped the formalities.

Dan Lester hopped in the front seat and slammed the door. "Hey, nice car," he commented and then, to make sure of his financial arrangements, he said firmly, "Hundred bucks."

Carl eyed his companion with unmasked contempt. "Right, after you get me to Silas Packard. Now which way?"

Dan Lester motioned to the right. "Follow that road out of town," he said.

They rode in silence for a few miles. Dan Lester switched on the radio, and twangy country music filled the car.

"Turn that noise off," Carl said to the toe-tapping Lester. "I gotta ride with you, but I don't have to listen to that crap."

Dan Lester scowled and then changed the station defiantly to a local news report.

"Off. No goddamn hillbilly music and no Hicksville news. Got that?"

Impatiently, Carl snapped the dial, and Dan Lester stared sullenly out the window.

Minutes later he jerked his thumb, motioning Carl to change direction. "Left, over that bridge, up into them hills," he said.

As they climbed into the foothills, Carl began to see why Tom Randall wanted the property so much. With gently rolling slopes and beautiful views of the valleys, the land was ideal for a retirement development. Suddenly Lester said, "Hold up, right here." The road was narrow and unpaved, and the car jolted to a halt.

Dan Lester got out, walked to a split railed gate that blocked their path, and fumbled with the heavy chain that was wrapped around the gatepost. The rusty padlock gave way, the iron links clanked against the wood, and he swung the gate wide, motioning for Carl to drive through.

Back in the BMW, Lester pointed toward some trees. "Go down there."

Carl shifted in his seat behind the wheel; only vacant land spread out on both sides as far as he could see. *Hope this guy knows where the hell he's goin'*, he thought, eyeing his companion. He glanced in the rearview mirror at the gate receding behind them. "What do those two letters in the circle stand for?" he asked.

"Silver Spur, name of the ranch. Used to be a fuckin' showplace in the thirties. Made some silent movies out here," Lester told him. "Old Silas was quite a horseman, raised some fine quarter horses in his day."

"Jesus, Silver Spur sounds like the title of a John Wayne flick," Carl said. "Does the old boy still raise horses?"

"Nope, just keeps a couple. Almost to the house now, just around the next turn."

The BMW bumped through a clump of bushes, twigs scraping its sides.

"Great for the paint job," Carl growled. "Bill that to Randall, too."

"This is it?" Carl asked. "Looks like one good wind would blow the whole place down." He stared at the dilapidated buildings. "You'd think the guy'd be happy to unload this."

"Park over there," Lester ordered, and Carl pulled the car up in front of a long, low clapboard house, a cloud of dust settling around them. From a gravel walkway, crumbling concrete steps led up to a small porch. A screen door, off its hinges, stood propped against the rotting wood siding, and weather-beaten shutters hung at various angles next to the dirty windows. A few yards away, a pair of horses idled by a corral fence swishing flies. Behind them stood what remained of a barn, bales of hay stacked next to it partially covered by a tattered tarpaulin.

"Wait here," Dan Lester commanded.

Carl watched from the car as Dan Lester pounded on the front door. It swung open, and a shaggy haired old man talked with Lester and gestured toward the car, shaking his head.

Better not have come all this fuckin' way for nothin'! Carl swore. Hot, impatient, he put the window down, but the pungent smell of hay and horse manure nauseated him.

"Hard to believe this place was ever beautiful. Nothin' but a pile of shit now," he said, mopping his face with his handkerchief. "Only clean thing here." He smoothed the linen cloth and shoved it back into his pocket.

He heard the door slam, ending Dan Lester's interview with Silas Packard. Then Lester leaned in the car window. "Says he don't want to talk. No need to, he won't never sell the Spurs."

Carl jerked open the car door and got out. "I didn't come out here to hear that. He'll talk to me," he said. "Get out of my way, Lester." He pushed past his guide.

Almost losing his balance, Dan Lester glowered at his most recent employer. "Won't do you no good to try. Old Silas ain't about to be shoved around by no city boy smart-ass like you," he sneered.

With a few quick strides, Carl Foster was up the steps and across the sagging porch, knocking on the paint-chipped door. When he received no response, he called out, "Mr. Packard, I know you're in there and I'd like to talk to you for a few minutes about your ranch." His tone was friendly, persuasive.

"Go away. Don't want nothin' from nobody. You're all a bunch of goddamn land-grabbers," came the gruff reply.

Carl thought quickly and then tried again. "Not this time, Mr. Packard. I represent a firm that's interested in preserving your land, its natural, unspoiled beauty."

The door opened a crack, and a stale smell of bacon grease, whiskey, and sweat made Carl step back.

"I said get lost, Sonny. Not interested." Suddenly Silas stood framed in the doorway, a double-barreled shotgun aimed directly at Carl. "Get off my porch and take your fancy-pants ass outa here."

Carl's knees quivered, but he stood his ground. *Jesus, I knew this guy was eccentric, but this is unreal*, he thought. *If the old bastard shoots me full of holes, he and Shifty will both claim I was trespassing.* Carl found his voice. "Now, Mr. Packard, just a few minutes of your time. I know you'd be interested in my company's proposal." *Not ideal conditions for negotiation*, he thought. But he plunged on, "You'd stay on here with plenty of surrounding acreage, and the whole ranch would be restored. We're prepared to offer you a large cash down payment and one-third more than fair market value for the land, plus water rights." He threw in the water, suddenly remembering the Clark Construction Company's purchase of forty dry acres. Hell, it had cost them a fortune to dig wells on that land. Randall would have his balls if he pulled a mistake like that.

The shotgun never wavered, and the steely old eyes stared hard at Carl Foster.

"Not selling, not talking; now git before I unload old Lucy here into ya." He patted the gun fondly.

Carl opened his mouth for one more try, and he heard the gun cock. Silas Packard was a man of his word, and Carl Foster knew he had lost this round.

"Okay, Mr. Packard." He found his voice. "But think about it. We're talking big money here and a chance to get your place fixed up, maybe even get some prize horses back in that barn again." *Any gimmick to get this guy's attention*, he thought. *Hell, I can find some nags somewhere for a good price to sweeten the deal.* His mind was racing, and he thought he detected a glimmer of interest on the old buzzard's face when he mentioned the horses, but it faded quickly. The gun poked closer to him.

"Get outta here. Answer's no—now, always. Off my land. Don't got nothin' to say to none of you corporate types. All a bunch of rattlesnakes in suits."

"If you change your mind, want to talk, I'm at Pine Bluff Lodge. Name's Foster. Okay, okay, I'm leaving"

Lucy's muzzle poked through a crack in the door. Hastily, Carl backed off the porch and returned to the BMW.

Dan Lester lolled, smirking against the side of the car, rolling a cigarette between his grimy fingers. His expression plainly said, *I told you so.*

Chapter 25

WHEN THE PHONE RANG THAT night in his Pine Bluff bungalow, Carl Foster shuddered. He knew what he would hear before he picked it up.

Tom Randall's voice crackled over the line. "Got something going with Packard yet, Foster?" were his first words.

Just put the screws right to me, Carl thought but answered, "I went out to see Packard. Talked to him. That was a real accomplishment in itself," he said, remembering his recent encounter with the crusty cowboy. "Mean old reclusive buzzard."

But Tom Randall wasn't interested in any excuse; he hadn't had to stare down Lucy's barrel.

"Where did you leave it, Foster? Is he considering our offer or countering?" he demanded.

"Like I said, I went out there to the Silver Spur ranch, but it's no go. The guy won't sell, not for any price. I'd stake my job on that."

"You already have. Listen, Foster, that old boy has no heirs. If he kicks off out there without a will, the government's going to step in, and all those luscious acres are gone for us. You're supposed to be my hotshot negotiator, but I don't see any deal. You're not on a paid vacation up there. You've got work to do. Figure a way to convince Packard; smoke out something that'll move him. Next time we talk, I want to hear you've got a deal pending on that land."

Tom Randall slammed down the phone.

"Damn it, this sale isn't gonna happen. Accept it, God damn you," Carl Foster yelled over the dead line. He sat on the bed staring angrily at the disconnected instrument he still held in his hand.

Janice came out of the bathroom brushing her hair, "What're you hollering about? Was that the phone?" she asked. "God, it's hot in here," she complained, not waiting for his answer. "My skin feels like sandpaper. Everything is so dry. I took a walk while you were gone today, but it was too hot and dusty to go very far. Came right back. You know this dump doesn't even have a pool. I've never heard of a motel without a pool. God, I hope you'll be done here soon so we can get out of this lousy place."

"I'm not in a mood for your complaints," Carl snapped. "Put it this way, Janice, your free meal ticket is gonna end if I don't come up with a way to punch this deal through. You got that? My job's on the line. I gotta get a shower and some sleep."

At two in the morning, Carl sat up suddenly wide awake. He should call Tom Randall and wake the bastard up to thank him. Randall had given him the idea, and a plan was beginning to form in his mind. He'd have to get hold of Lester tomorrow, arrange for his services one more time. That'd be easy—if the dollars were there, shifty Dan would be too.

Lying next to Janice, careful not to wake her, Carl Foster began to feel better and better as he worked out the details of his scheme. First, another trip to Nellie's, locate Lester. He'd show Randall a thing or two about cutting a sweet deal. Just before dawn he drifted into a fitful sleep.

Dan Lester wasn't hard to find, but he was hard to hire for a reasonable price. In the end Carl, had to go up a thousand. But it would be money well spent—insurance, he reasoned, their guarantee that the Packard land would be bought.

"You know what to get?" he questioned Lester.

"Yeah, but I need some dough. Hundred bucks oughta do it."

Reluctantly, Carl made him an advance. "Rest paid on completion," he reminded Lester.

"Got no wheels; you'll have to drive."

Carl nodded. He didn't like that part of the bargain. "Just quit talkin'. Get the stuff so we can get going. I want to be back at the lodge before dark."

An hour later, Dan Lester ambled down the street with a worn duffel bag and two small boxes.

"That all you need?" Carl questioned.

"Don't take much," Lester answered. "Not makin' a fuckin' bomb, ya know. Open the trunk. Or do ya want this stuff in the backseat?"

Carl winced when Lester slid into the car next to him, an overpowering odor of stale tobacco and sweat accompanying him. "You need a flea dip, Lester," he said.

His companion responded with a loud belch, adding a foul smell of garlic to the already sickening stench.

"Regular smart-ass, aren't ya?" Lester said, giving Carl a menacing look. "Least I don't take a bath in no sweet pussy perfume like some I know." He sniffed, coughed, and then spit a stream of tobacco juice out the car window.

"Jesus, are you trying to suffocate us or what?" Carl Foster turned up the air-conditioning, grateful for the blast of clean, cool air.

They rode in silence toward the Silver Spur Ranch, with Carl congratulating himself on the brilliance of his scheme. God, this job couldn't end soon enough. His plan couldn't fail. The old guy would have to get out, be begging to sell, and he'd be right there, ready to buy when the price was right. Hit that bastard Randall up for a raise after this one, he promised himself, slowing the car to round a sharp turn.

"This far enough?" He looked over at Lester. "Don't want to take the car in too close."

"Nope. Keep goin'. I gotta drag all that stuff ya know," was the gruff reply.

"Should have four-wheel drive for this," Carl complained as the BMW jostled along.

"Stop over there." Lester pointed at a small clearing. "I won't be long. Wait for me," he said, scrambling out of the car. "Open the trunk," he ordered, glaring at Carl. "Now gimme my money!"

"When the job's done."

Lester dropped the duffel bag in the dirt. "Now or I don't go."

Carl hesitated, but he knew Lester meant it. "Okay, half now."

Wavering, Lester looked at the roll of bills Carl held out to him.

"Shit," he pocketed the cash, "I want the rest as soon as I get back." He disappeared into the dense stand of trees surrounding the clearing. Carl Foster waited until Lester was well out of sight and earshot before starting the motor. Carefully, he turned the car around and then headed across the meadow back onto the road. A hot, dry wind blew dust and leaves across the windshield. He pressed down hard on the accelerator.

"God, with all these potholes, I can't make any time." He cursed impatiently.

"Janice better be ready. I'm not waitin' for anybody to get out of this hellhole."

Chapter 26

His conversation with Carl Foster had made Tom Randall more determined than ever to acquire the Pine Bluff property. Confident he would soon be purchasing it, he was already projecting when he would break ground. Foster was conniving and often unscrupulous but a wizard at the bargaining table; he always brought in the best real estate at the right price. As Tom studied the plot map and aerial photos of the terrain, a clear picture of the already completed project began to form in his mind. Quickly he jotted down notes, sketched site layouts, and made production outlines. His enthusiasm mounted as he worked, and later that morning, he called his team of engineers and architects together. He spread an assortment of rough plans, drawings, and maps across his wide, polished wood conference table. Eagerly he addressed them, pointing out the desirable location and its easy accessibility from the city.

"It'd be simplest and most cost-effective to cut access roads in from the main highway here and here." He pointed to the map. "We can bypass the Silver Spur ranch altogether, work around it if we have to."

"Better to level it; it's too central, Tom," John McGrath advised.

Practical, cautious, John McGrath had engineered Randall Development projects for years. His conservative voice had guided Tom's father when the company was a fledgling, but this morning, Tom frowned at the older man's advice. He didn't want any roadblocks, and tearing down that ranch could be a major one.

"We'll have to lay it out the best way we can with the package Foster brings in. Hopefully, he'll get it all, John. But if we have to leave a piece of the pie on the table for that old boy up there, we still won't be hurting. That's a lot of prime acreage, and if we don't get greedy, maybe we can work Silas Packard out gradually. If we have to build around him, we will. Hell, maybe we'll even capitalize on him—fix the ranch up a bit, make it a real attraction. Remember, a lot of old movies were shot out there."

John McGrath shook his head, unconvinced, but a murmur of agreement went around the room.

"I want to cut the land into one- or two-acre parcels with a level pad for each mobile home unit, run in basic utility and water lines," Tom continued. "No frills. Build only a few structures—clubhouse, fitness center, pool, maybe a pitch-and-putt golf course. With a low budget, we can get off the ground and start selling right away."

"What about models?" John McGrath asked, still looking dubious.

"We'll put up three or four—decorated, furnished to scale—just for show. Throw up a few outdoor patio additions, but when it comes to purchase price, we stick to the bare bones unit. That's what we're selling. We want to appeal to the little guys who've dreamed all their lives of owning a retirement place in the country. We'll need to spend some money on advertising, but the place will sell itself. All we'll have to do is get the people up there." He flipped on the intercom to the outer office and commanded, "Denise, get me an appointment with Sandy Winters." He switched off the intercom and turned back to the group. "Sandy's the one we'll need to kick off promotions."

The day sped by with more meetings with project and sales managers to generate ideas for launching the Pine Bluff venture. Sandy Winters was fast and efficient, outlining a preliminary advertising portfolio including brochures, periodical ads, and media coverage.

"We need an appealing name, one every retired couple will want to identify with and want a piece of," Tom told her. "Catchy, simple, not elegant or sophisticated. This is for the moms and pops who want to kick back in the woods." He nodded as he listened to her suggestions on the other end of the line. "Sounds good already. Talk to you more tomorrow." Smiling, he hung up the phone. It had been a very satisfying day, the kind he really enjoyed. Start-up always gave him a thrill. The planning, the creativity—that was the best part of every project.

He got up and walked to the antique sideboard where he stored a few bottles of aged whiskey for special occasions. He poured himself a drink. "A toast." He raised his glass to his finally quiet office. "To Pine Bluff or—what was the name Sandy Winters had suggested?—Whispering Pines. To Whispering Pines," he repeated, taking a long sip of his drink. "Nice sound to it. I like it."

The scotch slid down smoothly, and he returned to his desk, looked over a few files, and made some last-minute notes for his next day's meetings before leaving for home. A good ending for the day, dinner out with the boys. He was actually looking forward to it, even without Elloree. Absently, he switched on his small portable television to catch the evening news while finishing his drink and packing his briefcase.

"My God," he gasped staring at the picture that had snapped into focus. An aerial view shot from a hovering helicopter showed vast acres of pine trees aflame with great black clouds of smoke billowing up from them.

A news commentator was dramatically reporting live from the scene. "I'm out here in Pine Bluff where a fire is burning out of control, a raging inferno."

Tom Randall leaped to his feet and jerked open the door to the outer office. Denise looked up startled as he spoke, "The whole goddamn place is going up in smoke."

She followed him into his office, and silently, they watched the rest of the shocking broadcast.

Two hours later, Tom Randall sat slumped in his office chair, his head in his hands. All phone lines were down, and his attempts to contact Carl Foster at the Pine Bluff Lodge had failed. The news coverage continued to report on the rapidly spreading fire as it engulfed the area. *Suspected arson*—the words pounded in his head.

"Jesus, the guy couldn't have done anything so stupid. Not gone that far. Sweet Jesus, don't let it be Foster," he muttered aloud to his vacant office. "All that's turned up so far is a burned-up car. Didn't even say what kind," he reassured himself. "Couldn't have been Foster. But sure as hell, whether it was Foster or not, there'll be investigations for months, maybe years. All that beautiful land will be parched and my plans for Whispering Pines gone up in smoke with it."

Dejectedly, he listened to the latest report from the hillside, where the blaze was continuing to race unchecked down into the valley. The camera zoomed in on a smartly dressed newswoman looking absurdly out of place surrounded by the smoldering ruins. Beside her, a whiskered old man sat astride a big bay horse. "And this is Silas Packard," she said, waving toward the mounted figure. "His Silver Spur Ranch was saved when the wind miraculously changed course. How did you feel when you realized the Silver Spur would be bypassed by the fire?"

Microphone in hand she turned to interview the man on horseback, but he had trotted out of the camera's view.

"Lived out on his ranch alone for years, bit of a recluse," she explained. "But I'm sure he'll want to talk with us about this. Mr. Packard, can you tell us just what you were feeling when the fire was threatening your ranch?" she called after his retreating back.

But the only picture was of his faded plaid shirt and sooty Stetson as his horse plodded out of sight.

Tom Randall finally left his office for home at 9:00 that night. He knew all he could do now was wait. From all indications, Carl Foster was still in the Pine Bluff area, but where he was or if he was even alive was unknown to anyone at Randall Land Development. Latest reports from the fire scene had included known fatalities, but none had sounded like Carl Foster

Tom knew he had no way to communicate with the Pine Bluff area so staying later would accomplish nothing. Denise had offered to stay and keep trying to get information for him, but he had sent her home. Silently, alone in his office, he sat staring at the recurring televised pictures of the now scorched, blackened landscape that, just that morning, he had dreamed of turning into Whispering Pines. Finally he stood up still watching, hoping to hear some news that would ease the growing dread that he felt. When at last he turned off the set and locked his door, he hesitated in the empty corridor of the Randall building. Looking around him, he thought of the years his father and he himself had spent building the business.

From somewhere in the dark interior he heard another door close and vaguely wondered if Carston Kramer was keeping a nightly vigil as well, watching the same station for some evidence that Carl Foster had no involvement in the disaster. But when he rode the elevator down to the parking structure, it was empty except for his own car. "Must have been the cleaning staff. Not Kramer," he muttered, sliding behind the wheel. "Guess I'm on my own on this one." He grimaced as he switched on the ignition, turned his Jaguar out of the garage, and headed home to Pilgrim Road.

The moment he rounded the corner and the old house loomed into view, Tom was alarmed. The place was ablaze with lights. The long, circular driveway was blocked by a fire engine, ambulance, and two police cars. He hardly took time to apply the brakes and switch off the motor before leaping out of his car and racing up the drive. Bursting through the heavy oak front door into the entry hall, he found Mildred Clive sobbing as two police officers helped her to a chair.

Through a thick haze of fear, Tom heard himself say, "I'm Tom Randall. This is my home. What's wrong? Has there been a robbery, an accident? Mildred, are you all right? For God's sakes, Mildred, stop crying and tell me what's going on here."

Through broken sobs, Mildred cried out, "You didn't come home; you didn't come. I tried to warn you."

Tom turned helplessly to the officers and spread out his hands in exasperation. "I couldn't get away. Couldn't get home tonight. I told them I'd take them to dinner, but there was a crisis, a fire out at Pine Bluff. Couldn't get away," he repeated, looking at them helplessly, unable to admit even to himself that he had forgotten his promise to the boys until the moment he swung the car into Pilgrim Road and saw the house flooded with lights.

"Mr. Randall, please sit down." One of the police officers took his arm and attempted to guide him to a chair, but he wrenched free. "My God, man, tell me what it is," he shouted.

"It's Paul," Mildred Clive shrieked. "I found him in the cellar, the steep stairs, the dark, a rope, the tipped over chair." Tears streamed down her ashen face, choking her words.

Tom Randall's knees buckled, blinding fear turned into engulfing blackness, and he pitched forward into the relief of unconsciousness.

Chapter 27

THE FLIGHT HOME SEEMED ENDLESS to Elloree, and the more Mark talked about his plans the quieter she became. Finally, the fasten seatbelt sign flashed on, and out of her cabin window, the lights of the city sparkled up through the misty night. Moments later, the plane was bumping along the runway; then it roared and shuddered to a halt. Excitement and eagerness flooding his face, Mark was out of his seat and into the aisle before the aircraft stopped.

"Look toward the terminal, El. See if you can spot Joan Mills. I called ahead to have her pick us up."

"Yes, I see her. She's there by the window."

"Good old Miss Mills, always prompt. God, that woman's a machine." Mark Williams smiled his approval.

He helped Elloree on with her coat and struggled into his own jacket in the midst of the pressing crowd of passengers. "We're meeting at my place. Joan Mills has made all the arrangements for us."

Elloree looked over at Mark standing next to her, his massive shoulders blocking the cramped aisle. *He is a giant*, she thought as she watched him impatiently shifting his weight from one foot to the other, ready to sprint for the door. *And he does accomplish gigantic things.* She flashed him a winning smile, gathered up her briefcase, and eased forward next to him through the surge of travelers.

"Okay, Mark Anthony, let's go meet your subjects—listen to them cry, 'Hail,'" she said, taking his arm as they were pushed and jostled toward the terminal.

Joan Mills proved to be not only a prompt and capable driver but an efficient party planner as well. As she neatly maneuvered her compact economy car in and out of the crowded airport traffic, she outlined to Mark what she had arranged for them.

"I have plenty of Brut champagne on ice, assorted cheeses, smoked salmon, and canopies—enough food, I'm sure. And your bar was well stocked, so I only had to order a few extra mixes." She hesitated and looked over at him. "I hope everything will be all right, Mr. Williams. By the time we arrive, the staff should be on the way."

"Hell, that'll be fine. Sounds like a grand spread, doesn't it, El?"

"Perfect." Elloree smiled encouragingly at Miss Mills's precise profile studying the road.

"Thank you, Mrs. Randall."

It seemed a long time since anyone had addressed her as Mrs. Randall, and now her husband's name sounded a little strange to her.

"Mark, I really must call home as soon as we get to your place. I tried before we left New York but got no answer." Concern clouded her face.

Mark reached over and patted her hand. "No worried face tonight, El. We're the returning warriors remember? Besides, they probably all went out to a movie or to get ice cream or something."

"You're probably right, Mark. But still, I'd better call."

He frowned but nodded his agreement.

Joan Mills turned carefully into the drive leading up to the Park City Towers. Colorful lush planting and trees illuminated by hundreds of tiny twinkling lights lined the narrow roadway. Two high, ornate, wrought-iron gates marked the Towers's entrance.

"Pull in over there." Mark motioned to a vacant space in the large visitor parking area. "Don't know where I put my damn key," he said, rummaging through his pockets. "Don't suppose you have one?"

Joan Mills handed him her key ring. "The largest one, marked T."

Mark grinned. "I knew you'd have it. Thanks. Now, let's get the party rolling." He ushered the two women up the walkway and through the gold-framed, etched-glass doors into the lobby. Marble floors, mirrored walls, and huge potted palms greeted them as they walked to a waiting elevator. Climbing toward the twentieth floor, Mark breathed a sigh of relief. He was home, Elloree was still with him, and as they passed each floor, he felt more relaxed, even a bit triumphant. It had been a damned hard battle to win over Polouski, and he deserved to celebrate. He felt jubilant with Elloree by his side, sharing their success. Over the past weeks, she had become more and more important to him and his future plans for Wishes. He glanced over at her and smiled. He wanted her with him to help him recount their accomplishments to the Wishes staff.

The view from Mark Williams's condominium on the twentieth floor was what had sold him on the place, and tonight it was particularly spectacular. The entire city spread beneath his windows glittered with a million lights blinking up at them. He had quite willingly turned the entire apartment's furnishing over to a decorator but with one stipulation. Nothing must block any part of the panorama.

"Like sitting on top of the world," Elloree said, gazing out on the cityscape below.

"Tonight I am. Wishes, you, and me—on top finally, where we belong." Striding to the bar that curved around the far corner of the spacious living room, he reached for the champagne resting in a silver ice bucket. He popped the cork, and the frothy liquid cascaded down the bottle's side. He poured three glasses, handed one to Elloree and another to Joan Mills, and then lifted his own in a toast.

"To you, El, and to Wishes."

She smiled and lifted her own glass. "Thanks, but it really was Little Susie. And, Mark, now I must make a call." She set her glass on the bar. "I'll only be minute or two," she promised.

"Okay, in there. It'll be quieter." He motioned toward the bedroom as the door chimes sounded, heralding the arrival of the Wishes top staff. "Don't be long. You've got to be the one to tell 'em how you bagged Polouski."

Elloree shut the door, sank down on the bed, and reached for the phone. She quickly dialed her home number letting it ring a long time, but there was no answer, no message recording, nothing. Puzzled, she replaced the receiver, checked the time, and then dialed again but with still no response.

"Hey, are you coming?" Mark called, tapping on the closed door. "The show's about to start." He poked his head in and waved a stack of order forms in his hand. "These are what everybody wants to see and you, too. Come on!" He took her by the hand and led her into the crowded room. A cheer went up.

"What'd I tell you? Elloree and Little Susie just put Wishes on the map." He poured champagne for them all and raised his glass. "To Susie and to Elloree, the two most important women in my life. And to Leonard Polouski, the meanest son of a bitch of them all."

Chapter 28

IT WAS LATE THAT NIGHT when Elloree and Mark Williams finally said good night to the last of the Wishes crew. They had celebrated, toasted, talked of the past, dreamed of the future, and retold the many stories of their successful New York trip. And now Elloree was weary; her tousled, honey-colored hair fell across her face, and she brushed it back impatiently trying to banish the fatigue. She roused herself from her comfortable position on the sofa and squeezed her tired feet back into her shoes.

"I have to go home, Mark. I've already stayed much later than I should've. But you did deserve all their applause, and I wanted to share in it with you."

He smiled his craggy grin at her, helping her into her coat. "I'll drive you home if you really think you have to go?" His question hung between them.

"Thanks, Mark. I do have to go." Ordinarily she would have resisted his offer and asked him to call her a taxi, but tonight she was too worn out to argue.

She held onto his arm and leaned her head back against the smooth mahogany paneling as the elevator descended to the ground floor. He guided her through the deserted lobby. "Too late even for old doorman, Sam. I thought he slept right there." He pointed to a well-worn chair in the corner and then punched in the security code and ushered her out into the cold night air. A full moon slid among the clouds, casting milky shafts of light across the vacant parking lot.

"We had a hell of a trip, El. But now our work is really beginning," he said. Although exhaustion played around his eyes, his voice was strong and commanding.

"I know, Mark," she said. "But tonight I go home. Tomorrow we can begin to plan."

"Okay, you win. Tomorrow." He looked at his watch. "Hey, it's already tomorrow, and so …"

"No," she said. "No more tonight. It's time we put Wishes to bed. And ourselves, too."

"Damn shame," he muttered. "I just wanted to kick around a few ideas."

She laughed as he helped her into the car. "No more ideas, Mark, not tonight. Tomorrow will be soon enough."

They rode in silence, and the car slid easily in and out of traffic as they headed toward Oak View. Elloree always marveled at the never-ending stream of cars on the crosstown parkway. She vaguely wondered where they were all going in the misty night and if their passengers were all as tired as she was. She didn't ask Mark how he knew the way to the big old house so well.

Had she asked him, he could have told her of one night long ago when he had wanted her desperately—wanted her with all his being, so much so that he had belted down scotches like soda pop, slammed into his car, and driven out into the suburbs. Only to sit staring into the darkness up the long driveway on Pilgrim Road cursing himself for being such a damn fool. He had sat there a long time that night and then finally driven away, the longing still pounding in his head. Perhaps it was at that moment that he'd realized his fierce drive and iron will could never bring him all that he wanted.

But tonight, as Mark guided the car into Pilgrim Road, he thought about himself, Elloree, and Wishes with a new confidence of his position with her. Over the last months her work, Wishes, had become more and more her life, and he, after all, was Wishes. He was taking her home tonight but hoping it would be for the last time. She had no place in this provincial world anymore. She belonged with him at Wishes, and he was sure that she knew that too now.

He pulled the car to the curb at the driveway entrance and switched off the ignition. "I'll walk you up. It might be better if we left the car here," he said.

"No, I'll go on from here alone, Mark. I'd rather." *I don't want any scenes*, she might have added, but she didn't need to say it.

As always Mark read her thoughts. "Don't put it off, Elloree," he said in a quiet voice, his words edged with emotion. "You're going to have to choose."

Elloree turned toward him, tears clouding her eyes. "Choose, Mark? I've already chosen. You know that. Before I left for New York. Maybe when you first called that Saturday morning a hundred years ago. I really don't know when. Maybe the day I went to that damn league luncheon and watched Aggie Marsh devour her friends." Her hand was on the door handle, but before she got out of the car, she said, "I'm glad you won, Mark. You deserve it."

"You won, too, Elloree. Think what you won, what you've accomplished. Can't you see that?"

"No. I have a strange, overwhelming feeling tonight, an eerie sensation of loss." And then she smiled and brushed her hand across her eyes. "Don't listen to me. I'm just very tired. I'll see you in the morning but a little later than usual, if you don't mind."

"Right, you do that. Get some rest. Then we can start working on that next line. Don't you like the cartoon character idea? I think it has a hell of a lot of possibility." Once again his face was animated by his thoughts of business. "You'll be fine after you get some rest," he assured her. "I'll just sit here and watch until you're in the house. I can see well enough through the trees. Flash the porch light when you're in, okay?"

She nodded and he reached across to her and clumsily kissed her on the cheek. "Goodnight, El."

"Goodnight, Mark. I'll flash the light. Thanks." She laid her hand gently against his rough, unshaven jaw, and then she was gone into the blackness up the driveway.

The house was cloaked in silent darkness when Elloree slipped through the heavy oak front doors. From the shadows, the sound of the grandfather clock's ticking echoed in the stillness. Quickly, she switched on the hall chandelier and then flashed the porch light for Mark. The children had to be sleeping at this hour, but she wondered about Tom. For a moment, she hesitated, listening to the steady *tick, tick*. Then suddenly, the silence was shattered as the clock chimed the hour. The ponderous bonging reverberated throughout the old house, and a sudden unreasonable stab of fear shot through her. Something was wrong, she sensed it. The entire house seemed to vibrate with it.

She shook her head, struggling to calm her pounding heart. "I'm being silly, imagining things," she whispered softly into the gloom. Then from somewhere in the back of the house, she heard sounds, muffled voices. Tom must be in the library watching television, she reasoned, moving toward the stairs.

Talk to him in the morning; that'll be soon enough. Just too tired to face him tonight. She clung to the banister for support as she climbed the steps.

Halfway up the staircase, the library door jerked open. She paused, peering through the dim light at Tom walking slowly toward her. Stubble covered his face, and his always impeccable clothing was soiled and disheveled. His hand holding a half-finished drink trembled, the ice cubes clinked against the glass, and the brown liquid splashed the carpet as he walked unsteadily toward her.

For a moment, she thought of fleeing to the refuge of her room, but then slowly she descended the stairs to confront him.

"I flew in this evening, Tom," she said in a tired but steady voice.

"New York buying is finished. All the big accounts signed. We did well. Wishes will be international. I tried to call you but got no answer." She spoke quickly, trying not to look at him, knowing this was the moment to say, *I really must move out, Tom. We must separate for all our sakes.* But the words would not come.

Suddenly as she peered into his face, she realized the swollen puffiness there was not from drink but from tears. A desperate sadness etched his look and enormous unmasked grief filled his eyes.

"Elloree," he spoke her name softly, not in anger. "Elloree, you've come home too late."

She swayed against the banister; the gnawing fear she had felt in the hall engulfed her. A terrible cloak of gloom pervaded the house, like someone had died. Death—that was it. Death.

"Oh my God," she whispered in a frightened voice, clutching the wrought-iron railing to steady herself. *Someone is sick, one of the children. Not death. Sickness. Please God, just sickness, and I am home in time*, she prayed silently. *I have to be.*

"Come, sit down, Elloree." He guided her into the living room.

In a daze, she slid down onto the velvet cushioned sofa, afraid to hear his words. His face filled with pain and anguish, lacked all hostility. She had expected anger, jealous reprimands, many things but never the agony she saw in his eyes. He sat beside her, took her hands in his, and slowly related the events of that terrible evening.

"I've scheduled the funeral but waited until you could be reached to arrange the final details."

She barely heard his words. They seemed to come from some place far away, washing over her in a merciless flood. The entire room swam before her eyes, and she felt like she was drowning. She gulped in air, attempted to focus her eyes, and forced herself to listen to what he was saying.

"I tried to contact you, left messages, but you were always out. Timmy needs you, Elloree," he said with a sudden fierce intensity. "You must not leave him. You must stay, help him come to grips with what's happened. His world has been shattered, and he's all that matters now—not you, not me, just him."

"Tom, I never got the messages. Never got the messages," she repeated over and over, tears streaming down her cheeks.

He took her hand. "I loved you, Elloree, but I hated you for leaving us, not wanting us. But I don't hate anymore. It's over. Something died inside me when Paul died," he said simply. "I'm as much to blame as you are, and I'm sorry for you—sorry for us both. If we'd had the courage to face what we were doing to ourselves, to them, it all might've been different."

He rose, head bowed, shoulders stooped. He looked years older, and his hands shook as he helped her gently to her feet. "Tomorrow we can talk, Elloree. What's left of tonight, you must try to sleep."

She clutched his arm, choking on her sobs. "Don't leave me alone, Tom. I can't bear this."

"I know," he answered simply. "I can't bear it either."

It was dawn before grief and exhaustion finally forced Elloree into a shallow, restless sleep. In her dreams, she was at the park once more with Paul and Timmy flying kites. *Clouds are free, Mommy; only clouds are free,* Paul was calling gaily, dashing toward her, arms outstretched.

When she awoke, the sun was streaming through her window, and Tom sat slumped in a chair next to the bed. She stirred, stretched, and then remembered the night before and where she was.

"Oh, God. It's real, isn't it, Tom?" she whispered, not really wanting him to answer.

Chapter 29

For Elloree, the next six months passed in a blur of unimaginable pain. Any attempts to restore normalcy to life in the old Pilgrim Road house failed. Timmy remained withdrawn and sullen. His once lively, winsome personality had vanished, and he was constantly in trouble at school. He ignored his friends, refused to join in his usual activities, and retreated deeper and deeper into himself.

Elloree could not bear to lose him as well as Paul. She lived through the agonizing days only to reach Timmy, help him to heal. As the weeks slowly passed, she doggedly planned outings to please him, brought him special treats, and did anything she thought might bring a smile back to his troubled little face. But he did not respond. The doctors encouraged her, telling her that with time, counseling, and grief management therapy, he would begin to recover.

One bright, warm autumn day, Elloree decided to try a trip to the park again. The fall colors were especially vivid; every tree was dressed in spun gold or burnished orange, and the air was crisp and breezy. The park had always been one of Timmy's favorite places, and she hoped she wasn't imagining the hint of enthusiasm she thought she saw cross his small, quiet face. Bundling him into a jacket, she gathered up a ball and baseball glove for catch.

"Come on, Tim. It'll be fun. I'll throw you a few. You can catch. Maybe some of your friends from school will be there, too."

"Okay," he answered listlessly, "if you want to." His gaze seemed to penetrate right through her, focus on the wall behind her. The therapists had cautioned her not to antagonize him. The slightest confrontation would create more stress and sink him into deeper depression. She longed to pull him to her, fold him into her arms, comfort him, and tell him things would be fine. But how could they be? Paul was dead.

Since the funeral, Timmy had not uttered a word about Paul. His mind had blocked out those painful memories, erased any part of the past that included his brother. But Elloree was tormented by memories that flooded her mind daily and haunted her dreams at night. She found no comfort in the accident report that claimed Paul had simply lost his footing on the stairs in the darkness and plummeted headfirst onto the concrete floor below. Death had been instantaneous—a broken neck, multiple head injuries. But why was he going to the basement alone at night? She asked herself the question over and over again. And why had a rickety old chair been dragged beneath a beam and a rope clumsily knotted around it? What demons had plagued her son's mind that night? Over and over, she read the note she found scribbled across his school notebook, "Nobody lives here anymore."

A heavy burden of guilt gnawed at her, sapping her, leaving her limp and helpless to stem the tide of her grief. *If only I had been less selfish, Paul would be here with us today*, she thought sadly, turning into the park entrance.

"Not many visitors," she remarked casually to Timmy as he stared bleakly out the window.

"What'll it be—catch or the swings and slide first?" She tried to sound enthusiastic.

"I don't care," he answered dully.

"Okay, then it's catch. Come on, I'll race you to the drinking fountain."

"I don't want to."

She looked at Timmy's small dejected form as he plodded next to her, head down, feet dragging. So much of her artwork had been drawn from her own vivacious children. Since her return from New York, she had not been able to sketch another little figure. Her one conversation with Mark Williams had ended in a futile attempt to explain why she could not come back to work. He had implored her to return to Wishes and once again lose herself in her creative world. But she could not bear to even look at her artwork or think of resuming her career. Mark did not understand. Wishes was on the threshold of international expansion, and she was walking away—away from her triumph, away from him. He'd tried repeatedly to convince her, but this time she'd refused him flatly. Timmy needed her, and she needed to be there for him. Together perhaps they could begin to mend. Nothing else was important to her.

Mother and son crossed the park, Timmy trudging despondently behind her, and for a while, they played catch. Elloree threw the baseball as hard as she could, smacking his glove with a thump. Timmy had always giggled with delight when he caught the hard thrown ones, but today he was silent, melancholy. Her arm ached, but still she pitched the ball to him.

"I'm tired. I don't wanna throw anymore." Timmy tossed his mitt belligerently on the ground at her feet.

"Okay, do you want to try the slide?" Elloree patted his shoulder affectionately, but he shrugged her hand off angrily.

"It's all right, Tim. I'm tired too," she said, smiling encouragingly at him.

"I don't wanna play anymore. I just wanna sit." He plopped himself down on the grass and turned away from her. But she joined him, sitting cross-legged on the ground, and tried once more to draw him into conversation.

"I think the Yankees look pretty good for next season. They traded for some really big hitters as well as strong pitchers."

"Uh-huh."

"Their first baseman is supposed to be a hotshot from the Red Sox. He batted .350 last year. They're hoping he'll be a big homerun hitter."

Daily, Elloree combed the sports magazines and newspapers searching for bits of information to interest him.

He looked over at her apathetically. "Maybe he'll win the league for 'em. I don't care." He stretched out on his back, pillowed his head on his arms, and studied the sky intently.

Elloree sat quietly watching him, searching his face for a clue to unlock the misery that must be there. Since Paul's death, Timmy had not shed a tear. Living through those terrible days dry-eyed and silent had forced his pain deeper and deeper. The doctors and counselors had told her that, if only he could cry, bring suffering to the surface, he might then begin to heal.

They sat in silence in the long, damp grass beneath the trees.

Be patient. Time—give him time, Elloree told herself.

The breeze came up, the afternoon light faded, and the park was almost deserted. Then a sudden gust of wind sent a shower of colorful foliage down around them. Bunches of brightly painted leaves scuttled across the grass and dotted the sky as the gusts spread them across the park. Suddenly, laughing and giggling, two boys burst from behind a clump of bushes. With rosy cheeks and stocking caps pulled down over their ears, they dashed across the park chasing the falling, swirling leaves. Their high-pitched cries floated on the air.

"There goes one. I'll get the big, gold ones."

At first Timmy gazed at them indifferently. Then abruptly, he sat up. Alert, he watched the boys attentively, as if remembering something from long ago.

"I'm gonna get these. You get your own, buddy," the one boy shouted into the wind, shoving the other aside as he dove to the ground clutching a fistful of leaves. They rolled in the grass tussling together and then clamored to their feet and dashed among the trees.

Timmy sat silently staring at the playful boys. A small tear rolled down his cheek, and he sobbed. Then the tears gushed, running down his smudgy face, dropping onto his hands that were clenched tightly around his knees. Elloree sat motionless, afraid to speak, fearing his weeping would stop. Great racking sobs broke from him, shaking his narrow shoulders, and slowly Elloree reached out to him, gathered him into her arms, and comforted him. Quivering, crying he nestled in her lap like a wounded bird, and she soothed him as only a mother can calm her aching young. She stroked his tousled red hair, rocking him gently back and forth and cradling him in her arms.

When his tears finally subsided into sniffles, he looked up at her timidly. A hint of a small smile played around his lips. "There are clouds," he pronounced solemnly, "lots of clouds." He pointed to the sky. "Some of them look like animals. There's a dog over there with pointy ears and bushy tail. Do you see him?" he demanded.

She nodded. The tightness in her throat kept her from answering, but she squeezed his hand in response.

"And there's Paul, right there beside the doggy. I can see him. Don't you see him? Paul is up there with my cloud animals, Mommy. They're playing together. They're free, and so is Paul."

Elloree gathered him closer. "Yes," she whispered. "I do see him. And we'll always see him, you and me. Always."

His hand, tucked tightly in hers, squeezed her fingers. "Let's go home, Mommy."

For the first time, she knew the real magic in those words.

"Yes, Tim, let's go home."

PART III

London

And, through and over everything,
A sense of glad awakening …
A last long line of silver rain,
A sky grown clear and blue again.

~ Edna St. Vincent Millay

Chapter 30

Mark Williams put down the phone and stared out the window. His conversation with Elloree had been unsettling, but he was more determined than ever not to let her drown in her grief. How had he just put it? "You can't bury yourself alive, go on punishing yourself. Are you going to wear that goddamned haircloth shroud forever?" he had roared over the wire.

And his harsh words had hit home. Elloree knew she needed to hear them, but she was not ready. It was too soon; her wounds were still raw and deep. But as always, Mark was insistent. He had called again the following day, his message brief and firm. "I'm coming over tomorrow morning to take you into Wishes for a few hours. Be there at ten. Won't take no for an answer."

Timmy was back in school full-time and making good progress now. He still needed her, but it wasn't Timmy keeping her home, isolated in the big house on Pilgrim Road. She was uncertain of her own feelings about Wishes or anyone. For months, she had shut out all thoughts of her work. And Mark was right—her sorrow had consumed her. She did not allow herself to think of New York, Mark, and launching

Little Susie. Wishes had become one of the nation's fastest-growing companies, but she was no longer a part of it. She coexisted with Tom, watching him withdraw further and further away from her into himself. They both focused on Timmy, trying to pull him from his despair and, in so doing, ease their own pain.

The next day, punctual as promised, Mark Williams pulled into the tree-lined drive on Pilgrim Road. He hesitated only a moment before bounding up the front steps and punching the bell.

She forced a smile when she opened the door to greet him, but her dull, tired eyes and pale, drawn face showed the strain of the past months.

"My God, it's good to see you," he said, reaching for her hand and gently squeezing it. "Ready?"

She nodded slowly. "Only for a little while, Mark."

He beamed his lopsided grin at her. "That a girl. I promise we'll take it slow." He helped her into her jacket and then down the steps to his car.

They were both quiet on the drive into the city, sharing the silent camaraderie they had always known together. But as the car pulled into the Wishes parking lot, Elloree shuddered and clutched her handbag tightly.

"I don't know if I can do this, Mark," she said solemnly. "I just don't know. I feel so shaky."

"It's, okay, El. I won't let you stay long. I'll take you right home if you really want me to," he told her, but his eyes pleaded with her to try.

"All right, Mark. I'll give it a try."

Then they were inside the sprawling, gray granite building that still housed Wishes and the elevator was jerkily taking them up. When the doors opened, Elloree stepped out timidly like an apprentice on her first day. But Mark quickly steered her down the corridor toward his office, and as they walked, it seemed to Elloree years had passed, not just a few months.

"I thought you'd come in here with me today so we can look over some things." he said, guiding her through the outer office past Miss Mills.

Joan Mills looked up from her desk and smiled warmly at Elloree. "Good morning. It's nice to see you back, Mrs. Randall. I'll just be a minute, bring you both some coffee," she said, retreating down the hall.

Once seated in a chair in Mark's office with a steaming cup of coffee, Elloree began to relax in the familiar surroundings. Mark shuffled through the piles of papers and memos on his desk. He glanced over at her, studying the drawings spread across the table behind him.

"Recognize those?" he asked.

But she shook her head. "No, I guess I don't remember doing these."

"Look closely, El. They aren't your designs. They're renderings of the cards Leonard Polouski showed us in New York."

She picked up one then and looked at it intently. "You're right—a good copy but definitely not mine."

"The simplicity of subject and purity of color isn't there. Not yours, not ours," he said.

She turned around to face him, and before she could ask the question, he answered. "Tenner, Alex Tenner," he snarled with disgust. "The guy sold us out, leaked our ideas to a competitor. Played both sides of the fence, the slimy bastard. He knew Little Susie was gonna go over big, and his jealous ego couldn't stand it. I knew right after we came back from New York. Or rather my suspicions led me to do some investigating."

Elloree's eyes widened. "I knew he didn't like me, resented me being put in over him, but to go so far, Mark." She shook her head.

"How he thought he could get away with it, I don't know. But we had a little conference about it," Mark said angrily, tugging at his tie, loosening it from around his thick bull neck.

And Elloree winced, picturing the slight, flaccid Alex Tenner confronted by the rugged, indomitable figure before her.

"You might say," Mark continued, obviously relishing the memory, "we had a bit of a ball crusher. Loathsome son of a bitch. Never seen a grown man blubber like that," Mark scoffed. "Jesus, I thought he was gonna get down on his knees and beg. Not a pretty sight."

"Mark, you didn't—"

"Naw, I wanted to whip his effeminate ass, but I just put the screws to him professionally. Nobody steals from Wishes. He won't be working for anyone very soon. He's finished in this town and in this business. You can bet on that," he said with grim satisfaction.

Before she could ask him more, a gentle tap on the door interrupted them and Joan Mills walked briskly into the office.

"Nigel Harrison is on the line. Do you want to take the call now or return it later?"

"I'll take it," Mark said, reaching for the phone on his desk.

"Williams here; glad to hear from you, Harrison," Mark barked into the phone. "There's someone I want very much for you to meet while you're over here. I know your time is limited, but could you fit in lunch before your flight tomorrow? Fine. We'll be there. See you tomorrow." He replaced the receiver, knowing Elloree had heard every word and was now waiting for an explanation.

"I'd like you to have lunch with me tomorrow, meet Nigel Harrison," he said quickly.

"I don't think I should, Mark. I can't consider coming back to work right now."

Mark was silent for a moment, knowing pressure would be a mistake. But then he persisted, "Nigel Harrison's over here from England for only a few days. I contacted him in London before he left, and he promised he'd get in touch with me. I didn't think he'd have the time, but I should've known he'd call if he said he would. The English are like that—word's their bond sort of thing. Anyway, he's meeting us for lunch tomorrow at the Terrace Room—twelve o'clock noon."

"There you go again making plans for me, Mark. But I simply can't come. Timmy needs me; you know that."

"Of course you can. Do you good. You can't just sit home and rot. Your boy needs you to be whole and healthy," he said quietly. "Don't go on punishing yourself. We need you here, too, El. We need to start work on another blockbuster new package, as well as a sequel to the

Little Susie line. Our buyers are going to be looking for another hot-selling series."

She knew there was truth in his words, and slowly she answered, "Okay, I'll try to make it for the lunch tomorrow. But now I should go home. I'm exhausted, and I've only been here such a short time."

"Take you home right now," he said, satisfied he was one step closer toward getting her back to Wishes. "Lunch tomorrow. I'll pick you up. Be real glad to have you on board. Want to see what you think of Harrison."

And once again, she was swept up by his boundless enthusiasm.

Chapter 31

Nigel Harrison was punctual, precise, and very British. He was also one of the most attractive men Elloree Randall had ever met. Dressed in a perfectly tailored, Saville Row suit accented by an Italian silk tie, he had the appearance of an aristocratic nobleman, but it was his sky-blue eyes, deeply set in the finely chiseled features of his face that held her attention. His wavy, chestnut-brown hair streaked with silver-gray highlights was neatly cut but fell slightly onto his forehead, giving him an unexpected boyishness. He had a genteel but relaxed manner, although his speech clearly reflected Oxford schooling. And Elloree found herself immensely enjoying his easy conversation and spontaneous quick wit.

"Only here for a few days this trip," he said. "But I was delighted when Mark invited me to join you for lunch today. I especially wanted to meet the lovely and talented lady responsible for creating Little Susie." He smiled warmly at Elloree, and she blushed at his flattery.

"I was a part of Wishes," Elloree said quickly. "But I'm not working at the present time."

Nigel Harrison smiled again at her but did not ask why she was no longer at Wishes. And Mark offered no explanation, plunging eagerly into an outline of his latest ideas.

"We're working on a new line but plan to keep expanding Little Susie simultaneously. Next month, we're moving into our new distribution center. State-of-the-art equipment will allow us to ship much more quickly and efficiently. Six months ago, we closed escrow on three more warehouses adjacent to the Wishes home offices, and we have offers in on the remaining ones in the surrounding area. With those facilities up and running, we'll pull our manufacturing, printing, and distributing all together into one big complex. The final phase will move in our Select Products plant and Fixture Center."

"I say, that's splendid; your plans for growth are first-rate. Glad you're planning to keep Susie going," Nigel said with approval. "That wee tot is all over England now. Caught on like a *Punch and Judy* show, just like Polouski predicted; every little girl in the country wants a Susie doll or outfit."

At the mention of Polouski, Elloree frowned and shifted in her chair, hoping Mark wouldn't relate her encounter with the man.

But for once, Mark Williams was tactfully discreet. "Tough sell that guy, but sure knows his business."

"Yes, he does know retailing," Nigel Harrison agreed. "He's done a good job for us. A bit unorthodox in his approach sometimes, but a superb judge of what's marketable. Shrewd buyer—he has an uncanny ability to predict volume and recommend advertising. He suggested we get you to come over to England to handle some promotions." He smiled hopefully at Elloree.

"I'm considering starting a string of independent shops specializing only in Wishes lines—not just cards and party supplies, but books, dolls, gifts, and maybe a coordinated clothing line. Home furnishings, linens, window treatments—create the Little Susie living style," Mark said.

"That's a very appealing idea. With the right locations, I'm sure it would be successful," Nigel responded enthusiastically.

A ripple of excitement went through Elloree as she listened. The combination of Mark Williams and Nigel Harrison would give Wishes another huge potential for growth.

"The timing's ideal for us both," Mark continued.

"I couldn't agree more. How soon can you come to England?" Nigel asked Elloree. "I'd be most happy to arrange accommodations, provide a car, all that sort of thing, you know. Please think about it." He glanced at his watch. "So sorry," he said, apologizing as he rose to his feet. "I must cut this short. I've a plane to catch. But I'll ring you next week, Mark. Do see if you can arrange the trip." He turned to Elloree, taking her hand. "So very pleased to meet you. I'll look forward to seeing you in England."

Then he was gone, striding across the restaurant, and she sat watching his tall, distinguished retreating figure.

"Quite the gentleman," Mark commented after they had left the Terrace Room and were threading their way through the late afternoon traffic. "Have to admire a guy like that. Born into it, fancy English title and all, but never flaunts it. One of the smartest, most hardworking businessmen I've ever come across. Too bad about his wife."

Elloree raised an eyebrow.

Reading her thoughts, Mark continued. "All over the papers a few years ago. The family holdings include a chain of upscale department stores throughout the UK and Europe. Hugely successful, due to Nigel. He's put them on the map. Works like a demon, since his wife was killed in an accident. The media over here really went after the story. You know how our press loves to get hold of anything about the Brits, especially ones with position and money. Surprised you missed hearing about it; the newspapers were full of it."

"I don't remember reading about it. How long ago was it? What kind of an accident?" Elloree asked, thinking of the charming, dignified man she had just met.

"Car, I think, but don't recall the details. Anyway, Nigel Harrison is one hell of an entrepreneur. Smart enough to team up with that bastard, Polouski. Gotta admit, they're as unlikely a pair as you could ever imagine. But hell, whatever works."

Elloree grimaced. "Just thinking about that guy, Polouski, makes my skin crawl."

"The son of a bitch's got a nose like a bloodhound for what sells.

Made major bucks for the Harrison chain. And just remember, you're the one who bagged him for Wishes."

"How could I ever forget?"

"You know Nigel Harrison is right, El. We should go across the pond and have a look for ourselves—see if there's the great potential for our specialty stores I think there is. Already tried the idea out here in the states. Just need the right locations. Can't miss," Mark said confidently.

He looked over at her, pleased to see her mounting enthusiasm as they talked about Wishes, their work, and Nigel Harrison's proposal.

Elloree had slipped easily into the conversation and, for the first time in months, felt the stirring of renewed interest in her work. But her grief sent a sudden crippling pain through her, and she withdrew into silence, sadness spreading across her face.

Like a curtain suddenly had been drawn between them, Mark felt her retreating into her sorrow. But determined not to lose her again, he persisted. "A trip to England would be good for you, El. I want you to think about it. Not a long one. Just long enough to check out some potential locations and put together some preliminary numbers. Promise me you'll think about it. That's all I ask."

Elloree did not answer. She had turned her face toward the window to hide her tear-filled eyes.

Chapter 32

While Elloree sat lunching with Mark and Nigel Harrison, Tom Randall was meeting across town with his company's head legal counselor. His opening remarks were not welcomed by his senior attorney, Carston Kramer.

"The Randall Land Development Corporation will not disclose their sending of Carl Foster to Pine Bluff or even that he was in our employ while up there. We'll deny any connection to Foster," he said determinedly. "You've got to keep us out of this whole Pine Bluff disaster, Kramer."

"Tom, your position is clear. You're up to your butt in shit," Kramer answered wearily. He'd been over this with Randall a dozen times in the last few weeks, and he was tired of his employer's refusal to face facts. "We're in the middle of an ugly sequence of events that can't be altered. There's just no easy way to come out of this smelling like a goddamn rose, Tom. It's known that Foster was up there and had been employed by the Randall Corporation. What we have to establish is that the guy acted on his own, without any direction or authorization from this company. That's gotta be our stand. Drum up some proof that he'd been let go and went up there to stir up trouble for us. Show he had a history of vindictive behavior, skirted the law. With all his past sketchy dealings, that shouldn't be hard to do. Dummy up some documentation if you have to. You've got to leave a paper trail that you want found and get rid of what you don't. Or as sure as I'm sittin' here, your ass is going to be in a sling for years."

Tom Randall glared at Carston Kramer and replied acidly, "I know damn well the position my ass is in. And I'm payin' you a goddamn fortune to tell me more than just that."

Carston Kramer's usually impeccably pressed pinstripe trousers were wrinkled from long hours of sitting at his desk, and his designer silk tie hung loosely from around his unbuttoned collar. His monogrammed, French-cuffed sleeves were rolled up to the elbow, and he was remaining calm with obvious effort.

Employed by the Randall Land Development Corporation for eight years, Carston Kramer had watched the company grow under the direction of Tom Randall. He had joined the legal team shortly after the old man had died and had heard many rumors about the differences between the two Randall men. He had gained respect for Tom's shrewd business judgment, and he'd aided him in pulling off some incredible deals in the past, often guiding him through legal minefields, but they were not going to easily side step this Pine Bluff fiasco. He knew it. Tom Randall knew it. The Randall Land Development Corporation was in the middle of a federal investigation and would be indicted unless the company could sever all connections to Foster—prove he'd acted independently on some kind of kamikaze suicide mission to take the company down with him. It was a long shot but the best one they had and no good at all if Foster's wife refused to play ball. But first, he had to convince his employer of just where they stood.

"Look, Tom," Carston Kramer continued, struggling for patience. "The Pine Bluff land development deal is dead—went up in flames with Foster. But the investigation is bound to drag on for a long time. Even if there's nothing but charred ruins left, the government boys are going to keep right on raking through it. Right now, your main problem is to figure a way to handle the wife, Janice. She's all too eager to talk to the press. Contingency lawyers are flocking around, assuring her they can mount an ironclad case against the Randall Company." Kramer shook his head. "God, I sure wish we'd never laid eyes on that bastard, Foster."

"Too late for wishes," Tom Randall snapped.

"Somebody's got to talk to the wife, try to head her off. Find out how much Foster told her," Kramer persisted firmly. "Then offer to console the grieving widow with a healthy pension and a substantial lump sum settlement to shut her up. If she'll deal, it's the best way."

Tom Randall glowered across his desk at Kramer, not happy with the advice he had just heard. "That fool Foster acted on his own. That's what killed him, not my orders. I'm not going to get hung out to dry because some smart-ass, ambulance-chasing lawyers set out to screw me."

Kramer studied his employer before responding. God, the guy looked positively gray from fatigue, aged ten years. The story about his kid really had been a shocker. Hell, he had two kids himself. *Jesus, how does somebody live with something like that*? He'd heard the story from Denise, Randall's secretary. Randall's wife was in New York at the time, gone back to work. God, with all their money, it must've been more than dollars that had sent her back into the workforce. And somebody sure shut down the media. Big bucks must've changed hands to turn that machine off. Only one short article in the newspaper had reported that the boy died in an accident.

According to the company grapevine, old Mrs. Randall had put out the story—held her own press conference the very next day. No room for scandal in her family tree. *God, what a piece of work that old lady is. I've seen some tough SOB lawyers but none of 'em could top her. Makes you wonder—wealth, prestige, for what? The article called it a tragedy with no hint the boy was unstable or having problems at home. Jesus, wouldn't a parent know before it got to that point. Scary.*

"Kramer." Tom Randall's voice sharply interrupted Carston Kramer's reflections. "Get hold of Foster's wife. Talk to her. See where she's coming from, and then get back to me." His tone was hard and flat, and he stood up abruptly, indicating their meeting was at an end.

When the door closed behind Carston Kramer, Tom Randall sat

heavily back down, swiveling his chair toward the window. He stared silently down on the busy city streets. Cars clogged the intersections; people, all of them in a hurry filled the sidewalks. "All in the great race," he muttered. "And for what? God, for what?"

Already the terrible pain in the pit of his stomach was returning and with it came the same sickening question that tormented his mind. Over and over, he had asked himself, had he gone home the night of the Pine Bluff fire would it have been different? And always the answer was the same—yes. But it was too late now. Paul was gone, and he could do nothing but live each day with the deadly guilt gnawing at him.

Business was Tom Randall's only escape, but this last week he had lost all enthusiasm for it. The disaster at Pine Bluff was a huge, messy affair that would take months, maybe years to clean up. Somebody from some investigative agency was constantly knocking at their door asking questions, implicating the Randall Corporation, attempting to fix the blame on him for the entire ugly incident.

"Should've let that one go—never pushed so hard for that project. Squeezed Foster too much, but who'd have guessed the bastard would do some damn fool thing like that?" he said aloud bitterly. "So much should've been different. None of it should've happened."

He switched off his office lights and walked despondently toward the elevator. He was too tired to work any longer, but he dreaded going home to the emptiness of the house on Pilgrim Road.

Chapter 33

A LIGHT DRIZZLE WAS FALLING, AND London's Heathrow Airport was shrouded in fog as United Airlines flight 106 made its final descent. The plane hit the runway with a jolt, shuddered, and then taxied smoothly to the gate. Entering the terminal, Elloree felt a surge of excitement in spite of her fatigue. Restless passengers moving up and down the aisles and a fitful, cranky baby's wailing had made it a long, sleepless trip.

Threading through crowds of travelers, Elloree made her way to the customs counters, where a ruddy-faced official stamped her passport and welcomed her to Britain. She was approached at the baggage claim area by a smartly uniformed chauffeur who greeted her by name and introduced himself. "Alan Jordon, Miss. I'll be drivin' ya to the Grovesnor. 'Ope ya 'ad a good flight," he said in a thick, cockney accent. "Only be a minute collectin' the cases." He disappeared in the crush of passengers but returned moments later carrying her two small bags. "Bit of a nip in the air," he told her, eyeing the tan Burberry over her arm as they threaded their way toward the exit.

Grateful for Alan's warning, she slipped into her coat, tying the belt snugly about her waist before emerging into the cold dampness. They quickly made their way to the parking area through lines of cabs and motor coaches. And once settled comfortably in the back seat of Alan's long, black Mercedes touring sedan, she felt herself relaxing as they sped down the highway toward London.

"Sir Nigel would've come himself, Miss, but he 'ad a meetin'. He asked me to tell you he'd come along straightaway after you've 'ad time to settle in at the hotel," he said, smiling in the rearview mirror at her.

Elloree leaned her head back against the soft leather cushions, enjoying the drive to the city.

"Good spot of traffic this time of day," Alan continued, maneuvering the car through congested roundabouts and busy thoroughfares.

"I'd never get used to driving on the wrong side of the road," she told him with a laugh. "Good thing I didn't rent a car and try to drive myself. I'd still be at the airport going around in circles."

As they wound through the narrow city streets toward the hotel, Alan pointed out historical landmarks and sight-seeing attractions.

"Natural History Museum straight ahead and the Victoria and Albert comin' up on the right. Real love 'tween them two, not like our modern royals," he sniffed disdainfully.

Elloree remained discreetly silent, recalling the latest steamy affair involving British nobility smeared across the American tabloids.

Alan turned the car into Park Lane and announced, "Just be a minute now to the Grovesnor."

Elloree gazed out of the car windows, captivated by the city view as Alan edged through the bumper-to-bumper traffic. Hyde Park's lush green lawns and spreading Chestnut trees stretched along one side, and stately, grand old edifices lined the other. Parked in a row like sentries standing guard, a string of identical black cabs blocked the hotel's circular driveway.

Alan pulled the Mercedes neatly through the entry portico and into the one remaining parking space directly opposite a wide, gold-framed, glass, revolving door. A florid-complexioned, portly doorman dressed in top hat and red morning coat helped her from the car and ushered her into the lobby. Alan followed with her bags, stacking them carefully on the luggage trolley by the reception desk. Thanking him and complimenting him on his expert driving, she fumbled with her purse. But he spoke quickly, "Not a shilling, Miss. Sir Nigel took care of all that. Enjoy your stay." He tipped his cap to her as he left

And she turned toward the desk to register. "I'm Elloree Randall," she said to the fashionably tailored clerk. A wave of exhaustion suddenly washed over her, and she hoped her reservation had been confirmed.

"Yes, we're expecting you. Your luggage will be sent right up if you'll just fill out this information card. The lifts are to the left, and 512 is in the east wing of the fifth floor." The clerk handed her a key, smiled, and then added in a clipped British accent, "Enjoy your stay with us."

When Elloree opened the door to her suite, she was greeted by the fragrant scent of fresh flowers. Perfectly framed by the drawn damask draperies, a large bouquet in a Waterford crystal vase stood on the table in front of the window. In the late afternoon light, the delicate pink and ivory blooms gleamed like iridescent porcelain. A small card elegantly embossed with the initials "NH" lay next to the arrangement and read simply, "Welcome to London."

She stood staring at the beautiful display of roses for a moment before surveying the rest of the room. Spacious with a high molded ceiling, the sitting room was furnished with period antique pieces and commanded a panoramic view of Hyde Park from tall, arched casements. A large four-poster bed with two rosewood side tables occupied one end of the adjoining bedroom. A carved Chippendale armoire and dressing table skirted in pale peach silk with matching upholstered bench created an elegant but restful setting. Double doors opened into a dressing area adjoined by a marble bath dominated by a huge porcelain tub and accented by gold fixtures.

The ring of the telephone interrupted her inspection, and Nigel Harrison's mellifluous voice came across the line. "Mrs. Randall, Elloree, so glad you're here. How was your flight? Not too tiring I hope."

"Not bad, just long," she answered.

"And the hotel, comfortable? I chose it because of its location. Close to Harrison House, shopping and all that." His deep rich laugh was exhilarating, banishing her fatigue.

"Everything is perfect. My rooms are lovely with a grand view of the park. And the flowers are exquisite. Such a nice welcome. Thank you."

"Glad they pleased you. I'm sure you'd like some time to rest. The time difference takes some getting used to."

"I didn't have much luck sleeping on the plane. I must be tired, but it really hasn't hit me yet."

"If I pick you up for a light supper in a couple of hours, would that give you enough time to settle in, take a short rest?"

"I'd like that very much."

"Fine, shall we say seven o'clock?"

"I'll be ready." Almost before the line went dead, Elloree sank down on the bed, pulled the soft satin comforter around her, and within minutes, drifted into a deep sleep. When she awoke, it was already dark outside, and she hurriedly dressed for dinner.

Nigel Harrison was waiting for her in the lobby. Seated in a high wingback chair before a massive stone fireplace where logs blazed, he sat studying the London *Times* financial news. He wore a charcoal gray business suit and conservative, burgundy striped tie, and he smiled and rose to greet her when she stepped off the elevator.

For dinner, Nigel had selected a charming English pub within walking distance of the hotel. The rain had stopped, and the cool, crisp air felt invigorating to Elloree as they walked along Park Lane. Red double-decker sight-seeing busses clogged the busy intersection, and skillful cabbies weaved their small black Austins in and out of the heavy evening traffic.

"Don't they have a lot of accidents?" she asked Nigel as two taxis sped by them, narrowly missing each other, almost colliding at the corner.

"Our London cabs are a bit of a British institution. All the drivers are tested carefully before they're licensed, and they can bring those cars around on a sixpence, as you'd say."

"I think you're referring to our American expression, 'turn on a dime.'" She laughed.

"Yes, quite, that's it, turn on a dime. That's very good. You people always seem to put the right twist to words," he said, smiling broadly. "Now, here we are, King's Arms, one of the oldest establishments in London."

Elloree gazed up at the pub's Tudor style facade, leaded glass casements, and window boxes filled with colorful flowers. A coat of arms hung above the entrance, and a mouthwatering aroma of freshly baked bread mingled with roasting beef greeted them when Nigel swung the door open for her. The King's Arms' two adjoining rooms were filled with round, wooden tables; red, velour upholstered chairs, and a long bar that stretched the length of the larger room. Nigel guided her to a quiet corner table, and once comfortably seated, she glanced around the pub with interest. The tables appeared to be occupied mostly by local business people chatting congenially over tall tankards of dark ale.

"Thought you might enjoy this more than the hotel. Food is good and the pubs give you a chance to sample some of our country fare. The menu's posted on that chalkboard over the bar. When you've decided, I'll place our order. Bit of an English fast food, eh? So there you are; that chap, McDonald, must've come over to England to get his ideas. Of course, we didn't have golden arches for him, only marble ones." He chuckled, enjoying his own joke.

She laughed with him, responding to his infectious good humor and relaxing in the comfortable, homey atmosphere.

They ordered fish and chips with mugs of rich, dark lager, and as he'd promised, the food was delicious. Their plates were piled high with crisp, golden fried potatoes and tender, flaky, lightly breaded white fish.

"About tomorrow," Nigel continued. "I have one early morning conference I must attend, and then we can spend the day looking at some areas I think would be first-rate for Wishes shops. I could pick you up about ten. Time enough for you to have breakfast?"

"Perfect," she responded eagerly. "I'd love to do that, and perhaps we could see some of the city highlights at the same time."

"We'll make time for that. Quite a lot to see actually, if you like history. We Brits do have some. Sometimes I think it's all we've got left of the old empire," he said wistfully.

On the walk back to the Grovesnor House Hotel, it began to rain again, a steady, damp drizzle, making the streets and sidewalks slippery. Nigel took her arm and quickly unfurled a large black umbrella.

"Carry one of these always. English weather is dashed unpredictable. Did you bring one with you? If not, we'd better pop into Harrison House tomorrow first thing and pick one up for you."

"I did bring one," she assured him. "But it isn't doing much good now at the bottom of my suitcase."

They laughed together as they made their way back to the hotel, sharing his umbrella's protection from the persistent drizzle.

Once back in the hotel, Nigel escorted her to the elevator and told her how much he'd enjoyed the evening.

"I had a lovely time, too," she said. "And I'm looking forward to tomorrow. I'll meet you in the lobby at ten," she promised, stepping into the waiting lift.

He smiled and waved as the polished brass doors slid noiselessly together. The car swiftly ascended to the fifth floor, and moments later, she was back in her suite. She hastily undressed, slid between the crisp sheets, and switched off the bedside lamp. Although thoughts of the trip, Nigel, and all the day's events drifted through her mind, she quickly grew drowsy and slipped into a deep sleep. And that night, she slept more soundly than she had in many months.

Chapter 34

Elloree awoke early the next morning, and in spite of the time change, she felt rested and eager for the day. She found the Grovesnor House dining room offered a traditional English breakfast of poached eggs, sautéed mushrooms, and toast with marmalade. As the waiter served her hot tea with warm milk and sugar, she glanced at the morning *Times*.

She quickly scanned both local and international news reports, but it was the full-page advertisement for Harrison House that caught her attention. A little girl in a lace party dress, straw bonnet, and Mary Jane shoes stood smiling beside a small boy in knee pants, bow tie, and blazer, offering her a bouquet of daisies tied with ribbons. Beneath the picture Elloree read, "Little Susie wear for Little Susies everywhere." She stared at the appealing layout and felt a rush of excited anticipation as she thought about the plans for Wishes that had brought her to London.

After breakfast, she wandered through the hotel lobby, stopping at the desk for sight-seeing brochures. Studying them with interest, she wished she had more time, but she had promised Timmy she would only stay a week.

Timmy. Elloree's eyes filled with tears at the thought of him. Although he had been improving steadily since that day in the park, she knew he was still mending. At least now she was able to talk to him, share in his struggle toward recovery. But this morning here in London as she waited for Nigel, Timmy seemed a world away.

And for the first time since that terrible night, she felt alive again, as if she had finally awakened from some dreadful, paralyzing nightmare. Mark had insisted she make this trip alone, and now she was grateful to him. He had been right; she needed this time to begin her own healing.

Browsing through the hotel gift shop, Elloree caught sight of Nigel Harrison striding across the lobby. Dressed in a cream-colored polo shirt, tweed sport jacket, and tan wool slacks, he smiled broadly and waved as she walked over to greet him.

"Good morning. Have a good rest and a spot of breakfast?"

"Yes to both questions. But I'm afraid I had more than a spot of breakfast. Many more like that, and I'll have to buy new clothes. Mine won't fit." She laughed.

"My car's right outside if you're ready? Ah, I see you remembered," he said, pointing to her umbrella.

"I almost didn't bring it. It's so bright this morning; doesn't look at all like rain."

"Could go either way today. Sun may be out now, but in England, there's always a chance of showers." He guided her through the busy lobby and out into the cool, bracing morning air.

"I hope I dressed warmly enough," Elloree said, buttoning her jacket against the chill as they walked.

"With your jacket and brolly, you'll be just fine," he assured her.

Walking briskly beside him in her trim wool skirt, white cashmere sweater, and beige suede blazer, she was a striking young woman, and Nigel Harrison found he was looking forward to spending the day with her.

They drove through London, and again, Elloree marveled at the congested streets and how easily Nigel maneuvered his Daimler through them. And she had laughed with him when she had started toward the driver's side of the car. "It just doesn't seem right," she protested. "You're on the wrong side."

"And I better jolly well stay on it if we're going to get there," he said, easing the car into the stream of black cabs and red double-decker buses that endlessly flowed through the city.

He took her on a brief sight-seeing tour, pointing out the highlights as they passed them.

"I wish I could stop to see them all, not just drive by," she exclaimed. "And Windsor Castle and the Tower of London—I'd like to visit them. I picked up brochures in the lobby." She dug into her purse, producing several colorful pamphlets. "This one takes a coach tour to Oxford and the Cotswalds. If only I had more time."

"I wish you did too. A week won't be long enough." He glanced over at her, relieved to see her relaxing as he drove. Mark Williams had not told him much, but enough to let him know she was going through a difficult time. But this morning, leaning back against the seat cushions, her blonde hair tumbling around her face, she looked young and happy. Her enthusiasm was contagious, and he felt lighthearted, eager to show her London.

When they reached Kensington High Street, Nigel pulled into a driveway behind a red brick building. "Not easy to find a place to leave the motor in the city. My friend, Jonathan Adams, owns this property and won't mind if I park here," he explained, pulling in between two small delivery vans. "Jonathan has acquired many of the buildings in this section, and what he doesn't own himself, he keeps a close watch on for his clients' investments. I want you to see some of the stores in this area. A few squares down, there's one that's soon coming on the market. Jonathan told me about it just last week. I think this shop would be in an ideal location for Wishes. Shall we take a look?"

Elloree took his hand as he helped her out of the car, and they walked up the street passing many attractive, upscale boutiques. She hesitated at the window of one displaying svelte mannequins dressed in elegant, stylish fashions. "Oh, for more time," she moaned. "How I'd love to go in there and try on that outfit."

"Well, why don't you? I'll be happy to wait for you," he told her, and she knew he meant it.

"Don't tempt me. If I get distracted like that, we won't get anything done all week."

"That wouldn't be so bad. Then you'd have to come to London again. You see, I have a plan; if I distract you enough, you'll have to come back soon."

They walked on up the street together, chatting easily about the various stores, their owners, and retailing. Nigel Harrison knew a great deal about the history of all of them, when they'd started, and how long they had been in business.

"What do you think of this one?" he stopped in front of a fashionable small shop, flanked on both sides by two much larger, trendier ones. "The clientele that comes here is the best in London. Located in this district, we'd draw the most moneyed customers. And I think we could negotiate a good price. If you and Mark approve, I can look into it straightaway. It's not yet widely known that the space is available, so we'd have to move fast. Have to take it 'as is,' of course. And it would require alterations to meet your needs but nothing major. The structure's sound and the location prime."

"It's a property in an ideal area. I can see that by just walking the few blocks we have," she said.

"This entire square has some of the most expensive shops in London. And if the pounds, or rather I should say dollars, are fair, you'd be wise to present an offer. Space like this doesn't come on the market very often, practically never. It's only through my friendship with Jonathan Adams that I found out about it."

She nodded in agreement. "I'll talk with Mark, impress on him that we need to move quickly if he's interested. But knowing him, he'll be ready to hop the next plane tomorrow to close the deal. He'll want to see some numbers, of course. But I'll put together a package for him right away, and if it looks as good as you seem to predict, he'll be eager to put down a deposit to hold it."

"Good show. Couldn't do better for Wishes, but we'll take a look in Mayfair just the same. Who knows, maybe we'll open another one there if there's any good space to acquire. After lunch, we'll pop over for a quick tour."

On their way to Mayfair, Nigel found another pub nestled between shops and rows of flats. The Black Swan offered simple but delicious dishes and a comfortable English country atmosphere.

"I think I could easily become addicted to the food in these places. That cottage pie was wonderful," Elloree told Nigel as he helped her into the car.

"Glad you enjoyed it. We English aren't often noted for our food. But I've always suspected it's a bit of a bad rap promoted by the French years ago," he said with a laugh as he turned the Daimler into the heavy afternoon traffic.

Mayfair proved to be another excellent area for a Wishes shop. With its narrow lanes lined with expensive, restored flats and clusters of small, exclusive shops, it was one of the most desirable neighborhoods in London.

"Both locations seem ideal for Wishes," Elloree told Nigel as they wound their way back through the clogged streets toward her hotel. "Thank you so much for devoting your whole day to me. You've obviously had to spend time researching these places. I wouldn't have known where to look—would've wasted days and found nothing."

"I've enjoyed every minute of it," he assured her as they turned into the hotel entrance. "Now about dinner." He glanced at his watch.

"Dinner?" she raised a questioning eyebrow. "Haven't you done enough for me today?"

"Not at all. A light supper after the show perhaps?"

Again she shot him a questioning look. "The show?"

"You can't spend a week in London without at least one trip to the West End Theater District. I have tickets for tonight. I selected the show because it's a real tradition here. Agatha Christie's *Mousetrap* at St. Martin's Theater is the longest playing production in British history. Originally, Agatha Christie wrote a short radio script called *Three Blind*

Mice for Queen Mary's eightieth birthday. Then some years later, she wrote the play based on it."

"I'd love to see it."

"Good, then the only thing we have to decide is dinner before or late supper after the show. Which would you prefer?"

They decided on the after-theater supper, and Nigel told her he would call for her at seven. "We'll take a taxi," he said. "Driving in the West End at night is a job better left to the cabbies."

Alone in her room, drawing her bath, Elloree reflected on the events of the day. London was a fascinating city, and the sites Nigel had shown her would be perfect for the new Wishes shops. She knew Mark would be pleased and impatient to move ahead with a cost analysis. She would have to prepare a preliminary package for him. Her mind was racing ahead with ideas as she slipped out of her robe and stepped into the tub. Sliding into the foamy bubble bath, her muscles relaxed as she soaked, luxuriating in the lilac-scented, soothing water. And for the first time in months, she felt excited to be part of Wishes again.

Chapter 35

In a smart, black knit dress with her hair swept up into a French twist, Elloree looked stunning when she greeted Nigel in the lobby for their theater evening. Her fair, classic features were complimented by the simplicity of her ensemble, and Nigel's throat tightened as he saw her wave and walk toward him. Appreciative glances followed them as they crossed the lobby together to the hotel entrance and the line of waiting cabs.

Taxis and pedestrians flooded London's West End Theater District, where neon-lit marquees advertised one after another famous musical and dramatic production. Their cab pulled sharply to the curb and halted with a jolt to avoid the swarm of theatergoers that spilled off the sidewalk.

"Never look, they don't," their driver muttered, stamping hard on the brake.

"Glad you're driving and not me." Nigel laughed as he paid him, adding a tip that produced a wide grin.

"Thanks, Gov. Enjoy the play," the cabby called, tipping his cap before jetting out into the endless flow of traffic.

Nigel guided Elloree through the throngs of tourists and playgoers to the stately entrance of St. Martin's Theater. The building had an early-1900 architecture that had been carefully preserved, but the interior had been newly refurbished. The lobby had been carpeted and repainted in a soft shade of mauve, and the once tarnished railings lining the balcony stairways had been refinished in a brightly polished brass. The view of the deep, wide stage had been greatly improved by the addition of modern footlights and banks of overhead spotlights. Large, comfortable loges, called stalls, had replaced the smaller, old ones that once had lined the front rows of the playhouse. A smartly uniformed attendant ushered Nigel and Elloree down the aisle just as the lights dimmed and the curtain was rising on the first act.

The Mousetrap proved to be as entertaining as Nigel had promised. Realistic sets, authentic costumes, and skilled actors blended together into a mystery that cleverly unraveled.

"The ending was a complete surprise. I never guessed who did it right up until the final curtain," Elloree enthused as their cab sped back across town. "No wonder the play's been such a success and run for all these years. Mark must see it when he comes to London."

"Remember what the lead actor told the audience," Nigel reminded her. "Don't reveal the plot to anyone before he sees it. That would spoil the suspense."

"I won't tell Mark," she reassured him. "But I don't often know something he doesn't, so I'll be tempted."

Nigel smiled at her, wondering about the two of them, Mark and Elloree, and their relationship. Obviously a strong bond existed between them, but Mark had insisted she make this trip alone. An unusual pair, Nigel concluded as he listened to her enthusiastic conversation about the show as they sat enjoying their light after-theater supper.

When they were standing once more in the lobby of the Grovesnor House, Elloree felt suddenly uncomfortable, searching for words to thank him. But he reached for her hand, held it gently for a moment, and then leaned forward, his lips brushing her cheek.

"I had a lovely time," he said. "You made it a special day and a wonderful evening. Thank you. I'll ring you in the morning. Good night."

The elevator doors closed, he was gone, and already the day was becoming a memory. But that night, Elloree drifted into a deep sleep with dreams of Nigel, Mark, London, and Wishes all entwined together into an odd kaleidoscope.

The next morning, the telephone's loud jingle abruptly woke her, and Elloree sat up rubbing her eyes and squinting to see the clock.

"I say, I hope I didn't wake you," Nigel's cheerful voice came across the line.

"Oh no, really, yes. I have to be truthful," she answered. "I don't know when I've slept so hard or so long. I just looked at the time and feel absolutely sinful."

"You deserve the rest, but I'm hoping to pick you up for lunch. Thought you'd like another look at the shop on Kensington High Street. I've arranged for a walk-through to give you a better idea of what it has to offer and how it could adapt to Wishes. Have you talked to Mark about the two locations?"

"I tried to call Mark yesterday, but with the time change, we're not connecting. I'll try this evening, probably catch him then. And lunch would be perfect. I'd love to see the shop again."

"Fine. I'll pick you up at noon."

She'd heard the enthusiasm in his voice, how pleased he'd sounded when she accepted his invitation. And she slipped out of bed, showered, and dressed, eagerly anticipating the day.

Their second trip to Kensington High Street convinced Elloree that the shop would be a sound venture for Wishes. Bubbling with excitement that evening, she gave Mark her report. He listened intently, asked for more details, and then agreed it could be ideal if they could negotiate a lease with the right numbers.

"Other than looking for space for Wishes, El, how is London? And how are you getting on with Harrison?" Mark demanded abruptly.

Surprised, she stammered, "I'm enjoying London immensely, and I'm getting along very well with Nigel Harrison. He's treating me like royalty."

There was a silent pause before Mark boomed, "You coming home on schedule? Not planning to stay over there any longer, are you?"

"I'll be coming back at the end of the week, Mark." And she was sure she heard a small sigh of relief from the other end.

"Good. Things are popping here. I need to go over more expansion ideas with you. Looked at another building that's come on the market close to us. It'd make a great shipping center. We could use more space, and word has it the outfit's in trouble, needs to bail out. We possibly could move some of the other departments. Even with the additional property I've acquired, we're cramped. I'm gonna throw a low-ball bid at 'em, see if they'll bite. And if they do, I'm gonna need your input on the restructure."

Same old Mark. She smiled as she replied, "I'll be home soon, Mark. But you and Wishes are managing just fine, I know."

"Like hell," he bellowed. "End of the week can't come soon enough. Meet you at the airport."

She replaced the receiver, suddenly feeling guilty over the days and hours that had passed with no thoughts of home. She dialed the overseas operator once more, this time placing a call to Pilgrim Road.

Timmy's high-pitched voice chirped, "Is that you, Mom? How's London? Is the bridge really falling down?"

"No, Tim, it isn't, but London's a wonderful place." She laughed. "And you're going to love visiting it with me."

"You mean it, Mom? I really get to come? How soon? How soon?" he repeated excitedly. And she could picture him jumping up and down at the other end.

"I do mean it, Tim. I'll be home Friday like I promised. We can talk about it then."

"Boy, I can't wait till tomorrow to tell Stevie McKensie," he squealed. "He thinks he's big stuff just 'cause his dad took him to the old ball game. Big deal! I love you, Mom."

"And I love you, Tim. I have to say good-bye now. Be a good boy until I get home."

Tears clouded her eyes as she replaced the receiver, but this time they were from relief and joy. Tim was mending, and maybe with more time and love, he would be all right. Maybe they both would.

Chapter 36

THE DAYS PASSED TOO QUICKLY, with Elloree cramming as much sight-seeing into her busy schedule as possible. She squeezed in a trip to the Tower of London, Buckingham Palace for the Changing of the Guard, and Westminster Abbey. Exploring the city, Nigel proved as excellent a tour guide as capable business advisor. He took her through all the major department stores and other retail outlets to see their greeting card sections. But by far the most impressive was Harrison House, the flagship of the Harrison international chain. Covering a complete block in downtown London, every section of the store reflected Nigel's unique planning and merchandising talents. As he ushered her through the departments with obvious pride, smartly dressed personnel acknowledged him with a differential reverence. He had built a company reputation for exceptional treatment of his employees, and Elloree could tell that they liked and respected him.

"They love you," she said as they were leaving the store. "They all do, you can see it on their faces."

"Not all, I'm afraid. But I do try to keep up morale within the stores, build pride into the staff."

"I've never seen a store like it, Nigel."

Slightly embarrassed but pleased by her praise, he added simply, "I do like my work. It's my life."

She gave him an understanding look but said nothing when she saw sadness cloud his eyes. But then he was smiling again as they walked together down Bond Street, and he told her about opening the first Harrison House.

"I've not seen anything already here in London like the Wishes shops we're planning," she told him after their last day of visiting their potential competitors.

"I agree," he said. "Between the three of us, we should be able to put together a unique, unbeatable package. I'm convinced the market's there, ready to be popped into. I'm dashed sure of it."

She smiled at his very British expression but raised a questioning eyebrow. How quickly Nigel had made himself a part of her planning for Wishes. She remembered the tone of Mark's inquiry when he asked how she was getting along with Nigel. Being in London working with him this last week had seemed very natural, like he already had become a part of Wishes. Together, they had accomplished all that Mark had outlined before she had left on the trip. Any reservations Mark might have about her working with Nigel would vanish when he saw the results. Whatever was good for Wishes was what Mark always wanted, and Nigel Harrison had been very good for Wishes already.

"We've only two more days," Nigel suddenly said to her that evening. "Unless you can arrange to stay longer," he added hopefully.

"I'd like to, but I'm afraid it's impossible. I have to get back," she said, feeling a sudden stab of regret at the thought of leaving London.

"I'd like to pick you up tomorrow morning, take you out of the city for the day. There's a place I very much want to show you. I can be at your hotel by ten. I have an eight o'clock conference, but I'll cut it short, get there earlier if possible"

"Sounds like another lovely day," she assured him, her curiosity aroused. "I'll look forward to it."

It was raining the next morning, a steady drizzle making the streets slick-wet as Elloree and Nigel drove out of London. The windshield wipers slapped back and forth, and they rode in silence, listening to nostalgic, old tunes on the radio. She leaned her head back against the car's leather seat cushions and snuggled deeper into her woolen cardigan.

"Are you cold? Shall I put the heat up a bit?" he offered.

"No, no, I'm fine," she murmured, letting the music float through her mind. "I wonder, when is the twelfth of never?" she mused.

He looked over at her, puzzled by the question. "The twelfth of never," he repeated. "I say, whatever made you ask?"

"You weren't listening—to the music, I mean. The song that just played on the radio is an old ballad; I haven't heard it for years." She hummed part of the melody. "I'll love you till the twelfth of never, and that's a long, long time," she sang softly. "Forever. The twelfth of never just sounds more romantic."

"I don't think I've ever heard it before, but the twelfth of never does sound like a long, long time," he agreed with a smile.

They lapsed into silence again, listening to the music as the miles fell away. Elloree gazed out at the passing lush, verdant landscape crisscrossed by low stone walls and dotted with rural cottages. At last the congestion of the city had given way to the rolling pastoral countryside, but Elloree felt a strained tension building in Nigel. His jaw was firmly set, and he tightly gripped the steering wheel as he wheeled the Daimler sharply around each curve. She shifted uncomfortably and tried to concentrate on the bucolic scenery, but her uneasiness mounted with every fast turn.

Suddenly, Nigel jerked the wheel of the car abruptly to the right. They skidded, cornered, and then turned into a winding cobblestone lane. Offering no explanation, he accelerated, and the Daimler sped down the narrow twisting ribbon. The gray, pattering rain had given way to a damp mist, and a few tiny patches of cloud-puffed, pale blue sky appeared as they rounded another curve. Nigel slowed the car, shifted into a lower gear, and they climbed to the crest of the sloping hillside.

In the distance, an immense manor house rose above the trees; its proud peaks and turrets loomed up out of the heavy blue-gray haze.

"What an incredible sight," Elloree gasped. "It's enormous but so beautiful, like something out of *Wuthering Heights*. It must belong to a duke or some nobleman."

"Certainly someone grand," he said quietly.

A deserted, gray, stone gatehouse flanked by crumbling rock walls marked the outskirts of the grounds, and a narrow, gravel roadway threaded through the trees up toward the palatial residence.

"It's more a castle than a house. Are we really going up there?" she asked as they passed through an imposing archway marked with a weathered bronze placard bearing a coat of arms and the name Chilton Manor.

"Do you know the Chiltons? Are you sure it'll be all right? It looks a bit intimidating."

"It's quite all right, really," he responded, relaxing his grip on the wheel and guiding the Daimler through the gates to Chilton Manor. To the right, a small lake rippled in the hazy afternoon light, and grassy emerald meadows stretched beyond. A great rolling lawn bordered by networks of neatly trimmed hedges and colorful flower beds spread down from the manor's entrance.

"What an extraordinary place. Imagine living here. How in the world would you keep from getting lost in your own house?"

"Yes, it could be a problem, especially for a small child." Nigel chuckled, pulling the car to a stop at the foot of broad, stone steps leading up to a pair of towering, carved entry doors.

"Are we expected?" she whispered, looking up at the sculpted granite columns of the stately portico.

"No need to whisper," he said taking her arm and guiding her up the steep steps.

"I always whisper when I'm in grand places," she said in a barely audible voice.

"Come on then. We must get you inside before you lose your voice completely."

Nigel raised the heavy brass knocker, and the doors suddenly swung open, revealing a vast, dim hall. He took her hand, and they stepped inside. High, arched, stained-glass windows cast shafts of light that played across the marble floor, and at the far end, a wide spiral staircase swept down from the upper stories. Enormous, age-faded tapestries depicting epic allegorical scenes hung on the thick stone walls, and a great, hammered-iron lantern dangled from the rafters.

Elloree blinked. Adjusting her eyes to the faint light, she stood waiting for some explanation from Nigel. Suddenly, a stooped, gray-haired woman appeared in the hallway. With one hand, she shaded her eyes and, with the other, smoothed her starched white apron as she peered across the threshold.

"Why it's you, Master Nigel. I didn't know you was comin'. Blimey, I didn't know you was comin'," she repeated.

"Never mind, Myrtle," he replied. "No need to fuss. I didn't know myself until last night."

She crossed the floor to them, her flat shoes slapping on the marble, her fingers twisting the ends of her apron. "Coo, and with a bonnie lass and me not ready. Not one of the rooms is made up proper. Not a fresh flower in the house," she wailed.

Elloree stared first at the old woman and then at Nigel.

"You live here," she blurted, her voice echoing through the vast, granite hall. "But you can't live here," she stammered. "You told me you live in an apartment in Mayfair. You pointed out the building when we were there."

"And so I did," he told her. "And so I do. I come here very seldom—in fact, hardly at all."

"But the name. The coat of arms," Elloree persisted. "Your name is Harrison, or is it?" she asked, her eyes widening.

"My mother. My mother was Lady Chilton. My father, Charles Harrison, was an American officer stationed here during the war. They were married only a few months before his plane was shot down on a special mission over Germany. It was the beginning of the war, and my mother, rest her soul, never changed her name, although she did give me his. I was the only thing the marriage brought her, I'm afraid."

Seeing Elloree's stunned expression, he paused, reached for her hand. "I'm sorry. I should have explained before I brought you out here," he apologized and then added quickly, "I didn't because I was afraid I wouldn't come if I thought very much about it. Just get in the car and drive was the best I could do. I haven't been here in quite some time," he finished sadly.

"I wondered when we were driving where we were going and why," she said.

"Come with me. I'll tell you about Chilton Manor if you want me to. And I'm sure Myrtle will work one of her miracles and prepare a tea for us."

The old servant nodded. "Better be goin' to the library, Master Nigel; only room I keep warm these days. Fire's already lit. Won't be a proper tea, but I'll bring it in there straightaway," she grumbled, shuffling off toward the kitchen.

"For Myrtle, it's never a proper tea," Nigel said, smiling at her retreating back. "And we better follow her directions and go to the library before our feet freeze to the floor," he said, leading Elloree across the dim, cavernous, gray stone hall.

Chapter 37

Late afternoon sunlight poured through leaded glass casements casting patterns and shadows across the library's richly hued oriental carpeting. Shelves filled with leather bound volumes stretched along the room's paneled walls and logs crackled in a huge open brick hearth giving Nigel and Elloree a warm welcome.

"How inviting," Elloree murmured, spreading her hands out to the fire and surveying the rows of well-preserved, rare, old books. "There must be hundreds of first editions in this collection. I'd like to read and study some of them."

"Perhaps one day you will," Nigel said, leading her over to a burgundy velvet sofa piled with crimson silk cushions. She sank into the plush softness, grateful for the room's warmth on the chilly afternoon.

"What a beautiful picture," Elloree commented looking up at a large, gilt-framed portrait of a young woman hanging above the fireplace. The artist had skillfully captured both movement and personality in subject and landscape. The girl's pink gown seemed to float, caught by some mystic breeze, and her head slightly turned as if to hear some distant faint strains of an evening serenade. With one hand gracefully outstretched, she stood poised, illuminated by twilight against a leafy, verdant background. Cascades of blonde curls framed her delicate, angelic features. "It's enchanting. The setting and elegance, it could almost be a Gainsborough," Elloree whispered to Nigel.

"You're whispering again." He laughed. "The picture's of my maternal great-grandmother. And it is. A Gainsborough I mean. The Chiltons always did go in for the portraits. There are many throughout the manor—another Gainsborough and a Reynolds but the rest done by lesser artists. Probably most of the others were painted by starving fellows from the local villages. Although they're all pictures of relatives, most of the names I've long forgotten, if I ever knew," he said, shaking his head. "I warned you, we Brits are steeped in family and country history. All these books have been here for generations. When I was a lad, I used to climb the library ladder searching for some daring adventure novel. But to my immense disappointment, all I ever found was more history and got into trouble for my efforts as well."

She smiled at him, imagining a curious little boy in knee pants swaying high above the library floor seeking some bold tale.

"You grew up here at Chilton Manor?" she asked. "I remember your comment about a child getting lost in the house. You must have on more than one occasion."

"Still do," he said with a smile. "Ah, now didn't I tell you Myrtle wouldn't let us down? She always says there's nothing in the kitchen and then produces the most amazing teas."

Clucking her disapproval, Myrtle came into the library carrying an immense silver tray laden with platters of delicious treats. She carefully laid the table before them with dainty bone china cups and saucers, finely engraved silverware, and tiny, embroidered linen napkins.

"Can't get the berries like we used to, Master Nigel," she complained. "The scones aren't the same without 'em. No sir, not the same," she muttered shaking her head.

The aroma of the hot steaming tea and freshly baked scones made Elloree realize suddenly how very hungry she was.

"It looks and smells delicious," she said.

Forcing a faint smile, Myrtle reached for the teapot's delicately curved handle. "Shall I pour?"

"No, no, Myrtle. That's quite all right. We'll take care of ourselves. Everything is as perfect as always."

"Then I'll be goin' to the kitchen if there's nothin' more I can get you," she said. At the door she hesitated. "Will you be wantin' supper this evening?"

"Yes, I think that would be quite nice, Myrtle. But no need to go to any trouble. Something very light will be fine after all this," he said, gesturing toward the plates piled with delicious delicacies spread before them.

"Just have to make do, that's all. Make do," she muttered, wagging her head from side to side as she closed the library door behind her.

"Dear old Myrtle," Nigel said. "She's the one thing that never changes here at the manor. There are never fresh berries for tarts or the right ingredients for pastries, but somehow she manages. All my life, as far back as I can remember."

"She's a marvel," Elloree agreed after the old woman had retreated to the kitchen. "Shall I?" she asked reaching for the silver teapot.

They settled back comfortably together on the sofa, sipping their tea and sampling the delectable cakes and scones.

Fascinated by Nigel's background at Chilton Manor, Elloree enjoyed listening to his childhood reminiscences. As he talked, she became aware of his deep love for the estate and wondered about his long absence from it. Then quite suddenly he grew silent, staring across the room, lost in his memories.

Elloree reached out to him, took his hand. "You don't need to tell me any more now. I understand. You've been gone a very long time. Feelings and memories must be flooding your mind," she said softly.

He held her hand gently, twining her fingers in his. "Yes, it's been a while, almost a year actually. For the first time since Elizabeth died, I felt I wanted to come back here, needed to. I wanted to share it with you, Elloree, because it always will be a part of me. I knew I had to come here, confront the past, make peace with it before I can have a future."

Elloree looked at him, deep compassion showing in her own troubled eyes. Suddenly, sadness filled the room, engulfed them both, and for a moment, they sat in silence, each remembering.

Then Nigel continued in a quiet voice, "My mother died here. She never remarried after my father's death. She raised me at Chilton Manor, and we shared some wonderful years together. My mother was a beautiful, accomplished woman," he said wistfully. "She entertained in the grand old style, surrounding us with scores of talented, interesting friends here at the manor. Although I was an only child, I wasn't a lonely, neglected one. Far from it. She gave me many opportunities but resisted Chilton tradition by refusing to send me off to boarding school. And I was endlessly grateful, spending my days here, attending Saint James private day school before going to university. But when she died, I came back to settle her affairs and ended up staying. It was to Chilton Manor that I brought my wife, Elizabeth, and she loved the estate almost as much as I did."

He smiled at the memory, rose, and poked the fire, sending sparks flying up the flue. He sat down and studied his teacup pensively.

"I thought I owed you some explanation," he said quietly. "Why I suddenly brought you out here."

"I think I know," Elloree said. "Or at least I think I understand."

"Elizabeth and I lived at Chilton Manor for eight years," he continued. "We were living here when Elizabeth and Susan were killed."

The shadows in the room deepened, although the heavy brocade draperies at the windows had been drawn back to let in the light. Dusk was fast giving way to nightfall as the two of them sat together in front of the glowing embers, absorbed in their own thoughts. Nigel roused himself, crossed the room, and switched on a lamp. The sudden glare illuminated the face in the painting over the fireplace, flickering across the golden, fragile beauty captured there.

"Susan looked very much like her," Nigel said looking at the portrait, "or would have if she'd lived. The same blue eyes, fine features, blond curls of the Chilton women." He turned away to hide the tears in his eyes. "Susan, my little girl, was in the car with Elizabeth. She was six years old." The words strangled in his throat.

Elloree crossed the room to him, took his hands in hers, and held them tightly, leaning her head against his shoulder. "Don't try to talk, Nigel. You don't need to tell me now. There's plenty of time."

He freed his hands, cupped her face in them, and gazed down into her eyes. "I want to tell you. I need you to know all there is, now," he said simply.

He led her back to the sofa, still clutching her hands in his, and continued in a soft, hushed voice. "There was a heavy mist that day. The fog lay across the Chilton meadow like a cold, wet blanket. I should've gone with them," he said fiercely, sitting up abruptly and turning away to hide his pain. I should've driven them myself, but I'd left early for London on business. Elizabeth always took Susan into the village on Wednesday for their weekly shopping outing together. They looked forward to it each week. Just the two girls, Elizabeth always said, on a 'wee spree' she called it. The fog was so dense they couldn't have seen the hay lorry. Elizabeth died instantly, but Susan lived for three days. I should've been with them, died with them." He held his head in his hands, his shoulders sagged, and he sobbed.

"You couldn't have known, Nigel. Even if you had been here." Elloree reached out to him, and he came into her arms. He shuddered against her, the cold dampness of his tears streaked her cheeks, and they clung together as the night deepened, surrounding Chilton Manor.

Chapter 38

THE LOGS IN THE LIBRARY grate had burned down to smoldering embers when Nigel stirred in her arms. He roused himself and pulled gently away from her, brushing her cheek with a kiss.

"I must show you to your room so you can bathe and rest before Myrtle springs another sumptuous feast on us."

As they climbed the winding staircase to the second floor, rows of Chilton ancestors peered out from their gilt-edged frames at them. Some wore serious expressions, others faint smiles, but all had the same high cheekbones and fair, aristocratic looks. *Generations of a handsome family now without an heir*, Elloree thought with a sudden twinge of sadness. *Nigel is the last, and he's a Harrison, not a Chilton. Lady Chilton honored her brief tragic union by giving her only son his father's name but in so doing ended the Chilton line. It could not have been easy for her. She must have been a remarkable woman, capable of great unselfish love.*

Nigel interrupted her thoughts by swinging open the door to a large, high-ceilinged bedchamber decorated in soft shades of dusty rose.

"Mother called this the Rose Room. Her favorite friends always stayed here."

Elloree gazed across the elegant room at the huge, carved canopy bed, draped in pale pink silk. A pair of fan-backed chairs upholstered in rich cranberry, floral brocade stood before the hearth, where a fire had been laid but not yet lighted.

"Better get this going. Take the chill off." Nigel struck a match, and the logs ignited, the flames immediately sending a flickering light dancing across the thick Aubusson carpet.

"I'm sure Myrtle has provided a robe and towels for your bath. Is there anything else you might like?"

"I can't think of a thing I could possibly need but a soak in a hot tub."

"Good," he answered, holding her hand to his lips and gently kissing the palm. "And thank you. Join me downstairs for cocktails when you're ready."

"I might get lost if I have to look for you."

"No you won't. I'll be waiting for you."

Softly, he closed the door behind him, leaving her alone in the Rose Room with the events of the day spinning through her mind.

When she had bathed and rested for a short while, Elloree dressed and went in search of Nigel. But when she descended the stairway, she found him waiting at the foot as promised.

"How on earth did you know exactly when I was coming down? Or have you been standing here for the last hour?" she asked with a laugh.

"A trick I learned as a nipper. The old place creaks when anyone walks down the upstairs hall or opens a door. Whenever I was up to mischief, I'd avoid discovery if I just listened." He grinned boyishly, taking her arm.

"I'm afraid I came unprepared," she said apologetically, looking at his fresh blue silk shirt, cashmere pullover, and neatly pressed gray slacks. "My daytime outfit has to stretch into evening."

"You look just perfect. After all, you couldn't have guessed where we were going, and I gave you no clue. I thought if I told you, I wouldn't be able to go through with it. Until the very moment we entered the manor, I was unsure about coming, but now we're here together, I'm very glad we came," he said, leading her across the hall into the great dining room.

A chandelier with hundreds of teardrop crystals and tiny candle bulbs hung from a high vaulted ceiling illuminating a long mahogany table that was flanked by straight-backed velvet cushioned chairs. On a massive carved sideboard a pair of tall Victorian candelabras stood lighted, their slender tapers casting a soft glow in the vast room. At the far end of the table, two places had been neatly set on a small lace cloth with a bowl of fresh flowers surrounded by a ring of flickering votive candles in hand-painted porcelain holders. A fire blazed in the grate, warming the cold stone walls and making pools of light on the marble floor. A bottle of Dom Pérignon chilled in an ice bucket, and two Baccarat champagne flutes stood waiting on a silver serving tray."

Nigel poured them each a glass of the sparkling champagne, raising his own in a toast. "To being here at Chilton Manor with you. And to feeling whole again."

She smiled, responding by lifting her own glass. "And to you. To us and this evening; may its memories last until the twelfth of never."

"Ah yes, your ballad," he murmured. "It will always remind me of today and you."

For a moment, the gentle tinkling of their crystal glasses was the only sound in the room as they stood, quietly sipping their wine. Then Myrtle appeared soundlessly from the kitchen, placing one delicious dish after another on the table before disappearing again without a word.

"It looks like dinner is served. Shall we?" He pulled back one of the chairs for her.

"Would you prefer red wine or white with dinner or perhaps more champagne?" he asked before joining her at the table.

"A little white would be nice."

Nigel filled their glasses, and once more they touched them together in a toast. Conversation flowed easily between them as they sampled Myrtle's culinary masterpieces.

"Myrtle is truly amazing, Nigel, and I can tell how very fond of you she is."

"Yes, she's been here many years. When I turned my full attention to my business after losing …" He hesitated before continuing, "After my wife was gone, Myrtle really took over the running of the manor. I poured myself into developing Harrison House. Building it was my salvation and has been all I needed, until now." His eyes locked with Elloree's, holding her gaze. "I shut out Chilton Manor and the past. I closed the door to Susan's room the day she died, left it as it was. I thought I would never want to return. But I was wrong. I wanted you to see it, to know me better and perhaps understand how much I want to work with you, be a part of Wishes. I knew I wanted to meet you the minute I saw your Little Susie line. Little Susie reminded me so much of my own Susan." And this time there was less pain in his voice as he sat studying Elloree's lovely face framed in the candlelight.

After they had dined, Nigel guided her once more into the library. A tray with a silver coffee service, delicate china demitasse cups and a plate of petits fours decorated with tiny, pink frosting flowers waited on the coffee table. And two cut-crystal brandy snifters had been placed by the fire to warm.

"Myrtle thinks of everything."

"She does," he agreed.

They sipped espresso from the tiny cups and nibbled on the pastries to please Myrtle. Outside, darkness had descended, the wind had started to blow, and a light rain pattered against the windows.

"That woman shows no mercy," Nigel moaned. "She's determined to kill us with food."

Moments later, the old housekeeper padded in to gather up their dishes and remove the tray.

"You'll be stayin' the night and goin' back to London in the morning?" she asked, hesitating in the doorway.

"Yes, in the morning or, to be more precise, about noon. No need to worry over breakfast, Myrtle."

But already she was retreating, grumbling over the shortages of fresh milk and eggs at the manor.

The fire crackled and the wind-blown rain pelted against the library's leaded glass panes, the strong gusts rattling the shutters. They sat curled up on the sofa sipping the warm cognac. Nigel told her more about the start of Harrison House, and she told him of her first days at Wishes. The grandfather clock in the corner suddenly chimed, and they looked at each other startled by the hour.

"This has been a wonderful day and evening," she said. "My whole week in London has been fantastic, thanks to you."

"And mine. But I suppose we'd better call it a night or Myrtle will be in here serving us breakfast."

Laughing softly, hand in hand, they climbed the stairs. He paused before the Rose Room door, looking down at her.

"I do thank you."

She put her fingers gently to his mouth to stop his words. "Hush," she said. "No need to thank me. I'm the one who should be thanking you."

Then she was in his arms, his kisses silencing her, his body pressing hers with fierce desire. He pulled her closer, his mouth traveling down the long, velvety smoothness of her neck.

"I love you, Elloree, I've never wanted anyone like I want you," he whispered.

And she felt her own passions soar as his hands caressed her. Urgently, his fingers fumbling; he unbuttoned her blouse, letting it drop to the floor.

"You are so beautiful, my love," he murmured, cupping her breasts gently, his lips and tongue sliding over them. Then easily he lifted her, carried her into the Rose Room, and laid her tenderly on the pink, silken softness of the bed.

Eagerly, hungrily she responded, helping him from his clothes. She stroked his muscular firmness and let her lips explore him. His every touch brought her to new heights of pleasure so that when, at last, they joined in one joyous burst of love, they lay together, hearts and bodies entwined, and drifted into a deep, peaceful sleep.

Nigel dressed in the faint dawn light, careful not to disturb Elloree. When she stirred, he tucked the downy comforter more closely around her. He gazed down at her long, blond hair tumbling around her face and her creamy skin, soft as new rose petals. How fitting she should be here in the Rose Room, he thought, longing to gather her in his arms again, kiss the satin smooth cheek and stroke the silky hair. But not wanting to wake her, he went silently out into the hallway.

Hours later, Elloree awoke, stretched, and then lay back against the pillows, remembering Nigel and their night together. A shaft of sunlight fell across the Aubusson carpet, dividing the room with a flickering white line. She slid out of bed and pushed back the heavy, pale pink brocade draperies. Below her window, the garden's brilliant colors were dazzling in the morning sun. Bathed by the night's rain, even the gravel paths threading between the flower beds and hedgerows glistened like pearly ribbons. As she opened the casement and breathed in the cool, crisp air, somewhere within the manor, a clock chimed, reminding her of the hour.

"Good Lord, it's already ten," she gasped. "I'll never be ready to leave by noon."

Hurriedly, she dressed, brushed her loose flowing hair, and caught it up into a ponytail with a wide, blue ribbon. She dabbed on lipstick, dusted powder across her nose, and quickly checked her reflection in the dresser mirror.

"Best I can do," she said as she left her room to go in search of Nigel.

Once again, she found him waiting at the foot of the staircase. Wearing tweeds and a chestnut-brown turtleneck, he smiled warmly at her, brushing her cheek with a kiss.

"We've a rare English sunny day to enjoy, and Myrtle's in the kitchen preparing to stuff us with breakfast." He took her hand and led her down the hallway toward the welcoming aroma of fresh brewed coffee.

Chapter 39

"Ummm, such a wonderful smell of coffee. I expected tea."

"Morning coffee was one of the first things I adopted from the Americans—maybe because of my father's Yankee genes. The day doesn't start right without it," he said with a laugh.

Myrtle was bustling about the large, bright pantry humming "The White Cliffs of Dover," and her lilting Scottish brogue floated out to greet them.

"Top of the mornin' to ye. Brought a wee bit of sunlight with ye, Master Nigel. The blooms are fairly burstin' in the gardens after the rains."

"I saw them from my window this morning," Elloree told her. "I've never seen such a beautiful display of color."

"Our spring is comin' later and later every year," she grumbled, turning toward the stove. "Even the seasons is changing wrong, not like they used to; April was always the fairest month. Aye, 'twas the fairest."

Nigel winked at Elloree as he pulled out a chair for her at the kitchen table and slid into one beside her.

"Now don't fuss, Myrtle, about serving us in the dining room. We're comfortable right here close to the coffee pot." He reached for a cup, filled it with the steaming brew, and passed it to Elloree.

Myrtle clucked her disapproval but placed a pitcher of frothy warm milk and a heaping bowl of sugar on the table. Her cheerful rendition of "The White Cliffs of Dover" soon gave way to more lamentations over the shortages at Chilton Manor.

"Nary a brown 'un," she moaned, setting gleaming white boiled eggs before them followed by a platter piled with toast, fried tomatoes, and fresh mushrooms. "And no strawberry preserves," she grumbled, plunking down a large pot of marmalade.

"It's fine, Myrtle. Quite perfect really."

"In every way," Elloree added. "Each meal has been delicious."

"Not a one right," Myrtle continued, shaking her head sorrowfully as she rummaged through cupboards searching for a missing ingredient to complete their breakfast.

"The old dear thinks we always should dine in grand style here at the manor. I'm afraid my casualness is a bit of an affront to her cherished formal ways. Clearly she'll never be serving us any fast food egg crumpets or whatever you call them in the states."

"Egg McMuffins." Elloree laughed as Myrtle reappeared, carrying a plate of warm biscuits slathered in creamy butter and a pot of fresh coffee.

"When you were just a wee bairn you went ridin' with Lady Chilton. Fox and hound huntin' all the way to Charring Cross, you went. Now those mornings we served a proper breakfast." She sniffed. "That's how it should be—proper staff, proper pantry," she pronounced, turning back to her stove and dishes. But soon the strains of "The White Cliffs of Dover" drifted again across the kitchen.

They finished their breakfast, lingering over a last cup of coffee and talking about their return to London.

"I'd like to show you around the old place before we leave if you think you can spare the time," Nigel said eagerly.

"I was hoping you'd suggest it."

"Since it's such a sunny morning, we could walk down to the stables, go out to the lake," he said uncertainly, suddenly looking down at Elloree's polished Gucci pumps.

"Myrtle, I say, don't suppose you could fix us up with a pair of walking shoes? Elloree and I want to hike down to the lake and the stables."

This time, the old servant disappeared from the kitchen without a word of complaint, returning almost immediately with a sturdy pair of oxfords.

"Might be a bit of a chill in the air," she said, producing warm woolen socks from her apron pocket.

Quickly, Elloree slipped on the socks and laced up the shoes.

"Not bad, not bad at all," Nigel complimented. "All you need now is a walking stick, and you'll be ready for a tramp through the heather across the ruggedest moors. Saved us once again, Myrtle. Thank you."

The old lady beamed and smoothed out her apron. "Now you be careful, Master Nigel. Likely to be a mite slippery out about the lake banks. The rain was heavy enough to wash away some of the paths."

"We'll be careful. Don't you fret about us. And after all that good food, we'll have energy to last for hours. All set, Elloree?"

She nodded, taking his arm.

They walked, chatting together, through the great hall. Suddenly Nigel stopped before a pair of high oak doors flanked by two pilasters crowned with two bronze Grecian figures. He hesitated for only a moment before pushing the doors wide and ushering her inside. Drawn jade-green damask draperies shut out the morning sunlight, and he snapped on the wall switch, flooding the room instantly with a blaze of light.

At least a dozen crystal chandeliers hung from the high, molded ceiling, accented by round sculpted medallions in gold relief. The splendor of the room brought a soft gasp from Elloree's lips as she stepped across the inlaid marble floor. Silk covered walls adorned by Waterford sconces and draped with medieval tapestries were illuminated by hundreds of tiny, dazzling points of light. Chilton Manor's grand ballroom was still resplendent, although closed off and unused for years. It's once elegantly displayed furnishings were pushed into corners, covered with dingy sheets, and its priceless Persian carpets lay rolled and stacked along the walls.

As Elloree stood with Nigel gazing out across the magnificent room, sounds of Johann Strauss seemed to echo from the past. And she envisioned bejeweled ladies in elegant gowns swirling gracefully in the arms of dashing gentlemen around the polished floors.

"It's just too beautiful," she whispered.

"No need to whisper. We're the only ones here, you know," he said sweeping her into his arms and waltzing smoothly around the ballroom floor.

When they stopped, a little breathless, still in each other's arms, he told her, "My mother used to hold a ball here twice a year during fall and spring. Always grand affairs, the last one was to celebrate my betrothal to Elizabeth. Mother was in declining health, but she insisted. The room hasn't been used since."

He switched off the lights, plunging the vast glittering chamber into blackness. Holding her close to him, he kissed her hair and cheeks tenderly.

"I haven't been through these doors in years, but I wanted you to see the ballroom, wanted to share it with you."

"I loved seeing it, Nigel. It's another part of you. The past is always with us, wherever we go. Whoever we are, it molds our future," she whispered, clinging to him. And for the first time, she felt her own pain fading.

Chapter 40

THE CLEAR, FRESH AIR MADE the walk to the lake invigorating. Holding hands and chatting, Nigel and Elloree hiked briskly down the muddy, narrow, tree-lined path. Wild flowers spread patches of color across the lush green landscape, and dozens of vividly marked ducks paddled along the lake's shallow banks.

"Over that ridge and through the next meadow is Withersby Castle," Nigel said, pointing across the lake. "Our estates join at the farthest reach of the pasture lands."

"Can't see the castle from here," he told her and then added, "The Chiltons and the Withersbys always have been connected, more by business than marriage. Except for Elizabeth and me; she was a Withersby. It was her grandfather who went out to India and made his vast fortune. My mother always said that old Bradford Withersby was seduced by more than the land in India." Nigel chuckled, recalling his mother's tolerant explanation of the old man's folly. "Took up with some Mahraj's daughter, my mother contended, although the Withersby gentry always insisted there was only pure English blood running through all their veins."

He looked wistfully through the trees in the direction of Withersby Castle before continuing. "Elizabeth had raven hair and dark brown eyes, not the fair Botticelli looks of most of the Withersbys. We knew each other as children, and it was assumed from a very early age that we were intended. She spent all of her holidays at the castle and much of the time she was here at Chilton Manor." He stopped talking, suddenly reaching for Elloree's hand. "I'm sorry. I'm going on too much about the past. I guess I've shut it out for so long."

"Don't apologize, Nigel. I want to know all that you want to tell me," she told him, squeezing his hand gently.

"The wind is coming up. You'll be cold. We'd better make our way over to the stables."

They followed a thickly overgrown trail through a large clump of chestnut trees. Their shoes made a mushy, spongy sound as they tramped through the wet, soggy soil. A sudden whir of fluttering wings broke the stillness as a flock of ducks rose from the bulrushes. Honking and flapping, they soared high in precision formation. Like a well-trained aviation squadron, they banked and flew out over the lake.

"I've never understood how anyone could gun them down. They're so beautiful, wild, and free," Elloree said, watching the birds until they disappeared over the far ridge.

"Caught a poacher out here once years ago. And I can tell you, I was tempted to take care of him myself, not wait for the constable to haul him off."

A sudden shrill whinny cut across Nigel's words. "Sulty knows we're on our way," he said, leading her out into a clearing where a long, low barn stood surrounded by fenced pastures.

"You still have horses," she cried. "I wish we could be here longer so I could ride with you."

"We only keep two now. Sultan's Pride and Harley are the only ones left," he said. A smell of hay and horses greeted them as they entered the dusky stable. At the far end, a loud snorting and stamping came from one of the stalls.

"That's Sulty, impatient as always." They could hear the horse pawing and moving restlessly as they walked through the barn toward him.

"I raised him from a colt." Nigel gave a sharp, short whistle, and the horse responed with a piercing whinny .

Sultan's Pride poked his beautiful, dappled gray head over the stall door and continued to drum the wooden slats with his hoofs. His ears pricked forward, listening for another whistle, and his wide-set, brown eyes peered through the dim light. Then recognizing Nigel, he gave a long, low whicker of greeting.

"What a magnificent animal," Elloree exclaimed. "He's an Arabian, isn't he?"

Nigel nodded. "A present from my mother," he told her, patting the arched muscular neck.

Sultan's Pride nuzzled Nigel's shoulder in return, pushing his nose into the man's chest, blowing and snorting his welcome. From his pocket, Nigel produced a bunch of carrots and held one out to Elloree as he gave some to the horse.

"Give him one, if he doesn't frighten you with his blowing and stamping. He's really very gentle, in spite of all his high-spirited antics."

Elloree laid the carrot across the flattened palm of her hand and felt Sultan's whiskered muzzle take it gingerly from her, and then he crunched it greedily between his big teeth.

"How you been, old boy?" Nigel continued to pat the horse's salt and pepper neck. Sultan bobbed his head, tossing his smoky mane and watching them with large, dark, luminous eyes.

"He has beautiful markings," Elloree said, peering into the stall at the proud, fine stallion. "I can see why you named him Sultan's Pride. He holds his head up so high, and he looks every inch a prince." She stroked the silver streak that spread from his ears like a pearly arrow down to his velvety pink nose.

"These aren't for you," Nigel said, producing two more carrots from his pocket and pulling them out of Sultan's reach. "Harley'd never forgive me if I left him out."

A large chestnut head with a white blaze face bobbed up and down in the next stall.

"He's a beauty, too," Elloree said, rubbing the mahogany neck. "And he's a big one, long legged. He must have a powerful stride."

"Harley was one of the finest hunters in the county," Nigel told her. "Bred for jumping. Nice easy gait and, in his day, soared over fences. He comes from a long line of steeplechasers. He was a gift to my mother from Sir Reginald Darnley. All the Darnleys raised horses, but Sir Reginald really went in for the racing. He was a bit of a rogue, I guess you might say, but was very enamored with my mother. Courted her for years. I think he really loved her, but she never would marry him. One Christmas, he surprised her with Harley as a gift. Sir Darnley named the horse Harley Davidson because of his love for fast cars and motorcycles—just one example of the old boy's brand of humor." He patted the horse affectionately, laughing at the memory.

"I remember on Christmas Day hearing the name Harley Davidson and dashing down the stairs in great anticipation, only to find a horse instead of a motorcycle. Big disappointment for a teenage lad," Nigel said with a laugh.

"You must have had a stable full at one time," Elloree said. She looked at the empty stalls lining both sides of the long, low barn.

"We did. My mother adored horses and loved to ride with the hounds. We hosted many hunts here at Chilton Manor while she was still in good health. But Elizabeth and I only rode together for pleasure and didn't go in for that sort of thing very much."

Elloree walked through an open door into a large tack room filled with saddles and bridles. A scent of oiled leather mingled with the sweet smell of hay and oats. In one corner, a small saddle and bridle lay partially covered by a royal blue horse blanket stamped in gold with the Chilton coat of arms. Her eyes rested on the tiny riding outfit.

"Those were for Tiddly Winks, Susan's Welch pony. He was her present on her fifth birthday," Nigel said, sadness clouding his eyes. "The pony died last year. Myrtle called me at Harrison House. Old Peter did everything he could to save him, but it was no use. Peter takes care of the horses and oversees the grounds. He's been with us almost as long as Myrtle," Nigel explained. "Now it's just Harley and Sultan left. Fortunately, they were spared from the virus that took the pony.

It was a bad year for livestock all over the English countryside. A lot of animals died. The veterinarian gave the disease some fancy scientific name, and now they've developed a vaccine for it. So hopefully Harley and Sulty are out of danger."

They walked out into the bright sunlight, squinting from the sudden glare. He took her arm and guided her over a fallen branch across their path.

"I'd love to show you more," he said. "But it's getting late. If we don't leave soon, we'll be caught in an awful London traffic snarl."

"I know," she said, "but I can't help wishing I could stay longer in this lovely place."

"You'll come back," he said.

They walked slowly away from the stables in the direction of the manor, neither of them wanting the day to end.

"If I know Myrtle, she's not going to let us out of here without feeding us one last time," Nigel said looking at his watch.

And as predicted, Myrtle greeted them in the hall carrying a tray.

"You'll have time for a wee tea in the library before you leave. Not a high tea at all, just some wee sandwiches, bread and jam," she said, setting her bountiful burden down on the library table.

They laughed and sank down together into the welcome softness of the sofa, feeling suddenly tired from their morning hike.

"There's no use arguing with Myrtle—never has been and never will be," Nigel said, reaching for the teapot.

Chapter 41

On the drive back to London, Elloree and Nigel rode in silence, lost in their own thoughts of old and new memories. The weather had changed once again. The bright blue morning sky had clouded over, replaced by patchy drizzles as they drove through the pastoral countryside. Nearing the city, the traffic increased, and Nigel watched the road carefully as he maneuvered the Daimler through the clogged streets.

"I'd like to make a brief stop at Harrison House before I return you to the Grovesnor," he suddenly said. "It won't take long." He looked over at her and she nodded. She was in no hurry for the day to end.

He escorted her toward the lifts through crowds of shoppers on the department store's busy ground floor.

"Our corporate offices are at the top," he said, pushing the button for number eight.

When the elevator doors snapped open, they were greeted by a smartly dressed receptionist. Nigel guided Elloree down a long hallway past rooms bustling with company personnel.

"Clair, we won't be needing a thing, thank you." He spoke to a tall, matronly brunette woman hurriedly approaching them.

"My secretary," he explained. "Intelligent and efficient. Don't know what I'd do without her. She keeps me organized. Ah, here we are."

They had reached the end of the corridor where a small bronze placard identified his office. He swung the door open and stood aside, and she stepped across a thick, crimson-toned oriental carpet into a spacious, walnut–paneled, high-ceilinged room. A heavy, carved mahogany Chippendale desk dominated the room's center, and at the far end, a wide plate glass window provided a panorama of London. All the landmarks they had visited together during the last week were spread below her as Elloree stood gazing down on the city.

"What a spectacular sight," she said. "No wonder you kept this floor for your offices. The view's a constant reminder of history and your important place in what's new."

"I never tire of it myself," he said picking up a file of papers. "Just take a minute to look this over." He jotted a few notes on a pad after flipping through pages and then tossed the folder back onto the desk. "All in order. I'm always amazed at my staff; don't give them enough credit." He pointed to the sheath of papers. "All ready for signature just as Clair promised. Now I want you to see the real reason I brought you up here."

He opened a door leading into the adjoining office, and they walked into a bright, freshly painted room. Light and airy, decorated in pristine white with pastel accents, the space had been converted to a well-equipped artist's studio. A shaft of daylight flooded through a skylight onto a large drafting table, and well-illuminated workstations were arranged around the room. On the walls, enlarged, framed copies of Elloree's first Little Susie designs were attractively displayed.

"I've followed the growth of Wishes, Little Susie's development, and made this collection. When you start on the London project, you'll need work space. Harrison House is the logical place, since we'll be working together."

"You think of everything," Elloree said, looking at him in amazement.

"But there's much work to be done first. I know how Mark operates, how thorough he is. And after all, it is his final decision."

"He's already convinced. I talked to him from Chilton Manor. He's very enthusiastic, wants to move ahead with acquiring properties in both the London locations we researched."

"Nigel, it's all happening too fast—Chilton Manor, us, everything," she said, turning away from the window to face him, her eyes filling with tears. "You don't know about me. I'm not free."

"But you will be, and I know more than you think, Elloree," he told her quietly. "I read your newspapers, too. And I talked with Mark Williams before you ever came over here."

"About me? Mark would never discuss anything personal about me with you or anyone. That's not something he would ever do." She frowned.

Nigel moved closer, gathered her into his arms, his voice softly reassuring. "It's all right, Elloree. We both know how difficult it is to come to grips with terrible grief and guilt. Take your time. You're still healing. I understand that." He kissed her forehead gently and then her lips. They stood locked in each other's arms for a long moment. "Just know I'll be here for you and this studio is yours, ready anytime you are."

"Thank you, Nigel," she said simply, dabbing at her eyes. "You've given so much to me already. Here in London with you, I've been happier, more at peace than I've been for a very long time. I know how much you've lost, that your courage to survive created Harrison House and all of this," she said, swinging her arm in a wide arc. "Building Harrison House has been your salvation, and making Wishes will be mine." She searched his face for reassurance and found only love in his eyes.

"I do understand, and I'll wait for you, Elloree."

"You're right; I am still mending," she continued slowly, searching for words. "After the accident, Paul's death, I felt like I was living with some awful, crippling disease and wished only that it could be terminal to end my pain. Then every morning, I awoke once more with the terrible realization that a part of me had been cruelly amputated; a piece of me was gone—not an arm or a leg but, far worse, a huge chunk of my heart had been torn out. I thought my life was over; I'd never be able to live with myself again. And now I am healing, but I know I still have far to go.

"You don't have to explain, Elloree." His arms tightened around her. "I love you. I want you here with me, but I know you have much to sort out. I don't expect you to give me an answer now. But I want you to know my feelings, how much I care for you," he said, looking deeply into her eyes. The afternoon light had faded, turning the chalk white studio walls to opalescent ivory. And outside, the evening's twilight glow was fast dimming to darkness as Big Ben's resonant toll reminded them of the hour.

They said their good-byes that night over a quiet dinner. Sensing her mood and knowing his own, Nigel selected the hushed elegant atmosphere of the Savoy Grill for their final evening together. And although both of them felt the sadness of her impending departure, they enjoyed the delicious meal, superbly served and accompanied by a fine, full-bodied wine. They lingered over coffee, and he ordered an aged Napoleon brandy for a final toast.

"Only thing the French ever got right," he said with a wry smile, swirling the light brown liquid in the crystal snifter and enjoying its heady bouquet. Then he touched his glass to hers, his eyes sparkling with love.

"To the twelfth of never."

She smiled at him, sipping the mellow, warm liquor and remembering Chilton Manor.

"For us, I hope it will be a long, long time," she said, reaching across the table to take his hand in hers. "I really do believe some things last forever, Nigel—the good and beautiful moments we hold in our hearts. The painful ones fade but give us the strength to go on to make new wishes."

The plane lifted easily off the runway, climbing abruptly into the misty, gray morning sky. It gained altitude and banked, leaving Heathrow Airport and London swiftly behind. Elloree leaned her head back against the seat cushion and listened to the flight attendant explain the safety procedures. Through her window, the British Isles below were rapidly shrinking into tiny, black dots in the steel-blue sea.

"I'll be back. I know I will," she whispered as her last glimpse of England was swallowed by the clouds. As the miles fell away, she closed her eyes, picturing Mark pacing at the airport, checking first his watch and then the flight schedule. The night before, his words had boomed through the static of the telephone connection and now were echoing through her mind.

"Can't get you back here soon enough. Things are popping and I need that new line. Goddamn it, let's get going, El."

"Slave driver," she muttered. But with a smile, she reached for her tote bag and laid a sketch pad across her knees. Within minutes she was making quick, sure strokes with her pen across the paper. Two children in old-fashioned riding outfits and a saddled pony filled the foreground. The small boy was handing the pony's reins to a curly-haired little girl, and beneath the picture Elloree scrawled, "Some gifts are forever." And at the top of the page in bold black letters she printed: "Tiddly Winks Greetings, a new division of Wishes, Inc."

About the Author

MARILYN HOLDSWORTH graduated from Occidental College with a major in literature. She has a background in writing and editing and is a Huntington Library Fellow. She created and operated her own greeting card company. She has visited the Kansas City Hallmark Center and made frequent trips to England to research her book. She lives in Southern California.

Praise for Pegasus

"Pegasus captivates audiences with an eye-opening and adventurous tale of love and wild mustangs."

—Albemarle Magazine.

"Pegasus is both a mystery-adventure and a romance. The combination, however, is a charming gift to readers. Even those of us who aren't particularly romantic can become enthralled as a relationship develops between mature, intelligent people."

—Ed Nelson, movie actor.

"I recommend "Pegasus" to anyone who wants a good story to take them away for a few hours, whether a lover of horses or not. You will enjoy the ride, much like an easy canter through the field on a nice, spring day."

—Marissa Libbit for Reader Views.

"Pegasus is a novel which shines light on the issues of animal abuse and exploitation. It is a compelling book and one that will appeal to all horse lovers, especially us Mustang lovers."

—Nanci Falley, The American Indian Horse.

"The writing style of author Marilyn Holdsworth is good, nice and fast paced, thus keeping the reader's attention and making the book a quick and entertaining read."

—Katherine Rizzo, The Equiery.

Praise for
The Beautiful American

“This book grabs the reader’s attention from the first page and won’t let you put it down till you are finished. The author has done her research to match the story line into some actual historical characters and happenings, which helps make the story believable and captivating.”

—Jon Mattheis, The Kindle Book Review

“Ms. Holdsworth holds nothing back as she delivers a well told story that entertains. If you love historical fiction, you’ll enjoy the trip back in time as much I did.”

—Vickie McKeehan, author of The Evil Trilogy.

“A great historical read! The descriptions were stunning. Author does a lovely job setting the scene for the time. Sweet character interactions…”

—Stacy Evans

“A story within a story awaits readers, with an antique dealer’s treasured find yielding a historical intrigue.”

—Mary C. Findley, author of Chasing the Texas Wind.

"Layers and layers of emotion takes the reader on a journey between past and present....it's best for you to dive in with an open mind and a willing heart. You won't regret it. Would I recommend this read? Oh yes, definitely"

—Andrea Kurian, book reviewer.

"A book that teaches you about courage, love and strength one thrilling page at a time. Holdsworth's writing is captivating and descriptive. A definite must-read."

—Pandora Poikilos,
international award winning author of Frequent Traveller.